"The dark suspense is
a breezy writing styl~
—Allison Brennan, N

Praise for ~

"Fast-paced mystery with a paranormal twist. Ms. Roberts delivers tight, crisp dialogue, an exciting plot, and true-to-life characters. If you like *CSI*, *Medium*, or *Ghost Whisperer*, you'll absolutely love *The Remains of the Dead*." —MyShelf.com

"Roberts has a unique gift: She makes talking to the dead as natural as talking to your neighbor over a cup of coffee. Sadie Novak, who cleans up crime scenes for a living, is a charming new heroine with a great deal of heart. . . . Here's hoping she comes back soon." —*Romantic Times*

"A fantastic debut! *The Remains of the Dead* is hip, clever, and fun. Don't miss this engaging story."
—Brenda Novak, national bestselling author

"A well-told mystery, a healthy dose of the paranormal, and a taste of potential romance will keep you guessing through the twists and turns. *The Remains of the Dead* leaves readers eager to discover where the next visit with Sadie and her friends will lead." —Darque Reviews

"*The Remains of the Dead* is a clever, humorous take on a fascinating occupation—a fast-paced, one-sitting read. A wonderfully flawed main character and unexpected story twists will keep you turning pages long into the night!"
—Stephanie Bond, author of the Body Movers series

"Wendy Roberts has created an incredibly unique amateur sleuth and a twist at the end of the book that I never saw coming." —Jana DeLeon, author of *Rumble on the Bayou* and *Unlucky*

"A fascinating, edgy series with a neat paranormal twist! A unique mystery with a great protagonist and an interesting cast of characters."
—Colleen Gleason, author of *The Bleeding Dusk*

Also by Wendy Roberts

The Remains of the Dead

DEVIL MAY RIDE

A Ghost Dusters Mystery

WENDY ROBERTS

AN OBSIDIAN MYSTERY

OBSIDIAN
Published by New American Library, a division of
Penguin Group (USA) Inc., 375 Hudson Street,
New York, New York 10014, USA
Penguin Group (Canada), 90 Eglinton Avenue East, Suite 700, Toronto,
Ontario M4P 2Y3, Canada (a division of Pearson Penguin Canada Inc.)
Penguin Books Ltd., 80 Strand, London WC2R 0RL, England
Penguin Ireland, 25 St. Stephen's Green, Dublin 2,
Ireland (a division of Penguin Books Ltd.)
Penguin Group (Australia), 250 Camberwell Road, Camberwell, Victoria 3124,
Australia (a division of Pearson Australia Group Pty. Ltd.)
Penguin Books India Pvt. Ltd., 11 Community Centre, Panchsheel Park,
New Delhi - 110 017, India
Penguin Group (NZ), 67 Apollo Drive, Rosedale, North Shore 0632,
New Zealand (a division of Pearson New Zealand Ltd.)
Penguin Books (South Africa) (Pty.) Ltd., 24 Sturdee Avenue,
Rosebank, Johannesburg 2196, South Africa

Penguin Books Ltd., Registered Offices:
80 Strand, London WC2R 0RL, England

First published by Obsidian, an imprint of New American Library,
a division of Penguin Group (USA) Inc.

First Printing, December 2008
10 9 8 7 6 5 4 3 2 1

Copyright © Wendy Roberts, 2008
All rights reserved

PUBLISHER'S NOTE
This is a work of fiction. Names, characters, places, and incidents either are
the product of the author's imagination or are used fictitiously, and any resem-
blance to actual persons, living or dead, business establishments, events, or
locales is entirely coincidental.

The publisher does not have any control over and does not assume any
responsibility for author or third-party Web sites or their content.

For my sister, Debbie, for her love and support. Also for Brent and our beautiful children, who lift me up.

Thanks to my editor, Kristen Weber, for her wise yet subtle suggestions and great encouragement. Deepest gratitude as well to my agent, Miriam Kriss, for always fighting the good fight and for believing in this series.

Theresa Borst of Bio Clean Inc. was a tremendous help with my trauma-clean research.

1

When she walked in, Sadie expected the sickening stench of ammonia that proclaimed the outwardly tidy bungalow a clandestine meth lab. She did *not* expect to be confronted by a vicious Rottweiler preparing to rip her to shreds. A step backward and Sadie found herself pinned against the screen door that had snapped shut behind her.

"Easy, boy," Sadie said, although it was doubtful the dog could hear her muffled voice behind her respirator.

The dog snarled, snapped, and inched forward. Thick ropes of saliva dangled from his yellow teeth.

Sadie's knees shook as she grappled behind her back for the door handle, but the sleeve of her disposable hazmat suit snagged and caught on the splintered door-frame. *Damn!* She tugged hard and stumbled when her arm came free. The dog lunged.

Sadie shielded her face with her arms and braced for the pain of teeth sinking into her flesh but felt only a mild shudder of revulsion. She looked around and realized the dog had sailed right through her and dropped to the ground outside the door.

With a hand to her pounding heart, Sadie blew out a relieved breath and stepped outside. She pulled off her respirator and watched the confused mutt as he attempted to right himself. Sadie now noticed the other side of his body. A large strip of flesh hung from his rear flank. Through the fatal wound, she could see the knee-high grass and weeds that covered the acreage behind the house.

"Hey, Fido, you're dead." Sadie chuckled, and wiped droplets of sweat from her upper lip. The sun was rising in the sky, and the temperature promised to reach ninety by noon.

When the mutilated canine charged again, snapping and snarling, Sadie merely closed her eyes and prepared for the skin-crawling disgust that flooded through her whenever the spirits of the dead touched her body.

"Talking to ghosts again?" Zack asked as he came around the corner of the house, carrying a stack of rubber medical waste bins.

"A dog," she replied, rubbing her hand over her short-cropped hair.

"A ghost dog?" Zack grinned, put down the bins, and straightened to his near six feet.

"Yeah. He scared the hell out of me."

"R-i-i-i-ght. The lady who mops blood, guts, and meth while talking to ghosts is afraid of a dead puppy."

"He's a big Rotty, not a cuddly puppy." She fanned her face with her hand.

"Dogs scare you, but dealing with human spirits is, apparently, a walk in the park." The lines around his dark eyes crinkled with amusement.

"I wasn't prepared. I forgot the cops had to shoot a guard dog when they raided this place."

"It happens. The dog was probably trained to protect the house," Zack commented.

"Guess you can't fault a businessman for protecting his assets," Sadie said.

"You can if that business is crystal meth." He combed his fingers through his dark hair, which was already damp with sweat. "Man, it's hotter than hell."

"Just wait until you're suited up. Nothing like wearing extra layers when it's almost ninety."

She tugged her hazmat coveralls from her chest and

blew some air down into her cleavage. She glanced up to see him watching. Months ago he would've had some embarrassing remark to make about her sweaty breasts, but now Zack just looked away.

Sadie stepped closer and reached to grab a couple of the containers at his feet. Zack went for them at the same time and their hands touched. Simultaneously they jerked their fingers away like they'd been singed. With an awkward smile, Zack hurriedly picked up some bins and walked past her to the back door.

Like awkward teens after a breakup, Sadie thought, rolling her eyes.

The silence stretched taut between them as they walked toward the back door. Sadie watched as the Rottweiler leapt in the air in a desperate attempt to tackle Zack.

"Oh, give it up," Sadie muttered.

The Rottweiler skidded to a halt. He tilted his head at Sadie in a look of comical bewilderment. The poor thing had no idea why his attempts to ward them off were futile. Sadie was at a loss about how to explain to a dead dog that he was, in fact, dead.

Zack and Sadie walked up the back steps together. Pausing while Zack got out his disposable hazmat suit, Sadie broke the discomfiting silence to chat about the estimated time involved in cleaning the meth lab.

Suddenly, they both glanced across the grassy field toward the sound of a vehicle kicking up gravel.

"There's a dirt road beyond that tree line." Zack pointed across the scrub of grass and the tall cedars that edged the back of the property. "I almost took that turn myself, but there's nothing else down that road. It's a dead end. Somebody must've made a wrong turn."

"Could be someone who's disappointed their meth supplier is out of business."

The city of Kenmore was a Seattle bedroom community, just up the I-5, in the northern part of King County on Lake Washington. It was quaint and picturesque. Not exactly where you'd expect a large methamphetamine lab. However, where you had acreage separating a home from nosy neighbors, anything could happen. With Seattle police cracking down on crack and messing up the meth, cookers didn't mind whipping up their brand of brain poison in a quiet community where they hoped to remain undetected.

"What is it?" Zack asked.

She strained to listen, then shook her head.

"Nothing." She prepared to slip on her headgear again. "I think I'll stop by the other scene later today to see how Jackie's doing." At his look she added, "I'm not checking up on her."

"Yes, you are." He held up his hands in a stopping motion. "That's all right. Scene-2-Clean is your company. You have the right to make sure your employee's doing a decent job on the first scene she's worked alone."

"It's not that I want her thinking I don't trust her, but—" She stopped again.

"But you don't."

This time she was sure she heard it. Turning, Sadie stared a couple dozen feet away, across the weed-choked yard, at an old wooden garden shed. A warm wind fingered the tall grass and a crow cawed from the top of a fifty-foot monkey puzzle tree.

"That's funny. I keep thinking I hear a—" She broke off and turned to Zack.

The look on his face said he heard it too.

When the sound came again, Sadie knew it was the muffled, keening cry of a newborn baby. A sound totally out of sync in the middle of nowhere around a closed meth lab.

"There's a baby in that shed," Sadie said, already down the steps and traipsing toward the building.

Zack caught up quickly. With a firm hand on her elbow he stopped her and turned Sadie toward him.

"Look, before the cops released this property to us for cleaning, they would've cleared the outbuildings,"

Zack said, his voice tight. "Whoever's in there showed up since then. Hell, they could've been dropped off by the car we just heard."

"You're right. Some methhead could be holed up with her baby waiting for this place to reopen for business." Sadie shrugged. "Then we'd better go tell her to do her shopping elsewhere."

Again, Zack grabbed her.

"We?"

Sadie nodded. "Yeah. We."

Determinedly, she shrugged off his hand and walked toward the shed. Zack joined her and they stamped down the tall dry grass as they angled across the yard. Grasshoppers jumped knee-high as the grass was disturbed. Sadie and Zack stopped walking a couple of feet away. Sadie blinked perspiration from her eyes.

"Okay, now get back," Zack hissed in her ear, and pulled something from the waistband of his jeans.

Sadie's eyes grew wide.

"Since when do you carry a gun when we work a scene?"

"Since you decided to let Scene-2-Clean mop up meth labs instead of just trauma cleans."

"Helping out Scour Power is temporary. Just until David Egan gets back in town."

"Then this is temporary too." He indicated his gun.

The infant's cries cut into their discussion.

"Just step aside, Sadie, and let me do my job."

She stiffened and spoke between clenched teeth.

"Hey, Zack Bowman." She waved a hand in front of his face as if waking him from daydreaming. "You're not a cop anymore and I shouldn't have to remind you that you work for *me*."

He rolled his eyes.

"Are we going to have a pissing contest right here? Right now?"

"Well, no, that would be silly because, um, you have better equipment for that."

"Fine. You're the boss. You go ahead," he whispered, stepping aside and indicating the door with his hand. "The person with that baby is probably a paranoid tweaker out of her mind from withdrawal. She's beyond caring about her kid and hoping to trade her baby for a dot of crystal. She's desperate and not above attacking whoever gets in her way."

Sadie cringed.

"Okay, I guess you *do* have more training in this sort of thing."

"You think?"

The baby's cries sounded frantic.

"Don't just stand there, Mr. Macho." Sadie waved her hand toward the shed door. "Do your thing."

"Stay outside until I tell you it's safe." His jaw tightened and his dark eyes hardened to bullets.

"Just hurry up."

Plastering his back to the wall of the windowless building, Zack slipped into cop mode like it hadn't been a couple years since he'd turned in his badge. Gun in both hands and in the ready position, he called out, "I'm armed! Throw down your weapons and come out with your hands up or I'll come in shooting!"

"That's a little extreme, don'tcha think?" Sadie whispered to his back.

"Shaddup."

There was no answering shuffle of movement or voices from within. The only sound was the continued muted wail of a baby. Sadie had a chilling visual of a drug-crazed freak holding a poor defenseless newborn. She nudged Zack's back with her finger.

"Go already."

In one quick movement, Zack booted open the thin door. Splinters of tinder-dry wood fluttered in the air. He disappeared inside and Sadie heard him suck in a gasp and blow out a loud curse. A beam of sunlight entered the doorway and lit the specks of dust in the air around Zack, but he blocked her view to what was beyond his frame.

Sadie hurried into the building, elbowing Zack aside. Her eyes took a few seconds to adjust to the dim interior. The smell hit her first. A peculiar and pungent barnyard scent. Her bewildered gaze went first to Zack's face, then zoomed in on what had captured his look of horror and disgust. On the opposite side of the ten-by-ten space was a makeshift workbench and on it lay the body of a goat. The animal had been eviscerated. It lay on its side, its thick, pale tongue protruding between lifeless lips.

Sadie's mind had a hard time coupling the sight of the slaughtered animal with the infant's cries cutting the air. Then she noticed a tiny fist rise from behind the carcass and she stepped forward.

"Stop!" Zack shouted in warning. "Don't go closer. We need to call this in. The carcass could be booby-trapped."

Sure, they knew from their training it was common for crankheads to protect their labs with trip wires and hidden pongee sticks (wood boards with large nails or spikes protruding upward), but they'd yet to encounter any tricky barnyard animals.

"A booby-trapped goat?" Sadie raised her eyebrows at him.

"Hey, it's a baby beside a mutilated goat." He threw his hands in the air. "You explain it."

Sadie could only shake her head. There was no explaining it, but she knew what had to be done. She crossed the dirt floor, swallowed nervously, then grabbed the coarse-haired animal and shoved it aside to get at a tiny naked infant wedged snugly between the goat and the wall. With rapid movement, Sadie scooped the baby boy from his dismal hiding place, noting that the infant's umbilical cord had been tied with twine. She unzipped her hazmat suit and pulled the sobbing child to her chest. He instantly curled against the hard buttons of her shirt, and his vulnerable body, tacky with blood and vernix, vibrated against her.

"Poor little guy," Sadie cooed, her voice thick with emotion as her heart tightened in her chest. "God, my own sister will be giving birth to a little human being like this pretty soon herself." She blinked back tears. "What kind of freak does something like this?"

Zack looked from the baby in her arms to the goat. He tunneled his fingers through his dark hair, shook his head slowly, and could only mutter under his breath, "Jesus . . ."

"Not quite," stated a female voice in the doorway.

Sadie whirled to see a robust woman with waist-length jet hair leaning nonchalantly in the doorway. Her emerald eyes were unnaturally bright and she wore a pale blue ankle-length sundress that was drenched in blood from the waist down.

"Is this your baby?"

"Not anymore," she said in a mockingly sweet sing-song voice.

"Who are you talking to?" Zack demanded, looking around.

Sadie shushed him as she instinctively bounced from one foot to the other, rocking the baby, whose cries had grown to stifled sobs.

"Who are you?" Sadie demanded.

The woman only smiled.

"All r-i-i-i-ght, I'll leave you to your ghosts," Zack growled. "I'm going to make the call."

"First, give me your shirt," Sadie said, her eyes never leaving the woman barricading the door.

Zack stripped to the waist and Sadie's eyes skidded uncomfortably away from his hard, muscled chest. He tossed her his T-shirt and left, walking right through the spirit of the woman still blocking the doorway.

Sadie's eyes narrowed as she scrutinized the woman's reaction. She neither flinched nor looked surprised when

Zack passed through. She knew she was dead and was apparently quite fine with it.

Swaddling the infant in Zack's shirt, Sadie kept her eyes on her guest. The woman didn't look like a drug addict. Then again, she wouldn't be the first person who had meth steal her life the first go-round.

"This baby looks like he was just born. Did you die in childbirth? What happened and what the hell is up with the goat?"

"I gave my son willingly," she replied with a simple shrug.

"Oh really? So you're dead and stoned out of your mind. That's just great. Well, party on," Sadie shot back. "But first, where's your body?"

"I don't need my physical self anymore. Soon all the power of the dead will go to the Alliance and that child will help. Besides," the woman replied, flicking her wrist as if it were no big deal, "I've gone to be with he who called me."

"No. No, you haven't." Sadie shook her head. She took a deep breath and slowly let it out before she attempted to reason with the spirit. "You haven't gone over. In fact, you seem to be stuck. I see it quite often. If you *had* gone to heaven, I wouldn't be able to see you."

"Who said anything about heaven?" She laughed roughly.

When the woman focused her gaze back on Sadie, her green eyes flickered and momentarily blazed, glowing bright bloodred.

The hair on the back of Sadie's neck prickled with fear.

"Okay, I'm out of here," Sadie announced with false bravado.

Fear tasted acrid in her mouth as she made to exit, the baby gripped tightly against her chest. Since the womanly apparition made no motion to step aside, Sadie took a breath and walked through.

She prepared herself for the grotesque nails-on-blackboard feeling she experienced at the touch of the dead. Instead, the moment her body contacted the spirit's, an agonizing scream left her throat. Sadie felt like she was being bathed in acid. As if her skin were melting from her bones.

2

Sadie was abruptly yanked forward through the doorway and tugged against Zack.

"Are you okay?" His eyes were wild as they scraped over her. "You looked like you were having some kind of a seizure."

Sadie's mouth opened and closed wordlessly. In stunned silence she glanced down at the baby, who only whimpered softly in her arms. Anxiously, Sadie looked over her shoulder. The ghost was gone.

"I'm okay. I think."

"You think."

"Yeah. You can let go of my arm before you snap it in two."

Zack released his grip.

"What was all that about?"

"I have no idea." Sadie shook her head. "You called the cops?"

He nodded.

She swayed a little on her feet and he grabbed her elbow to steady her.

"I'm okay." She tightened her grip on the squirming infant in her arms.

"You are definitely *not* okay."

"I'm just a little warm." She pulled away. "Since when does Seattle get to ninety for a whole week in May?"

Sadie shifted the baby in her arms. "And who knew a baby could give off this much heat?"

"So you're blaming global warming and a newborn for the fact that you look like you're going to pass out?"

"Yeah. I think I'll just go sit in the van and run the air-conditioning until the cops get here." She took a step away, then stopped and said over her shoulder, "Don't suppose you have a bottle of milk on you for the baby?"

"Nope."

"How about an ice-cold beer for me?"

He smiled. "Later. I'll even buy."

Sadie climbed into the Scene-2-Clean van and with trembling fingers started the ignition. She blasted the AC, careful to keep the baby turned away from the blowing air. Her thoughts were a jumbled mess as she tried to come to terms with the ghost in the shed.

"Your mom isn't the kind of spirit I'm used to, kiddo," Sadie told the baby boy.

Using the tip of her finger, she touched the tight dark curls covering the vulnerable soft spot on the top of his head. "Jeez, what the hell happened to you?"

His reply was a snuffling cry as his mouth routed and searched in jerky movements against Sadie's chest.

"Sorry, little guy," Sadie said with a sigh. "You're definitely searching in the desert there."

It wasn't long before police and EMTs arrived on the scene with lights blazing and sirens blaring. Sadie was both relieved and a little hesitant to turn the child over to a paramedic.

"He's hungry," Sadie said.

"We'll take good care of him."

Detective Carr arrived from King County's Major Crimes Unit. He had a deep frown that only got deeper as he questioned Sadie and Zack. The pair described what they'd heard—the vehicle leaving the area—and what they'd seen; the baby and the goat in the shed. The freckles across the detective's cheekbones looked all wrong on his hard face. He blew out a hot breath and walked off to examine the scene with the other officers before bringing Sadie and Zack back inside the shed.

"And the baby was stuffed between the wall and *this animal*?" Detective Carr asked for probably the fourth time. "Just lying there?"

"Yes," Sadie and Zack replied together.

He shook his head with a look of disgust.

"The whole world's just going to hell."

The detective's shirt was darkened with sweat. He patted the sparse red hair at the top of his head as he stared from the goat to Sadie and then back again, as if the answer were somewhere between the two.

Sadie felt exhausted and weakened from her heated exchange with the ghost.

"I've got to get out of here," she said, a hand on her stomach as she glanced nervously around.

"It's the heat," Zack explained to the detective. "We'll just wait outside."

"Yeah, go ahead," Carr said dismissively.

They stepped out of the shed, and Sadie looked around at the swarm of officers and investigators on the property and let out a low whistle. To the uninitiated it looked like chaos, but each person was tending to a precise task.

"This is a big deal," Sadie said.

An officer shouted something from the far reaches of the grassy area near the tree line.

"It's about to get even bigger," Zack said, his tone dire.

Snippets of conversation reached them as the officers gathered in a knot across the yard.

"They've found a body," Zack said.

Sadie closed her eyes and let out a low breath.

"Find out if it's a young woman with long black hair, wearing a blue sundress that's soaked in blood."

Zack folded his arms across his chest and glared at her.

"You and I both know if that's the ghost you saw in the shed, there's no way I can walk over there and ask that question without getting thrown in jail."

"I'll get you out no matter how many years it takes." Sadie winked, but when Zack continued to scowl, she added, "Okay, just forget it."

Sadie's pocket began to vibrate and she fished out her cell.

"Just wanted to see if you needed me at the meth site when I'm done here?" asked Jackie, another employee of Sadie's bio-recovery company.

"You're done?"

"Not yet."

"Don't bother coming out here. Something's going on. I've got a feeling the cops will be closing off this scene and we'll be backing off," Sadie said.

"What's up?" Jackie asked excitedly. "Did some crackheads show up?"

"Nothing like that. I'll tell you about it when I swing by and help you finish up."

"You don't have to do that. I'm fine here."

"I'm already on my way," Sadie said, ignoring Jackie's protests.

After she hung up, Sadie looked at Zack.

"Bet you want to hang out here and watch the show."

"Maybe for a while, if you don't need me elsewhere?" He tore his eyes away from the scene unfolding across the yard to look at Sadie. "Does Jackie need help?"

She shook her head. "Wrists slit in a tub is beginners' work. If she can't handle that one on her own, we might as well fire her. But since we're done here, I'm going over there anyway. Just because . . ." She let her words trail off.

"Because there's something about Jackie that bugs the hell out of you," Zack finished.

"Not really." *Except the way she looks at you like she wants you alone, naked, and covered in whipped cream.* Sadie felt herself blush and cleared her throat.

"She may not be perfect, but don't be looking for an excuse to fire her. People aren't exactly standing in line to work in a job where you clean up blood, guts, and meth labs," he stated evenly. "Don't hang over her shoulder. Just let the girl do her job."

"I know. I will." Sadie watched the Rottweiler attempt to gnaw on Zack's ankle. "I so need a break from this place."

The hound gave up on Zack and charged Sadie again. She only let her shoulders drop with a sigh.

"Don't suppose Mace would work on a dog spirit, would it?"

Zack only offered her a world-weary look. Sadie caught a glimpse of the black metal buried in his waistband.

"I hate seeing you carrying a gun."

His square jaw hardened and he sent her a dry look. "As long as we're decontaminating meth labs instead of mopping up body parts, I'll be bringing it along. I don't need to be armed to sweep up the dead. They don't shoot back. Cranked-out freaks looking for crystal aren't as reliable." He nodded at her. "You're licensed to carry a concealed. You should pocket your Ruger when you work these jobs. You never know when a meth cooker is going to return to the scene to resume his work and be pissed off that you're trashing his supplies."

"I've seen too much blood spilled from bullet wounds," Sadie said softly. "Guns creep me out."

He looked to the heavens. "This from a woman who talks to dead people to help them go over to the other side." He pointed a finger in her direction. "You can bet your ass Egan doesn't walk onto these scenes without protection, and I'll bet he doesn't let any of his crew work a job unprotected either." He regarded her coolly. "And speaking of Egan, we've been covering for him for two weeks and it was only supposed to be one. Call him."

"I have. I've left messages."

"Try again."

Sadie nodded and walked back to her van, which was parked in the driveway. The growling dog followed her, gnashing his teeth and nipping at her heels. She turned to him.

"Look, Fido, you're dead. You need to think about sniffing hydrants and chasing poodles in the next dimension. Take a moment and walk toward the light or the glowing dog bone or wherever it is that dogs go when they leave this place behind."

He sat down and whimpered up at her.

The medical examiner's vehicle pulled up in front of the house. It would be a while before they removed the body. Across the field, detectives were busily tending to the business of death. When the ME workers passed by, Fido bounded after them, eager to chomp on someone else's legs and frustrated at his lack of success.

Sadie climbed into her van and steered out of the Kenmore area. Within minutes she was merging onto the I-5, heading south to Seattle. While on the way, she multitasked and dialed David Egan, owner of Scour Power meth-cleaning service.

"Hey, Twisted Sister, great to hear from you," he answered. "Bet you've been busy."

That was an understatement.

"Nice of you to answer the phone," Sadie said drily. "I've been trying to reach you for days."

"Sorry. My cell doesn't work too well where I am."

"And that would be where?"

"Out of town."

"Can you be more specific?"

"I'd rather not."

Sadie sighed.

"I know I asked you to help out for only a week," Egan said hastily. "But if you can give me a little more time, I'll be back up to my elbows in meth and you can go back to being strictly a blood 'n' guts cleaner."

"When?"

"Soon."

She groaned.

"Look, my employees are pretty much handling the load of both companies. Your guys aren't helping. We just attempted a meth job, but that fell apart, so I scheduled a few days for squat." She told him briefly about the situation. "Luckily, I've got that dripper job in Kirkland next."

"I'm missing all the fun. How come my guys aren't helping out?"

"When I've called on your crew, they haven't returned my calls for work." She paused before finishing. "I heard they're flying solo. They said they hadn't been given enough jobs from you lately. Sorry about that."

She didn't add that his guys complained Egan had only sporadically given them work over the last month and they were sick of waiting for him.

"Shit, I was afraid that might happen," Egan said, but didn't sound overly concerned. "Ever since Seattle PD made it a priority to shut down cookers, business has exploded and new meth-cleanup companies are popping up all over. My guys aren't stupid. They've got the certification to tackle the jobs on their own, so they don't need me. You were right when you told me last year I should pay my guys more to compete with those start-up companies. Guess I figured they'd stick with me out of loyalty."

"If business was so big, you should've delegated if you were too busy."

"Yeah, I was busy fixing up my mom and dad's place. Renovations can take over your life," he grumbled. "I should've just handed the jobs to my guys and I still would've gotten the cut. It was stupid of me to expect them to wait around."

"Speaking of stupid," Sadie began. "If Thuggy tries to get paid for working that job last week, make sure you remind him that showing up drunk when the job is half-completed doesn't mean he'll get paid."

"Damn. I didn't know he was a drinker. Maybe he's just off the wagon."

"If the smell of him is any indication, then he fell off that wagon and it dragged him through a brewery as it pulled out of town."

"He didn't abandon ship like my other guys?"

"Guess the rest of your crew didn't want to work with a drunk any more than I do."

"I'll talk to Thuggy," Egan said seriously. "You need him. He's only been with me a short time, but he's good. Your partner was the one who recommended him."

"Zack? Really?" That gave her pause. She'd have to remember to ask Zack what was up with that. "Maybe it's hard to believe anyone named Thuggy could ever amount to much," Sadie chuckled.

"*Thuggy*'s short for *Thugwold*."

"That's even worse."

"He's always willing to be the first one in to deal with the dangerous chemicals before anyone else gets inside."

In Sadie's mind Egan was confusing suicidal tendencies with work enthusiasm.

"Throw him a bone and keep him busy so I'll have at least one guy on my team when I get back," Egan asked. "I planned on cutting back on the jobs, so maybe one guy is all I need. You did trauma clean on your own until you partnered with Zack Bowman. You got lucky with him. So to speak." He laughed.

Sadie cringed at his implication.

"Zack and I aren't a thing. He works for me."

"None of my business," Egan said.

"Get your ass back soon," she told him sincerely. "I can't continue to cover Scour Power's meth jobs and still give trauma clean the support it needs."

"I'm not saying you owe me, Sadie, but . . ."

But she did. He'd backed her last year when a client had accused her of being a thief.

"I haven't forgotten," Sadie said. "I can cover for you for a few more days."

"That's all I'm asking. I'll call you in a few," he said, and disconnected.

Sadie tossed her cell phone into her purse and concentrated on driving. After a couple weeks on the meth side, cleaning death scenes would be nirvana. Sure, methamphetamines were bigger business in Seattle than murders, suicides, and unattended deaths, and quite lucrative, but it wasn't as rewarding. Sadie felt more comfortable helping the dead go over to the next dimension while she made sure those left behind weren't traumatized any more by having to clean up the remains of their loved ones.

In the case of meth labs, those left behind didn't need sympathy. Nope. They wanted you dead.

3

When Sadie pulled the van up to a townhome complex, she ignored the curious gazes of neighbors out tending their small patches of grass frontage. She banked the van at the curb outside an end unit. Jackie spotted her through the window and came to greet Sadie at the door.

"Wow. You're blond," Sadie said by way of a greeting. Then because she realized her shock over the brunet-to-platinum dye job possibly made that remark sound rude, she added, "It looks nice."

"Thanks," Jackie said with a smile. "I just felt like a change. Zack said he almost didn't recognize me."

Sadie bit her tongue.

"I'll help you finish up," Sadie offered, nodding toward the townhome.

"I'm finished, but you can help load up the biohazard waste tubs." She looked past Sadie. "So, Zack didn't come with you?"

"No, he stayed at the other site. Too bad you're already finished here. We didn't accomplish anything at the other place. I was hoping to help you out a little." Sadie didn't bother to hide her disappointment.

"Nah, you were hoping to look over my shoulder." She put up a hand and smiled. "That's okay. First job on my own. I get it. Anyway, the good news is that I can help out with the cookers."

Jackie absently scratched her arm using her right

hand, which was completely missing the ring and baby fingers. Sadie was tempted for the umpteenth time to ask her employee how she lost the digits. However, since the disfigurement didn't affect Jackie's work, Sadie was uncomfortable asking the question and Jackie had never volunteered an explanation.

"Would you prefer I do the drop at the storage unit?" Jackie asked.

Sadie tore her gaze away from Jackie's fingers and just shook her head.

"No. We've been pulled off the meth job."

"Oh yeah? What happened?"

Sadie told her employee all about what had transpired regarding the baby in the shed and the body found in the field. She left out the ghost thing, since Jackie didn't know about her boss's unique ability.

"Holy crap! That's something," Jackie said, her eyes wide. "What kind of crazy takes a newborn and sticks it next to a gutted goat?"

"The kind of crazy that usually keeps us busy mopping blood," Sadie grumbled. "But instead the lunatic is costing me a job."

Inside the cramped town house, Sadie and Jackie worked together to load up the medical waste bins. When Jackie hefted the last red rubber bin, she said, "Go ahead and check."

"Check what?"

Jackie smirked. "You didn't come all this way just to tell me about the baby and goat thing. You could've told me over the phone. Go ahead and make sure I did a good job."

Sadie frowned. "It's not that I don't think you're capable."

"Yeah, I know. You're just a control freak," she laughed mirthlessly, and turned to leave.

Sadie did go into the master bath to check and was surprised to see an elderly man sitting naked in the bathtub. His wrists had deep gaping slits.

Sadie nodded a hello.

"You can see me?" he asked in a warbly old man's voice. "Ah, damn. It didn't work, did it?"

"You're dead, if that's what you mean."

"But how can you see me, then?" He frowned and looked confused. "And talk to me. That other gal, the one with the missing fingers—she just cleaned around me like I wasn't here. Kinda weird having a young blond chick like that seeing me in my birthday suit."

Sadie tunneled her fingers through her short-cropped highlights and shrugged.

"You're dead. I can see the dead. Although, truthfully, I can't see suicides, so I gotta ask, what really happened here? Who killed you?"

"Nobody!"

Sadie sat down on the lid of the toilet and faced him.

"You might as well fess up and tell me who you're protecting."

He shifted uneasily and Sadie kept her eyes respectfully on his face instead of his withered, naked body.

"If you can see me, how can I be dead?" he asked, neatly sidestepping her question.

"I just can," Sadie replied. "Ever since my brother died, I've been able to talk to the dead and help them find their way to the other side." She folded her arms across her chest. "You didn't kill yourself, did you?"

"Of course I did!" he shouted angrily. "You can't just waltz in here and accuse me of being a liar!"

"No harm, no foul, if you had help, you know," Sadie stated matter-of-factly. "But, like I said, I've never been able to see the spirits of suicide victims. Not even my own brother, even though I'd give my right arm for that. It might be because suicides already know how to get to the other side, or else they're just anxious to get there—they don't pause in the here and now."

"That's crazy talk," he muttered.

"You're talking to me and you're dead, so, yeah, it's crazy talk," Sadie replied with a half smile.

"I have an inoperable brain tumor. It's the size of an orange." He tapped the side of his head. "Damn thing's been slowly eating me alive."

"That must've been really difficult for you and your wife."

"You don't know the half of it. Last month Martha had to put me in diapers. Then she had to start feeding me. Some days my hand couldn't find my own damn mouth." He shook his head from side to side and then his tone grew wistful. "We had a good life together, you know? It wasn't all sunshine and roses, but we did all right. We agreed that when the time came, she'd let me choose how to go."

"So you asked Martha to help you end your suffering?"

He sighed.

"I was supposed to do it myself. We'd put aside enough of my pills to make it easy, but that damn son of mine found my stash and flushed it. He whined about how miracles happen and I should just hang on. As if this were all about him." He rolled his eyes. "He always was a selfish kid."

"So Martha had to slice your wrists for you? How did you manage to make it look like a suicide?" Sadie asked curiously. "Usually the first thing the cops check is whether the cuts have hesitation marks, whether they're left to right and all that."

"We watched enough crime shows to know what they'd be looking for. We're not stupid." His eyes challenged her to say otherwise. "I wrote the note. Then Martha climbed into the tub behind me. I wanted to do it myself. Leave Martha out of it. But my hands shook too much and then, well, I guess I turned chicken. She put her hand over mine. I fought her for a second—"

"You changed your mind, but Martha went ahead?" Sadie asked with an edge.

His eyes flashed angrily.

"She did what she had to do. Even sang 'Amazing

Grace' as I went out." His tone softened. "She's got the voice of an angel. You're not going to make trouble for Martha, are you? I only had another month in me, tops."

Sadie rubbed the back of her neck.

"My job is just to help you go on over. You can't stay here."

"I thought there'd be a light or something, but . . . nothing."

"Sometimes you get held back. I'm not sure why," Sadie said quietly. "Try to take a deep breath and close your eyes. You just have to want it. Let go of what's here."

"I'm worried about Martha. I never even showed her how to balance our checkbook."

"Maybe your worry is what's keeping you here. Do you want me to talk to your son about that? About making sure Martha's financial details are worked out."

"Yeah." He nodded. "That would be good."

Sadie watched him close his eyes. She could tell he was trying, but although his outer edges shimmered slightly, he didn't fade.

"Anyone in your family go before you?"

"My brother, Ted, died two years ago," he said. "His heart went."

"I bet Ted's waiting for you. Close your eyes again," she said softly. "Picture your brother in your mind. Listen to his voice. Feel his touch. His arms are embracing you and—"

She stopped short and watched his essence glimmer, then slowly dematerialize. Within seconds there was nothing to see but a well-scrubbed bathtub.

Sadie turned to leave and was startled to find Jackie standing in the hall eyeing her curiously.

"Talking to yourself again?"

"Guess so," Sadie replied. She nervously cleared her throat and nudged her way past her employee.

Wordlessly they locked up the house and loaded the remaining bins in the back of the van.

"I've noticed you do that a lot on the job," Jackie commented as she leaned nonchalantly against the side of the van.

"What?" Sadie asked, digging out her keys and pretending she had no idea what Jackie was talking about.

"Talk to yourself. Zack says it's nothing to be worried about. He says you're just a little eccentric and that it's no big deal. I'd be lying if I didn't say it freaked me out a little."

Eccentric! Sadie stiffened. It made her sound like an old lady who lived alone and talked to her cats.

"Everybody handles stress differently," Sadie said curtly, and her eyes cut to Jackie in a way that told her to just drop it.

Jackie nodded, but her brown eyes regarded Sadie warily. She looked like she was about to speak and thought better of it. Sadie wasn't about to have this conversation with Jackie right now. Hell, maybe not ever.

"Feel like working another job after this slice 'n' soak?" Sadie asked.

"Sure. Bring it on," Jackie said confidently. "I want as much work as you can throw my way."

Sadie reminded herself that this was exactly the kind of enthusiasm that made Jackie a valuable employee. The fact that Jackie flirted with Zack didn't make her a bad worker. It only made her female.

Just keep telling yourself that, she thought.

"We've got release to do a job in Kirkland. A dripper. Zack and I were going to work it alone in a few days, but since the meth job is out of our hands and you're done here, there's no reason why we can't all go," Sadie remarked.

"Awesome!"

Um. Not for the dead guy.

"I heard about that one. Biker dude shot, then bled out through the boards at their clubhouse before anyone noticed, right?" Jackie asked.

"Bikers?" Sadie asked.

"Yeah. Fierce Force. You must've heard of them."

"Sure. Seattle's Hells Angels wannabes. How do you know this Kirkland place was their clubhouse?"

"It was on the news," Jackie said. "Supposedly they held meetings there, but then started using it as a meth house."

"Meth and bikers. I guess it's not exactly a stretch," Sadie remarked. She snagged a pen from her pocket and scribbled out the Kirkland address. "You can take your time. Grab a coffee or a bite to eat. I'm going to drop off the med waste bins at storage first, then go back to the Kenmore house to pick up Zack."

"I could pick up Zack. I don't mind."

I just bet you don't.

"I'll do it," Sadie said. "The cops there may have more questions for me anyway and I'd rather get that over with."

That was true, but Sadie had no desire to run into the freaky ghost she saw there earlier.

She climbed into the van and drove. She retrieved her voice mail messages, noting two from her mother, both nagging about arranging a baby shower for her sister. She didn't feel like dealing with that. Instead, she cranked up the radio and sang along while she passed cars on the I-5. Snow Patrol was just singing the last lines of "How to Be Dead" when Sadie steered the van back onto the meth-lab scene, now turned into a murder scene.

Not a lot had changed at the property while she was gone. It was still a hub of activity. She climbed out of the vehicle, leaving behind the AC and stepping into a wall of heat.

"You'll be happy to know that Baby Doe is doing fine," Zack reported when he greeted her at the van. "He was a little dehydrated, but they say he'll leave the hospital in a day or two. If they can't find any living relatives, he'll go straight into the loving arms of a foster parent." He raised his eyebrows at her. "Smile. We did a good thing."

"I'm glad," Sadie said.

"Oh really? Tell your face that."

She looked beyond him toward the garden shed.

"What about the baby's mother?"

"She wasn't as lucky." Zack leaned in to whisper in her ear. "Like you said, she was wearing a blue sundress. Long black hair. Lots of blood. Word out here was she had an impromptu C-section."

Even though the topic was ugly, Zack's warm breath on her ear tickled and caused her to blush. He still wasn't wearing a shirt and being in this close proximity to his naked chest made Sadie's nerves ping. She joked to cover up.

"Guess having you hang around your ol' pals helps, huh? Look at all the information you picked up." Sadie smiled. "A couple years off the force hasn't hurt your connections." She heard movement behind her and turned. "What the hell?"

A television reporter and his camera crew had arrived on the scene and had a camera focused on Sadie and Zack from just a few feet away.

"Hey, back off," Zack snarled, his angry stride eating the ground until he was inches away from the reporter.

"Sadie, is it true you discovered a baby inside the body of a dead goat?" the young journalist shouted over Zack's shoulder.

"What part of *back off* don't you understand?" Zack asked heatedly.

"No comment, Scott," Sadie replied, waving an officer over by shouting, "Hey, we've got a couple of vultures who've crossed the line."

Scott Reed stepped closer and grinned wolfishly.

"A vulture? Now, that hurts."

Zack blocked Scott until a uniformed officer ordered the reporter and his crew back behind the police line.

"Creep," Zack said.

"He's just doing his job," Sadie said with a shrug.

"Yeah. Sure. Like the time he misquoted you, remember that? You came off sounding like a cold, unfeeling bitch about that teen suicide we worked a couple months ago."

Sadie's blood heated at the thought.

"Technically he didn't misquote me. I said every teen thinking about suicide should have to clean one. And I meant it. I just didn't know Reed and his crew were within earshot and had a camera lens zoomed in for a close-up."

Zack said something, but Sadie didn't hear. She was too focused on the shed behind him. Leaning against the outbuilding was the figure of the woman in the blood-soaked sundress. Her stance was casual, but if looks could kill . . .

"Let's go," Sadie said to Zack. "Jackie's meeting us over at the dripper scene in Kirkland."

"I got someone I want to talk to. I'll be right with you," Zack said, walking down the driveway and stopping to talk with a uniformed patrolman from the King County Sheriff's Department.

Abruptly she turned on her heel to go back to the van. When she reached the door, she glanced to the side and noted that mangled Fido was lying in the shade of the house. His head was on his paws and he looked depressed. Of course he was missing probably a third of his body, so he had every right to be an unhappy puppy. Sadie walked over and crouched down to his level.

"Wish I could help you, boy," Sadie said, her voice low. "My specialty is helping spirits walk to the light, but I don't know how to apply that to dogs."

He leaned in and licked Sadie's fingers. She shuddered and pulled them away. Then the dog got to his feet and turned to look in the direction of the shed, toward the womanly ghost. A growl started deep in his throat and turned to a snarling bark as Fido suddenly charged. The dog bolted across the field toward the shed, but the lady in the bloody sundress faded before he reached her.

"Dueling ghosts," Sadie muttered, leaning against the shade of the house. "This just keeps getting better."

"Hey, Novak, you all right?" Detective Carr's deep voice asked.

"I'm okay. Just needed a moment out of the sun."

"Yeah, nothing like working a scene like this in the heat."

The man stank of grime and sweat. It wasn't even noon and his antiperspirant had already given up.

"Why would someone cut a baby from a pregnant woman and put it in a shed with a dead goat?"

"Sadie, even if I knew, it's not like I could talk to you about it. You know that." He frowned over at a detective in the field who was calling him over. "No sense in you and Zack hanging out here. We know where to find you both if we need to."

"Okay, we're headed to that dripper scene in Kirkland next."

"The biker house, huh? Have fun," he said sarcastically as he turned and walked away back toward the shed.

Weird ghost lady still wasn't back. Sadie knew, though, that she wasn't gone for good. She'd be back and Sadie didn't want to be around to talk to her. She didn't feel at ease until they were in the van and driving toward Kirkland. She'd much rather deal with an old-fashioned scene of body decomposition than a freaky ghost with red eyes any day.

When they pulled up to the scene, Jackie was already parked in the driveway. She was sitting in her car blasting heavy metal so loud that her car vibrated.

"You'd think she'd go deaf," Sadie mumbled as she turned off her vehicle and pocketed the keys.

"I've heard you listen to U2 that loud," Zack countered.

"Not in a customer's driveway," Sadie replied. "Besides, U2's different. It has to be loud."

Zack chuckled and they climbed out of the van and walked toward Jackie's car. They watched a minute while Jackie played drums on her steering wheel. Her missing fingers didn't interfere with her drum solo.

"One of these days I'm going to ask her what happened to her hand," Sadie said.

"It's not a secret," Zack said. "I asked months ago. If you want to know, I'm sure she'll tell you."

"I guess since it doesn't interfere with her work, I'm not comfortable asking."

"Then I'll tell you. A few years ago she had a gambling problem. Owed debts to the wrong people. They pinched off a couple fingers with gardening shears to teach her a lesson."

"Holy crap!" Sadie gasped.

"She doesn't gamble anymore."

"Wow." Sadie shook her head. "That's what you'd call an extreme twelve-step program."

Jackie still hadn't noticed they were standing beside her car, so Sadie walked up to the driver's side and rapped loudly on the window. Jackie jumped and cursed before she turned off her vehicle and opened her door.

"We ready to go?"

"As long as your ears aren't still ringing," Sadie replied snarkily.

"I'm good." She smiled behind Sadie. "Hi, Zack," she added; batting her eyelashes.

Oh, give me a break, Sadie thought. She walked away before rolling her eyes.

There was a carport attached to the small Craftsman home and Sadie designated that area as their safe zone, where they would don and doff gear and store supplies. Together they unloaded the van and brought their equipment to the carport area. Since Sadie had already been inside to take pictures for the insurance company and her own records, she filled them in as they went.

"Basic body decomp. Big guy shot in the chest and left to rot in the kitchen."

"Place has had a few transformations," Zack said. "Seattle's reigning biker gang, Fierce Force, rented the house and used it as a meeting place for a couple months. Then they used it to make meth."

"So are we dealing with both a meth-clean and decomp scene?" Jackie asked.

Sadie shook her head.

"David Egan's company, Scour Power, got the call to clean up the meth lab. It was pronounced clean, but then a guy got shot here and was left to rot, so now it's our turn."

"The body was lying around in this heat?" Jackie let out a low whistle. "They probably had to pop his bloated body just to get him through the doorway. I've always been curious about guys who choose to get involved in bike gangs. Seems like such a loser thing to do."

Sadie was still thinking about Jackie losing a couple fingers for a gambling bet and figured Jackie knew a thing or two about being a loser. She cleared her throat roughly.

"Yeah, well, he was somebody's son and maybe somebody's brother," Sadie said more harshly than she intended. "Let's just get in and get the job done."

She didn't like to talk about the victims before a job. It made closing herself off emotionally a lot more difficult. Jackie, on the other hand, loved to chat and give opinions on the people who passed. It was one of the little things that bugged Sadie about her employee. She watched Jackie bend over in her short-shorts, exposing part of her perfect ass as she slipped her feet into her hazmat suit. That was another thing that bugged Sadie, but she wasn't quite ready to admit it.

Wordlessly the three suited up in the disposable Tyvek suits, goggles, shoe covers, cotton glove liners under their latex gloves, and full-face respirators with P100 cartridges because it was a body-decomp scene.

Sadie unlocked the house and was first to step inside. She shooed away the flurry of flies that greeted her, and looked around. Zack followed, but Jackie stayed outside the doorway and handed supplies from the safe zone into the house until they had everything they needed.

Even without the stench of decomp the house would never have made the cover of *House Beautiful*. Instead of the usual window coverings, all the windows were covered with tinfoil. However, the tacky choice in home decor provided them with a working area that was probably fifteen degrees cooler than the ninety degrees outside. Still, it wasn't long before Sadie, suited up to the gills, felt like her shoes were filled with sweat.

The medical examiner had ruled the cause of death a bullet to the heart. Sadie looked at the man's ghost and had a hard time believing he hadn't died of an ink overdose. The burly biker dude's arms and chest were completely covered in tattoos. He had a gaping hole where the bullet entered, but the rest was pure ink. In the center of his chest, buried in a forest of black, springy chest hair, was a large flaming *O* surrounding a double *F,* the emblem for the Fierce Force biker gang.

The ghost sat with his butt perched on the kitchen counter, wearing nothing but an ugly pair of puke green boxer shorts. Sadie would've loved to deal with him and send him on his way to the next dimension, but she couldn't approach him in front of Jackie. Instead, she tried to ignore the man as she worked at scrubbing his sloughed skin and liquefied remains off the faded linoleum.

When it was time for a break, Sadie and Zack were first to step outside and doff their gear.

Sadie quietly told Zack about the resident ghost.

"Ugly, huh?" Zack joked after hearing Sadie's description. He hadn't always accepted Sadie's talent as fact, but he'd come to the point where he couldn't deny her gift and had stopped looking at her like she was a total loon. At least most of the time.

"Ugly is right," Sadie whispered as she tossed her gear into the waste bin on top of Zack's. "He's covered in tats and is as hairy as a gorilla. The tattoo in the middle of his chest is the Fierce Force emblem you told me about before."

"The fiery *O* and two *F*s?"

"Yeah." She blew out a long breath. "I need a break. It's the heat. And I can't take the pressure of him staring at me inside that house with you two there and—" She stopped, frowned, and tilted her head as she stared at the back door of the house.

"Who the hell is she talking to?" Sadie demanded.

Before Zack could reply, Jackie opened the door, exiting the house to step into the carport where they waited outside. She had her cell phone pressed to her ear and was just finishing a call.

"Just a few bucks until payday," Jackie said into her cell phone.

She took one look at Sadie's lethal glare and came to an abrupt stop in the doorway.

"I'll call you back," she told the person on the phone, and clicked her phone off.

"What the hell do you think you're doing?" Sadie demanded. "You were on the phone!"

Jackie shifted uncomfortably from one foot to the other under Sadie's venomous glare.

Sadie pointed to Jackie's hand. "You just used your cell phone in a contaminated area."

Jackie looked down at her phone and then up at Sadie.

"It was just a friend and he—"

"I don't care if it was the pope." Sadie's voice rose in anger. She pointed to one of the forty-gallon medical waste bins at her feet. "Dump it."

"I'll clean it," Jackie said, her full lips pinching into a tight line.

"You handled that phone with your gloved hands. Your gloves that were just touching any number of blood-borne pathogens. The body fluids in that house could be swimming with every kind of disease there is:

HIV, hepatitis C, E. coli"—she ticked them off on her fingers—"not to mention salmonella, herpes, and tubercle bacillus and a hundred others. Any of those friggin' diseases could now be on that phone!"

"I said, I'll clean it."

"Your cell phone would never survive the kind of cleaning it would need and you know it. This is basic stuff. It's bio-recovery one-oh-one. Jeez, have you forgotten all of your blood-borne-pathogen training? We shouldn't need to have this conversation."

Jackie opened her mouth to speak, thought better of it, and two-pointed her phone into the red bin. Then she hurriedly stripped down out of the rest of her gear until she was standing in her cutoffs and tight T-shirt. She tossed her gear into the container with her phone.

"I'm starved. There's a McDonald's a couple blocks away. We can take my car," Jackie said, already walking away.

"Sounds good," Zack replied, but his eyes were on Sadie. "She screwed up. We've all done it."

"Really? You never did. I never did."

"But we could have." He slipped out of his hazmat suit to his jeans. Sadie had given him a company Scene-2-Clean T-shirt to wear, but it was too snug. You could count the ripples on his washboard abs. Sadie made a mental note to suggest he wear the company shirts every day.

"That was a junior mistake." Sadie realized she was nearly shouting and lowered her voice. "Go with her. Bring me back a burger," Sadie told him in a softer tone. "I'm going back in to deal with Gorilla Guy."

"A minute ago you wanted a break. Now you want to keep on working?"

"You'd rather I talk to the dead in front of Jackie? You and I both agreed that I should keep that little skill to myself so she doesn't walk out on Scene-2-Clean like every other employee in the last six years."

Not that those others left because of Sadie's ghost-whispering talents. They mostly couldn't handle mopping up the dead day after day. Few could.

Sadie took a calming breath and slipped out of her own gear down to an oversized T-shirt and nylon running shorts.

"Take her to McDonald's. Buy her a burger, then take her to the nearest store and buy her a new cell phone. Get her an upgraded phone and put it on your company credit card."

He smiled.

"You're a good boss."

"I guess we're all entitled to one screwup." Sadie looked pointedly at Zack. "This one is hers."

"I'm sure she gets that."

"A little reminder from you wouldn't hurt. She l-i-i-i-kes you," Sadie said in a childish singsong voice. "I bet she's hoping you'll ask her to the prom."

He rolled his eyes and looked embarrassed.

"See you after lunch."

Once Jackie's Prelude had pulled out of the driveway, Sadie made her way to the company van to get a bottle of water. She climbed into the back of the vehicle, reached into the cooler, and dug out the coldest one from the bottom to take with her. When she stepped out of the van, Sadie nearly walked right into a huge black man dressed in camouflage pants and a stained white T-shirt.

"Thuggy!" Sadie gasped. Her hand went to her throat, where she could feel the pounding of her pulse against her fingers. She blew out a breath. "Jesus, you scared the crap out of me."

"You never called me back," he said, stepping even closer so she'd have to face him. "You said you'd call when you had another job."

"Yeah, well, I don't need you on this site. How did you even know where to find me?"

"I helped Egan clean this place before as a meth lab, remember?" Sadie knew that for a big man who looked like he got his clothes out of the bottom of a Dumpster, he could be charming. He blinked at her with eyes that were surprisingly warm and friendly.

"Nice of Egan to tell you about the job, but did he also tell you that I don't work with drunks?" Sadie asked stiffly.

She stepped around the large man and could feel the anger radiate from him.

"I'm not drunk now. And I wasn't drunk then. I got into a scuffle and got a beer bottle smashed against me. Got attacked by a crank user on a job." He pointed to the side of his head. "Got the stitches to prove it. That's why I smelled like booze when I showed up on the job."

"I don't know. . . ."

"Talk to Zack. He'll vouch for me. The only mistake I made was showing up without changing my clothes."

"I've had enough mistakes today," Sadie snapped at him over her shoulder.

"Right. I heard about what happened at the other scene. It's all over the news. A goat, a baby, and some woman, huh?"

"Shit. It's on the news?" Sadie turned to face him.

He nodded. "Yup, they even showed your faces on a commercial for the six o'clock news."

"Whose faces?"

"Yours and Zack's. Oh, and I heard Scene-2-Clean mentioned on the radio on the way over when they were talking about the scene."

"Great. Just great." Sadie groaned.

"It's publicity. It can't be all bad." He smiled. "It's not like you can take up an ad in the *Times* saying, 'Need Uncle Joe's remains mopped up? Call Scene-2-Clean.' "

"True."

She walked over to the carport area and prepared to suit up. He looked ready to join her.

"Like I said, Thuggy, sober or not, I don't need you

on this job. Zack and Jackie are already working this one, since we got pulled off that scene this morning."

"I really need the work."

Sadie heard another voice and glanced over at the door leading from the carport into the kitchen. Gorilla Man was staring out the little window in the door, shouting at the top of his lungs, and waving his fists in the air.

"Crap," Sadie muttered.

"No, really, I need the work," Thuggy said sincerely. "Egan said you'd keep me on."

Thuggy couldn't hear the ghost freaking out, so he had no idea Sadie wasn't referring to him.

"Zack and Jackie have just gone for lunch. I don't need four people working this one scene," Sadie said, aware she was raising her voice above Gorilla Man's, but she couldn't seem to help herself.

"Okay, okay," Thuggy said, holding up his hands. "You don't have to get pissed."

Sadie blew out an exasperated breath.

"Fine. Call me tomorrow. I'll see if I can hook you up with something."

He looked at her strangely, nodded, and turned away.

By the time Sadie was suited back up, he was gone. She flung the door open into the kitchen and shouted loudly through her respirator.

"Shut up!"

Gorilla Man stopped in the middle of the temper tantrum he was having in the kitchen and he turned to face her.

"Are you talking to me?"

Sadie nodded.

"You can see me?"

"Yes. And hear you. No more yelling." Except she had to yell her reply so he could hear her through her respirator.

"But I thought I was . . ."

He looked down at the floor where his physical body

had lain for two weeks in the heat before the cops broke down the door. A younger officer was still being teased mercilessly about the number of times he'd thrown up in the bushes after just glancing inside from the doorway.

"Yes, you're dead," Sadie said. "I can talk to the dead."

One corner of his lip went up in a surly grin.

"Well, ain't this my lucky fucking day?"

"Right. Mine too. So, Mr. . . . ?"

"Snake." He nodded as his eyes looked her up and down. "Jake the Snake. It's kind of hard to hear you with that thing on your face."

"Sorry, Mr. Snake, but I can't take the respirator off. I've been hired to clean up what remains of your rotting corpse."

"You sure got the short end of the stick." He laughed. "What did you do wrong to get that job?"

"It's what I get paid to do. I run a trauma-cleaning company called Scene-2-Clean. The other thing I do, that's kind of a bonus for people like you, is that I can help you to move on. Somehow, your spirit has remained here in this place. As pleasant as your home is"—she gazed around at the tinfoiled windows, peeling paint, and faded cabinetry—"it's time for you to move on."

"Hey, this ain't my house. I was just visiting, so to speak. My buds, the FF, had valuables stashed here. I decided it would be helpful to have a little for myself, since I was planning on defecting. The FF don't take too kindly to one of their own jumping ship. Especially when they help themselves to some loot. But I had my reasons. Not that it mattered when I got caught. Boom! I was toast."

"Right."

He folded his arms across his chest and raised his eyebrows at Sadie.

"Damn. So I'm like a ghost or something?"

"Yeah." *A big, hairy, tattooed ghost.*

"So if I'm a ghost, how come you can see me?"

"I don't know the exact answer to that. After my brother ate his gun, I started doing bio-recovery work. I found out the dead could communicate with me."

"But nobody else can see me? Not even Thuggy?"

Sadie narrowed her eyes. "You know Thuggy?"

"I'm sure he's the bastard who ratted me out to the FF!" He slammed his fist on the counter, or tried to. He couldn't connect. "Hey, you know what? You *can* help me."

"That's what I've been trying to tell you."

"Not that ghost stuff. Look, do you really have to be dressed like a spaceman? You know they cleaned up all the meth shit here already, right? So you can lose the suit."

"Yeah, I know this isn't a meth lab anymore. I'm dressed like this because I'm a bio-recovery technician and, you know, the blood 'n' guts cleaning can be a bit . . . risky too."

"Huh. You think you're going to catch something from me?" He looked insulted.

"Forget that and let's focus on how I can help you," Sadie rushed on. She didn't want to be dealing with this freak when Zack and Jackie got back from their lunch. "I'll tell you exactly what to do so you can leave this dimension and go to your rest."

"Like hell!" he spit. "I'm not going anywhere. The FF is coming back here to get their shit and I'm going to haunt the hell out of them."

"But you know they won't be able to see you."

"Why not? I've seen all those scary movies. I'm going to be like the poltergeist from hell, man."

Oh brother.

"But you can do something for me anyway. I'm going to tell you where I've hidden all my stuff, and you're going to find my old lady and give it to her. Even if I'm not around to enjoy it, there's no reason why she can't have it for herself and our baby when he comes. And you should tell her it's time for our dog, Brutus, to get his shots next month. I don't want him to get sick."

Sadie felt a little dizzy as a sudden, potent realization hit her. This house was connected to the other scene. The one with the baby. The goat. The dog. And the dead lady with the red eyes.

"Your girlfriend was pregnant?"

He nodded, puffing out his beer belly with pride, as if it took more than his bodily fluid to create a child.

"She's big as a house. Going to give me a son any day now."

"Long dark hair to her waist? Dark green eyes?" Sadie asked, swallowing nervously.

He frowned. "You know Penny?"

"What's her last name?"

"Penny Torrez. Why?"

Because the cops would like the name of the woman given an impromptu C-section in a field behind a meth lab.

"And your dog, Brutus, is he a big old Rottweiler?"

"Yeah."

"And did Penny and Brutus hang around the meth cookery over in Kenmore?"

"Sometimes. I told her not to go inside the house. I didn't want her breathing in that shit with her being pregnant and all. She got together with a bunch of loony tunes and they had their weird meetings in the yard at night."

Sadie sighed.

"I've got some bad news, Snake." Sadie closed her eyes. "Penny's body was found in the field behind that house. She's dead."

"You're lying!" he roared.

"I wish I was."

A thunderous scream exploded from his lips, and in a rage, his hand formed a fist and he drove it at Sadie's face. His hand coursed straight through her, causing

Sadie to shrink with nausea from his touch. He wound up again.

"Stop that!" Sadie shouted. "Your son. Your baby. He was delivered just fine."

Snake stopped short of throwing another blow.

"My baby boy's okay?"

"He's beautiful." *Except that his little body was stuffed beside a dead goat and he may have his own miniature crystal meth addiction.* Sadie left all that out. "They'll give him a checkup and then I'm sure Child Protective Services will make sure he goes to a very good home."

A heart-wrenching sob broke from the large man's lips and he sank to his knees.

"We were going to be a family," he cried. "I told Penny we could make a fresh start. Maybe head down to California. I was getting outta the FF. Her away from those creepy Witigo nuts."

"Witi who?" Sadie asked.

"It doesn't matter." He covered his face with his hands and sobbed. "Nothing matters anymore. It's all gone to shit."

"But you can still be together," Sadie assured him. "Let go of this place. Go to be with Penny. She needs you."

He looked up at Sadie.

"How can I know that for sure?" he asked, narrowing his eyes. "You can't make that kind of promise. How do I even know she'll be in the same place that I'm going?"

It was a question Sadie had never been asked. She thought about Penny Torrez's red glowing eyes and looked at Snake with his freakish tattoos. Somehow she didn't think Saint Peter was standing at the golden gates waiting for either of them.

"I don't know," Sadie admitted. "But I do know you can't stay here."

"The hell I can't," he said defiantly. His essence was gone then, but his shape didn't shimmer. No shimmer meant he did not move on to the next dimension. He wasn't truly gone from this dimension. He was only invisible to Sadie.

Tired of dealing with Snake and grateful to be alone with blood, guts, and gore rather than biker-gorilla ghosts, Sadie got down to work. She was at the point where she knew she had to start taking out the floorboards in the kitchen when she heard Jackie outside the kitchen door.

Sadie got up and unlocked the door. Jackie was fully suited up again and ready to go back to work.

"I had to drop Zack back at the Kenmore scene. Detective Carr called his cell and asked for him," Jackie shouted through her respirator.

"How's he getting back here?" Sadie shouted back.

"Carr said he'd drop him." She nodded outside. "Your burger's in my car. By the way, thanks for the new phone." She paused. "Sorry I screwed up."

Sadie shrugged it off, then pointed to the cracked linoleum she'd been just about to lift. Jackie nodded, picked up a sharp tool similar to a crowbar. The house was built in the early 1950s and it didn't look like the faded yellow linoleum had ever been changed. All the cracks and curled corners of the old lino had allowed bodily fluids to seep beneath. The entire subfloor of the room would need to be removed wherever it was contaminated.

Jackie pointed to a baseboard. It was already loose and looked like it would come away easily. Sadie worked the tool into the crack between the trim and the wall, and the board popped off easily. Too easily. It was like it wasn't properly attached to begin with. Maybe David Egan's meth-clean company, Scour Power, had removed the board when cleaning the meth lab, but they should've done a better job than that.

Careful not to snag her gloves on the nails, Sadie lifted the baseboard free. Behind the eight-inch-wide piece of wood, the drywall had been oddly cut away. Sadie sat back on her haunches and stared at what looked like black plastic trash bags stashed inside the cavity where there should've been insulation.

Then she realized this entire part of the wall was newly painted.

"What the hell . . . ?" Sadie murmured.

Jackie came over to kneel beside her.

"Someone hid stuff in the wall," Jackie commented loudly. She nudged a plastic bundle with her foot. "Open one up," Jackie encouraged.

Sadie hesitated, then hooked a gloved finger into the plastic wrap and pulled it free. One tightly wrapped square package came away, but there were a whole lot more stashed there.

Jackie's eyes were bright, as if they'd just found buried treasure. Sadie felt another housecleaning job slipping out of her hands, convinced the walls were lined with drugs, not gold.

Jackie made ripping motions with her gloved hands. She wanted Sadie to tear into the packaging. It was the logical thing to do. Sadie's stomach was a knot of tension as she tore open the plastic.

When the bag split open, Sadie and Jackie simultaneously gasped in shock.

4

Jackie was whooping and hollering with excitement. Sadie rolled her eyes and began packing up their cleaning gear. Her employee helped, but the minute they'd brought the bins outside to the carport, Jackie tore off her respirator and laughed loudly.

"Oh my God, there's got to be thousands in there!" Jackie giggled. "Wow. I can't get over it!"

"I'll call it in," Sadie said with a dire tone after removing her own headgear.

"Oh. Yeah." Jackie nodded. "I guess this job'll be put on hold too, huh?"

"I wish we'd never opened up the walls until the rest was done," Sadie said, toeing the ground angrily. "And I wish I'd never opened the package and found that cash."

"But it's your job," Jackie insisted. "You're removing the boards due to contamination. Whatever was in the plastic could be contaminated too, so you needed to check." She grinned. "Besides, weren't you curious?"

"We don't get paid to be curious," Sadie snapped. "There are still supplies inside. While I make the call to the authorities, could you go back in and get the rest of the stuff?"

"Sure."

Sadie took a couple of bins and loaded them into the van. Then she took a seat behind the wheel and dug out her cell phone to call in their findings to the local law.

When she was off the phone, she watched Jackie bring a bin out of the house. She had almost completely removed her gear when she changed her mind and began donning it again before going back inside. She must've forgotten something.

I'll have to talk to her about double-checking before doffing her gear.

While Jackie was inside, a single motorcycle rider pulled up. He sat on his idling bike, staring at her. Sadie looked in the side mirrors of her van and watched him. Behind his matte black full-face helmet, Sadie couldn't see his face, but she felt his eyes on her. After a moment, he turned his bike around and took off in the direction he'd come.

A few minutes later, there was a sound in the distance. The unmistakable growing roar of a platoon of Harley-Davidsons headed their way. Sadie's throat clogged with fear. She saw Jackie had just made it outside with yet another bin. She picked up the container and walked with it toward the van. She looked unconcerned by the growing roar of the motorcycles until Sadie rolled down her window and screamed, "Run!"

Suddenly Jackie got it. She bolted the final few feet toward the van clumsily carrying the bin. Sadie helped her heave it into the back. The two jumped inside Sadie's vehicle. Just as they locked their doors, the hogs thundered up the driveway. Two cornered tightly around to the front of Sadie's van and a dozen surrounded them. She couldn't go anywhere. They were trapped unless she chose to back over some bikes and take out some tattooed thugs. Probably she wouldn't get far after that. She was pretty sure those who remained would take offense.

"What do we do? What do we do?" Jackie squealed.

"We lock our doors," Sadie said. Her voice was calm, but she was no longer perspiring just because of the heat.

To the left of the van was a black cherry Harley with

flame detailing on the tank. Astride the bike was a large, bearded man in faded leathers. Sadie watched as he swung his beefy legs off his bike and strode toward the van.

"Tell him we're just leaving," Jackie advised. "And tell him the cops are on the way because of the money."

"Yeah, I'll just tell this group of fine gentlemen that we uncovered one of their stashes of cash inside their old clubhouse and they're about to lose it all to the evidence room," Sadie whispered back sarcastically.

"On second thought, maybe we should be quiet about the money."

"You think?"

The beefy guy rapped his Neanderthal knuckles hard against the driver's-side window, and Sadie flinched.

"What the hell are you doing here?" the bearded biker dude shouted through Sadie's window.

"We were hired to do cleaning," Sadie shouted back. "But we're just leaving."

There was no way she was lowering her window, but the thin plate of glass gave her little comfort. She knew it wouldn't take these thugs long to break her windows and haul her and Jackie out for their own amusement. Swallowing the acrid taste of fear, Sadie slipped the gearshift into reverse but carefully kept her foot on the brake as she did, and she looked him in the face. Even though she felt she'd pee her pants from fear, Sadie's gaze never faltered. They stared each other down for a full minute. Then the ugly dude glanced around Sadie over to Jackie. His eyes scraped hotly over her body and he made a crude display of elaborately licking his lips before he returned his gaze to Sadie's.

"This here is Fierce Force property," he growled, and a fine spray of spittle hit her window. "This ain't a place for broads unless you wanna be *our* broads."

"Got it."

He tapped the window with a thick finger yellowed from nicotine.

"Don't come back."

With an abrupt nod of his head all the riders angled their bikes away from the property. Within seconds the roar of their bikes grew distant, but Sadie's hands still had a death grip on her steering wheel.

"Holy shit," Jackie breathed. "I thought we were dead meat."

Sadie could only nod. She didn't breathe steady again until the cops were on the property and Zack was with them.

"I leave you alone for an hour and you end up rolling in cash," Zack said, dragging his fingers through his hair. "And pissing off a platoon of career criminals."

"It was somethin'," Jackie laughed, leaning casually up against the hood of her car as if she hadn't just been shaking like a leaf along with Sadie. "We pop off the baseboard and there's all this plastic stuff. We opened one and it's money. Thousands. We can't believe it. Then the next thing you know, we're in the van surrounded by scary bikers, but Sadie here wasn't even fazed. It was cool."

"It was *not* cool," Sadie corrected, ticked off at Jackie's attempt to glamorize the situation. "Those bikers wanted to chew us up and spit us out. But first they would've had themselves a little gang rape party." Her voice caught. After a deep breath she focused on the business side. "Plus, this is the second job in one day that we've been pulled from. I'm losing money here."

"Guess you could've pocketed a few of those bundles from the wall and you would've been just fine," Jackie said. At Sadie's cutting look she quickly added, "Just kidding."

Jackie bent over to pick up her water bottle from where she'd put it on the ground. Sadie watched Zack as he watched Jackie. Her cutoffs rode up and revealed more of her firm, twenty-eight-year-old legs that disappeared into her frayed cut-offs. Sadie's thirty-six-year-old calves ached sadly in reply. It wasn't that she was out of shape. Sadie knew she could outpace Jackie on a long-distance run. She just didn't think Zack would consider another go-round in bed just because she beat Jackie in a marathon.

"Could you give us a minute?" Sadie asked Jackie.

"Sure. There are at least two cute cops around here who haven't taken my statement yet," Jackie said with a giggle. She sauntered away, adding an extra swing to her hips that made Sadie want to throw up.

Sadie turned to Zack. "The woman who was sliced open and left in the field, her name was Penny Torrez." Zack looked like he was daydreaming and Sadie had a feeling those thoughts were about Jackie. "Hello?!" She snapped her fingers in front of his face.

"Sorry," he said. "Got a lot on my mind."

"Tough. We've all got to work together. If you and Jackie would just roll up your hanging tongues and keep the drool off your chins for long enough to get the job done, I'd really appreciate it," Sadie spit.

"Excuse me?" He looked at her with a combination of amusement and anger on his face. "Huh. How about that? I swear your eyes are looking just a little green today."

She blushed from her head to her toes.

"As I was *trying* to say, the woman in the field—her name was Penny Torrez," Sadie said impatiently. "We need to find a way to let the cops know so they don't waste time searching for her identity."

"They already know. Her purse was found nearby. Doesn't look like any attempt was made to hide who she was, or else they didn't get a chance because we scared them off."

"Oh. Good."

"That's why Carr asked me to come back to the house in Kenmore. Torrez's rap sheet showed I was the arresting officer when she was picked up hooking."

"Wow. Small world."

"Yeah. Her name doesn't ring familiar to me, but she wasn't the only solicitation pickup I ever made."

There was a forced casualness to Zack's tone and Sadie got the feeling he was leading up to something.

"Is Carr worried about you cleaning the meth lab there, since you got a connection to Penny Torrez?" Sadie guessed.

"Not just that scene. He's considering getting me to back off all jobs linked to Fierce Force. That means this one too. Just in case."

"In case what?"

"My guess is the order came from higher up. Who knows what kind of case the feds are trying to put together against the leaders of the FF? They'll want to eliminate any possible conflict of interest that could blow their case."

"Conflict? What kind of conflict could there be when you aren't called in except by me to help clean up after all evidence is collected?" Sadie said, sounding annoyed.

"Look, Torrez was the old lady of an FF member. Her body was found outside an FF meth lab. Torrez had links to FF. I had links to Torrez." He shrugged. "It's not exactly brain surgery."

"Yeah, but it's stupid. If she was hooking, probably half of the force had links to her."

"Yeah, but half of the force wasn't encouraged to hand in their badge because of a drug problem," he said quietly.

"You became addicted to painkillers after taking a bullet for your partner," Sadie said indignantly. "That hardly makes you a meth addict. Besides, you're working for me now. I'm talking to Carr and telling him he can't treat one of my employees like this."

"Let it go."

"No, it's just not right and—"

"I said, let it go!" Zack shouted.

When she opened her mouth to speak, he stopped her.

"They need to protect the integrity of the case. I'm fine with it. As long as Egan is back handling his meth-lab cleanup company soon, this won't affect my working for you, right? So it's no big deal."

She nodded.

"Okay. Fine."

After a minute Zack relaxed.

"So Torrez's name—I take it a little bird told you."

"Actually, a big gorilla. I'm glad the cops know her name. I couldn't figure out how to explain that Torrez's dead, tattooed biker boyfriend gave me her name." Sadie looked over and watched the police coming and going from the house in full hazmat gear. "I should've gotten Jake the Snake to tell me about the money."

"Jake the Snake?"

"The guy we're mopping up at this location. Torrez's hunka hunka burning love."

"Right. Gorilla, tattooed biker dude."

"Yup. How much money do they figure was inside that wall anyway?"

"They won't know for sure until it's counted, but I remember seeing bundles of cash like that in evidence from a bank heist. If that wall is floor-to-ceiling with bundles of twenties, it could easily make a hundred grand."

Sadie let out a low whistle.

"We mop a lot of blood for that kind of cash and these guys make it selling crank to kids. Doesn't seem right. Snake said something about helping himself to some of the valuables."

"If he tried to make off with the FF's cash, that was probably what bought him a bullet in the chest."

"He wanted to start a new life with Torrez and the baby."

"Stealing from bikers gets you a death warrant and a life in hiding or on the run. Not exactly a riding-off-into-the-sunset ending."

"For a guy who handed in his badge, you've got a

big mouth," Detective Orr suddenly barked from behind them. Orr was a cynical cop who had a bulldog face and looked like he ate nails for breakfast without any sugar.

Sadie and Zack turned to face the detective.

"We can't talk about the money," Orr growled. "And neither should you." He looked specifically at Zack.

"It's not me you've got to worry about," Zack said, his voice deceptively casual, but Sadie noted the tightening of his jaw as he nodded to the street.

The Emerald Nine News van was just pulling up.

"Aw, shit on a stick," Orr grumbled, and headed off in the direction of the van, ordering some officers to accompany him.

"Let's call it a day," Sadie said, suddenly sick of the heat.

Just before Sadie dropped Zack off at his apartment in Bellevue, she remembered to tell him about her visit from Thuggy.

"He just showed up at the house out of the blue. Said he needs the work," Sadie explained.

"Use him," Zack replied, opening the passenger door.

"Are you sure?" Sadie frowned. "He showed up drunk at a scene."

"He got a beer dumped on him during a fight. He wasn't drunk."

"That's what Thuggy told me, but I thought he was feeding me a line."

"It's the truth. I did security with him for a short time before I came to work for you. He's a good guy. Use him."

With that last comment Zack closed the door, leaving Sadie shaking her head.

The rest of the drive home seemed to take forever. It was the dinner rush, but no cars near Seattle were rushing; they were doing the bumper-kissing-bumper crawl. By the time she pulled the company van into the garage attached to her house, Sadie was dreaming of an ice-cold vodka martini after a refreshing shower.

She stepped into her house through the garage entrance and stripped. The tiny hallway that was between the garage and the rest of her home had a shower stall next to her washer and dryer. She'd had it installed to prevent any part of her stinky career choice from entering the rest of her house. The clothes she wore went directly into the washing machine before Sadie jumped into the hot spray. She soaped, rinsed, and repeated every inch of her body to help wash away the grungy smell of Jake the Snake's decomposing corpse.

After scrubbing down, she snagged a clean towel from a nearby trunk, wrapped it tightly around her damp body, and opened the hall door. She quick-stepped into her bedroom.

And screamed.

"Jesus!" Sadie hissed, and stomped her foot in anger. "Dawn, you just about gave me a heart attack."

Sadie's sister grunted as she sat up in bed.

"Sorry, I came over to talk and decided to take a nap."

"Did you ever hear of calling first?"

"I left a message on your answering machine and your cell phone." Dawn yawned. "Besides, didn't you see my car parked a few houses down and notice that you didn't have to disarm your alarm system when you came in?"

Sadie frowned. No, she hadn't noticed. That wasn't good. She needed to be vigilant about that kind of thing. Last year getting in over her head in a murder-suicide cleanup had almost resulted in her own death.

"Whatever. That spare key I gave you was only to be used in case of emergencies. A nap isn't an emergency," Sadie snapped.

"I'm nearly nine months pregnant and Seattle's having a heat wave. Trust me. My need to nap comfortably *is* an emergency." Dawn swung her legs over the side of the bed and stretched like a cat. A cat with a pumpkin belly.

Sadie opened her drawers, pulled out clean clothes,

dropped the towel and dressed. When she turned, she regarded two large boxes in the corner.

"What are those?"

"We've been converting the spare room into a nursery. Those are the boxes I've been storing for you. Remember, I said I'd drop them off?"

"Oh. Brian's things."

"Yeah."

Sadie stared hard at the cardboard separating her from her dead brother's belongings and swallowed thickly.

"I know you've had a bad day," Dawn said softly. "Maybe I should just go."

"What do you know about my day?"

"Thanks to Emerald Nine News, all of Seattle knows about your day. I even recorded it for you."

"Oh, God." Sadie groaned.

"Your hair looked really cute on TV. I could tell right away that you touched up the highlights." She was walking out of the bedroom. "Let's watch it."

"Forget it."

"Really?" She sounded disappointed. "Mom and Dad have already called. Don't you want to know what they saw?" Her voice held a touch of amusement that made Sadie anxious.

"There's something you're not telling me," Sadie said, but Dawn only shrugged in reply. "Fine. Let's get this over with," Sadie relented.

They walked into the living room, where they were greeted by Hairy, Sadie's black-and-white pet bunny. Sadie scooped the rabbit onto her lap as she waited for her sister to rewind the tape. Dawn lowered herself carefully into the big armchair next to the sofa and hit play on the remote.

The scene opened to a close-up of reporter Scott Reed, using his most serious face. His wavy, sun-streaked hair was tousled by a light breeze, making him look like a model out on a fashion shoot, and his blue eyes glinted with star quality. He gestured to the house in Kenmore standing ominously behind him.

"A reliable source told us that the traumatic-incident cleanup crew from Scene-2-Clean were here decontaminating a clandestine meth lab when they made the shocking discovery." The camera cut away from twenty-something Scott Reed's chiseled features and zoomed in on the Scene-2-Clean company van. Beside the van Sadie stood offering Zack a broad smile of her own. The camera went for a close-up of the two of them and showed Zack as he leaned in to whisper in Sadie's ear. Sadie proceeded to toss back her hair in what appeared to be a flirtatious manner and giggled while gazing at Zack with a look of unadulterated adoration.

"Oh. My. God!" Sadie shrieked as she got to her feet. "Turn it off. I've seen enough."

"That was about all there was of you anyway. The cutesy reporter went on to talk about a baby found with a mutilated goat. Tell me that's not true." Dawn put her hand on her swollen belly.

"Never mind the barn animals. I looked like a love-struck teenager with Zack as my prom date!" Sadie cried. "I do *not* look like that. Please, tell me I don't look at Zack that way."

"Well . . ."

"Oh my God, just shoot me now!" Sadie screamed. She began to pace. "We were just joking around a little about him getting information and still having connections with the police. That's all it was. Really. Nothing more." She put a hand to her forehead and closed her eyes. "Christ, people are going to think we're cold and inconsiderate. It looks like we're joking at such a serious scene. Or worse, they might think we're lovers."

"You *did* sleep together."

"Once. It was a mistake."

"It was a mistake because you only did it once," Dawn pointed out. "Remember how things were before? He worked for you, but you could cut the sexual tension with a knife. Finally, the two of you came to your senses and gave in to what was obviously between you—"

"It was right after that freak nearly killed both me and Maeva at my place. It wasn't like we dated. I went to stay with Zack for a couple days because my place was trashed and—" Sadie stopped short. Memories of that time always made her think of Pam and thoughts of Pam always cut deep.

Sadie and Pam became quick friends when they worked together at the same grade school. Sadie had taught second grade and Pam was the special education teacher, but they'd been more than coworkers. Pam had been Sadie's shoulder to cry on when Brian died and a big supporter of Sadie's metaphysical talent. She'd been the kind of friend you could lean on, but she still gave Sadie a kick in the ass whenever she needed one.

Sadie was shaken from her memories of Pam by the fact that Dawn was still talking. She was saying something more about Zack.

"Look," Sadie said. "It was a bad time and Zack felt sorry for me. He slept with me out of pity and—"

"Pity. Right." She smiled.

"It *was* pity. Anyway. It happened only once and then Zack turned to ice and things got all weird between us for months. We're okay now. Finally." She reconsidered and admitted, "Well, sort of. But this!" Sadie waved her hands at the television just as the phone rang.

"Hello?" Sadie answered.

"I saw you on the six o'clock news," Maeva Morrison said over the line. "You didn't tell me you and Zack were back together."

"First of all, we were never *together,* so there's no way we could be *back* together. Secondly, channel nine caught us joking around at a scene and the reporter played up a sneaky angle. As a friend and a psychic, you'd think you'd be able to figure these things out yourself!"

"Okay, I get it. Calm down. You don't have to yell."

Sadie blew out a breath. "Sorry. It's been a long day."

"Yeah, and we should probably talk about that goat thing. I might know some stuff—"

"I don't want to talk about the goat. As a matter of fact, I'd be quite fine never hearing the word 'goat' ever again. Call me later. After I've had a couple of martinis."

"Better yet, how about I come over? You've got air-conditioning, right?"

Sadie rolled her eyes to the ceiling.

"I've got to go," she said, and disconnected.

Dawn was looking at her with a Cheshire cat grin on her face.

"Don't look all smug like you've got me figured out. I do not, I repeat, do *not* look at Zack that way," Sadie said vehemently. "That reporter just caught us at a weird moment and that's all."

"Uh-huh."

The phone rang again and Sadie recognized the number as belonging to their parents. Dawn reached for the receiver.

"Touch that phone and you can kiss any future napping here good-bye," Sadie warned.

"You'll have to talk to Mom eventually," Dawn said, and she yawned again. "You and I both know she expects you to throw me a surprise baby shower before I pop."

"What kind of surprise is it if you already know?"

"I promise to act surprised."

"How about we skip the shower, but I buy you an extranice gift?"

"No. I want a shower. Tacky decorations. Yummy food. The works." She got slowly to her feet. "I've got to pee. Again." She sighed and shuffled off down the hall.

"I've got to go. John's taking me out for Italian," Dawn said on her return. "I've had a craving for fettuccine Alfredo. Feel like coming along?"

"Thanks, but not tonight."

Sadie passed a couple hours first sharing a salad with Hairy and then going for a nice long jog. Her body ached on her return, but it was a good-to-be-alive soreness. She felt relaxed and settled down to watch mindless sitcoms. On a commercial break she'd just poured herself an icy martini when the doorbell rang. It was just after eight and Sadie assessed her guest through a peephole she'd had installed.

"I didn't think you were serious," Sadie said to Maeva when she opened the door.

"I never joke about air-conditioning when it's almost a hundred degrees in my kitchen." The woman with the sharp-angled features brushed back her black curls and stepped around Sadie to walk into the living room. She stopped, spread her arms wide, and sighed. "Bliss."

"Ya know, it's cooled off to about seventy-five outside. If you just opened a few windows at your place, it would be fine."

"Tried that, but there's no breeze and Terry's been working on new recipes for a wedding next month. Our oven's been on all day and all night. It's like a freakin' inferno."

"Oh, c'mon." Sadie rolled her eyes. "We both know that ever since you met Terry and he moved in, your life has been perfect."

"I'm not complaining," Maeva said, a smile playing on her lips. "But living with a caterer isn't all fancy desserts and gourmet meals." Maeva plunked herself down on Sadie's sofa and put her feet up on the coffee table. "Well, I guess it is that, but according to Terry, you can't use a microwave to bake. Practically everything he caters has to be cooked in a hot oven that's going almost twenty-four/seven." She bent and patted Hairy's head as he paused to wiggle his nose at her. "How's it hanging, Hairy? Be grateful your mom didn't find that goat alive or you'd have company."

"Ugh. Let's not talk about the goat," Sadie said, cringing in disgust.

"Yeah, except that's exactly why I'm here. To talk about the goat."

"I thought you were here for a martini and to suck up my AC."

"Those are just great bonuses." She glanced over at Sadie. "About that martini . . ."

Sadie went into the kitchen and returned with a fresh vodka martini for Maeva in a frosted glass. She handed Maeva her drink, then sat in the chair next to the sofa.

"Dawn was napping here when I got home. I think the heat's getting to her," Sadie remarked.

"The heat's getting to all of us, but Dawn must be really uncomfortable because she has a built-in furnace growing in her belly, making it worse for her. Speaking of her belly, when's the baby shower?"

"I kept hoping Dawn's friend Chloe would step up to the plate, but so far, she hasn't. She keeps using the excuse about how she just had a baby of her own a couple weeks ago, so she's not up to it."

"She's evil," Maeva said, smiling over her martini. "But Dawn's your sister. You should throw the shower."

"Yeah, so my mom tells me. Over. And over. But I'm busy as hell handling Scene-2-Clean and Scour Power. I have to schedule time to breathe. Besides, I'm not that good at this kind of stuff."

"It's not that big a deal. Just pick a day and I promise to help you with the details. It'll be great."

Sadie sipped her drink and eyed her friend from over her martini glass.

"You'll help? Really? We're talking a normal shower, right? No séances or trying to contact our ancestors from beyond the grave?"

"You know, some people actually *like* that kind of thing. That's why my business does so well."

"Only crazy people like that stuff."

"Madame Maeva's Psychic Café is not filled with crazy people."

Sadie looked at her pointedly.

"Well, not *only* crazy people." Maeva giggled. "Fine. If you insist, I'll help you with a normal boring shower. Nothing new age. I'll even get Terry to make the food. He can do cute little triangle sandwiches, appies, and canapés that will knock your mother's socks off."

"I've tasted Terry's cooking. If you're offering his services, you can consider it a deal." Sadie clapped her hands in delight. "I'll choose a day and let you know."

There was a moment of silence while they sipped their drinks.

"Now, about that goat . . ."

"Oh, God." Sadie blew out an exasperated breath. "It was a freakish thing done by some sort of a weirdo. The baby, thankfully, made it out alive and that's all that matters. Just drop it."

"I can't drop it. I've heard of this kind of thing before and so has Terry. We were at a seminar last summer—"

"A goat seminar?" Sadie said, wiggling her eyebrows.

"A paranormal workshop that also dealt with satanic cults and rituals." She shook her head from side to side. "This goat thing creeps me out."

"Is it barnyard animals in general or goats specifically that you have a problem with?"

"Not funny. The woman who gave the session on satanic cults told us about all kinds of crazy rituals by some wack jobs in her area."

"Which area?"

"She was from Dallas."

"We're not in Dallas."

"So what? Freaks can travel. It's not like Texas has the market cornered on goats. Anyway, she talked about a cult who performs rituals involving goats and babies."

Sadie put down her martini glass and gave Maeva her full attention.

"Goats and babies," Sadie parroted. Then she relented. "Okay. You've got my attention."

"Good. It was a type of baptism ritual welcoming new-borns into a life to be raised worshipping the dark forces."

"The babies . . ." Sadie swallowed thickly. "Did they die?"

"No. That's why there's been no media attention on this. She'd talked with people who'd left the cult and they described the ritual. The followers put the babies inside the body cavity of a goat only long enough for a few chants. Then maybe the Satanist sickos will have a round of blood to drink. After that, the baby is symbolically delivered from the goat and is said to be reborn from Satan."

"Ewww. That is the sickest and most revolting thing I've ever heard and as someone who mops up grossness for a living, that's saying a lot. Why the hell would they do something so stupid?"

"The followers believe the babies are given extra powers and that as they grow inside the cult, they'll share those powers with the group." She sipped her drink. "You know the goat has long been a symbol of Satan. If we're talking about the same kind of thing here, then you and Zack interrupted the ritual and took off with their prize."

Sadie closed her eyes against the vision of the woman with the evil eyes and whose ghostly touch was like liquid fire.

"She told me that she gave her son willingly."

"Who?" Maeva asked.

"The baby's mother. They found her body in the field and someone had cut the baby right out of her. Weird thing was, she seemed okay with the whole thing." Sadie looked at Maeva. "I figured she was either in shock or stoned out of her mind on meth."

"But she was dead?"

"Yeah and there was something major wrong with her."

"Well, yeah, if she was perfectly okay with someone

killing her to take her baby and stuff him next to a dead goat, she's got something missing up here." Maeva tapped her head.

"There's something else. Her eyes." Sadie shook her head slowly. "They turned really red."

"You're sensitive to evil just like most of our kind. Her eyes appeared red to you because your senses told you her soul was lost."

"What do you mean, lost?"

"It means you won't be able to help her go over. She's committed herself to evil. The people you've helped go over have gone toward light. She walks in darkness."

Sadie shuddered.

"She was blocking the entrance to the shed. I had to get out of there, so I picked up the baby and just walked straight through her."

"And when you touched her?" Maeva asked, focusing intently on Sadie.

"It was like being burned alive. I thought my skin was on fire. Zack pulled me out and if he hadn't . . ." Sadie's stomach roiled with nausea. "I don't know what would've happened if he wasn't there. He said it looked like I was having a seizure."

Maeva's face grew deadly serious.

"Listen to me." Maeva leaned forward. "This is scary shit. Don't get mixed up in it. Dark forces can drain you of your energy. Or worse."

Sadie put her hands in the air. "You don't have to tell me to stay away. I'm done with that place. Besides, the cops have taken over the scene now."

"That's good. Real good." Maeva sat back. "Only thing is, whoever was running that show, well, he considers that baby his own. You stole from him. There's a good chance he's mighty pissed at you."

"Stop trying to scare me."

"Fear can make you careful. You need to be very, very careful."

5

After her martini, Maeva stayed long enough to watch a *Law & Order* rerun and have a cup of decaf. Once her psychic friend was gone, Sadie went to her bedroom. She took one look at the boxes Dawn had dropped off, and decided she wasn't tired.

Crossing the hall to her den, Sadie powered up her computer and was halfway through a game of FreeCell when her office line rang. It was late, but death didn't have a time line.

"Scene-2-Clean," Sadie answered.

"Hi, Sadie, did you catch your beautiful face on Emerald Nine's *News at Six*?" Scott Reed's charismatic voice smoothed into her ear.

"Ass," Sadie snarled, and promptly hung up.

When the phone rang again seconds later, she let it go to the machine and soon heard Scott's terminally charming tone over the speaker.

"Hey, don't know what's got your panties in a knot, Sadie Sweets, but that on-the-scene coverage was pure aces. Not a bad word about you, and your company got great on-air buzz. Oh, and I thought the natural sunlight made the highlights in your hair look great." He paused. "Guess you don't want to hear my news about the baby you and Zack rescued, then. . . ."

Sadie snatched up the phone.

"What about the baby?"

"He's doing fine. Not a goat hair on his tiny little body." Without a pause he went on. "I heard about your other job today. What's up with that?"

"So you've got nothing new on the baby. You just tricked me into picking up." Sadie rolled her eyes and wished she'd never answered.

"I know the kid would've died of dehydration if you hadn't rescued him. Who knows how long a newborn can survive in this kind of heat? Now, about that Kirkland area job . . ."

"I've gotta go."

"Oh, c'mon, Sweets," he pleaded.

"It's Sadie, not Sweets," Sadie corrected. "I don't hear you calling Zack any sexist nicknames."

"He doesn't have your fine, um, attributes." He chuckled lightly. "I don't get it. Why won't you give me your spin on the biker house? You know damn well I've got other sources I can use for this info."

"Then use those sources, Scott. I don't talk to the media about my jobs. Ever. You know that."

"Then you leave me no choice but to do my own thing and point out the obvious."

A feeling of dread filled Sadie's gut.

"What's the obvious?"

"That Scene-2-Clean caught two high-profile jobs in one day. Both connected to Fierce Force. I'll let Jane and Joe America put two and two together and see if they come up with a conspiracy."

"Give me a break! Someone's got to clean up after Seattle's drug trade and I'm helping out Scour Power with some of the jobs they'd normally take on. Nobody's going to be stupid enough to think it's a big deal that Scene-2-Clean worked two Fierce Force cleanups, since everyone knows the gang has their fat fingers deep into the local drug trade. They probably have a dozen meth houses operating in and around Seattle. Besides, we've worked meth cleanups totally unrelated to FF."

"Ah, you're too smart for me." He laughed. "Still,

maybe the average Joe Six-Pack would be interested in another little tidbit."

When she said nothing, he continued.

"If I were the public, I know that I'd be curious about a company that cleans up crime and why certain people chose that line of work."

"Whatever," Sadie said coolly, but worry grew acidic roots in her belly. "It's no secret why I got into the biz."

"It would make a great human-interest story, but I'm not talking about you. I'm not so low I'd use your dead brother against you, Sadie." His voice grew soft. "You know, Sweets, if any other reporter caught wind of the little bit of spicy info I've got, they'd be quick to crank it out. I've known about Scene-2-Clean's dirty little secret and I've kept it quiet for months."

"You've kept nothing quiet about Scene-2-Clean, because there is no dirt," Sadie said, exasperated. "I run a reputable and ethical company. Everything's aboveboard."

"Hey, I don't mind keeping my mouth shut. I want you to stay in business a long time, Sweets. You look awfully sexy in a hazmat suit."

Sadie closed her eyes and sighed wearily.

"C'mon, Sadie, there's no harm in giving me a little something I can run with. You wouldn't be telling me anything that I won't find out tomorrow afternoon when the police hold their news conference."

"Then you don't need me."

"Hey, this biz is all about getting there first. Emerald Nine is number two in the six o'clock slot and we're hungry for number one." He paused. "Just tell me this, how much cash did they find inside the walls?"

"If there *was* anything found and police want to make it public, it'll come from them. Not me," Sadie stated evenly.

"You're not being fair. I need an edge. It would be a helluva shame if I had to go on air with an unflattering sidebar about Scene-2-Clean instead of real meat about a house still smelling of decomp that has walls lined with a ton of cash."

"It sounds a lot like you're blackmailing me, Scott."

"That's such an ugly word."

"Stop dancing around and tell me what you're talking about."

"Fine. Meet me for coffee so we can discuss things."

Scott Reed was tenacious as hell. Sadie suspected if she blew him off, he'd run some kind of mudslinging comment about her company. She decided not to take the chance.

"Fine. I'll meet you. Where and when?"

He gave her the address of a small coffee shop in Bellevue and half an hour later Sadie was parking her Honda Accord in the lot. Once inside, Sadie got a decaf latte because she was already on edge. When Scott showed up, he had a Mariners cap pulled down low over his eyes and was wearing faded jeans and a dark jacket. Nobody would've easily mistaken him for his flashy television persona.

He got himself a coffee and joined her at the corner table.

"Talk," Sadie said.

"Nice to see you too." He offered her a quick flash of his television smile. "How about some pleasantries like the weather? It's sure been hot. How many records do you think Seattle's broken with this heat wave?"

When Sadie only scowled, he leaned in and added in a throaty whisper, "Anybody ever tell you that you're sexy as hell when you're pissed off?"

Sadie frowned to cover her blush.

"You didn't ask me here to flatter me." She lowered her head to catch his gaze. "Or to stare at my boobs."

"No, but I take my perks where I can." He winked. After he sipped his coffee, he lowered his voice again to a near whisper. "Okay, we'll cut to the chase. I know the cops found cash inside the house today. I want to know how much."

"I don't know. The cops don't call me up and tell me stuff like that. I get called to clean up the mess. They don't call me with their press releases."

Scott shook his head. "I don't buy it. You've got connections." He sat back and grinned. "I'm sure all of Seattle would like to know why one of your employees isn't allowed to work Fierce Force cleanup scenes."

"What are you trying to say, Scott?" Sadie asked, fighting to keep her voice even.

"I'm talking about the one and only Zack Bowman." He sat back and wiggled his eyebrows at her.

"What about him?"

"C'mon, I'm sure it wouldn't be good for Scene-2-Clean if word leaked out that the reason Zack's no longer arresting whores for SPD is because he was fired for a Vicodin addiction."

Sadie could feel her control crumbling and her temper rising.

"That's a lie. Zack was never fired."

"Encouraged to quit. Fired. Do you really think Larry Lazy and Carole Couch Potato will make a distinction when they're stuffing potato chips into their face in front of the television?"

"Screw you."

"That's a pleasant thought. I'd love for you to give me one of the sexy smiles you only reserve for Bowman."

"First of all, stop with the ridiculous flirting. I'm probably ten years older than you and I'm not stupid. I will not be conned or blackmailed."

"First." He held up one finger. "You're only about five years older and I'm dead serious when I say your body just rocks my world." He held up a second finger. "Second, I'm not conning or blackmailing you. I'm giving you the opportunity to help me out and avoid some bad press for yourself." He reached across with the two fingers and lifted her chin. "Seriously."

She whipped her head away from his touch.

"Really? It sounds like you're prepared to go all tabloid on this and if that's the case, I don't think there's anything I can do about it." Her voice was tight with anger. She took a deep drink from her coffee. "You know, Scott, I always hoped you were above that kind of snake-in-the-grass reporting."

"I am," he said hastily. "And blowing Zack out of the water isn't the angle I want to go with. But I'm in a dog-eat-dog business here, Sweets."

Sadie thought about Zack's life being crushed by a few comments on the six o'clock news.

"Don't do it," she whispered with a catch in her throat.

He finished his coffee without meeting her gaze.

"I guess I really don't need you to tell me how much cash they found. I got sources in the police department to tell me that."

"Thank you," Sadie said, breathing a sigh of relief.

"But I'm working on something else you might be able to help with."

The way he leaned forward and his eyes gleamed with excitement, Sadie had a feeling she was about to find out what he really wanted.

"I'm working on an investigative series to expose Washington State's satanic cults."

Sadie choked on a mouthful of her latte and coughed for a full minute while Scott nodded appreciatively.

"Yup. That's exactly the kind of reaction I'm hoping for. I want all of Seattle choking in surprise."

"Surprise or disbelief?" Sadie cleared her throat and then smiled over her cup. "Your plan is to make Seattle-ites paranoid and suspicious that their neighbors are worshipping the devil?"

"Exposing Seattle's seedy underbelly is my kind of thing. Remember my series last year on school gangs?"

"I try not to watch or listen to the news too much. I get enough reality at work."

"Gotcha. But the rest of Seattle sure tuned in and our ratings were huge. This next segment I'm working on now is going to be even bigger. I could be in line for an Edward R. Murrow Award with this." His eyes were alive with ambition.

He'd eased back in his chair. Talking about his work brought a hardness to his face. He was only around five feet nine but had a thickly muscled build that filled the chair. Some of the movie-star look to him didn't translate off camera. His looks had a harsher edge without a camera lens to frame him.

"Well, I wish you much success with your witch hunt," Sadie joked. Anxious to get back home, she pushed. "Seriously, I see no way I can help with this."

"You should get informed, Sadie. For your own good," Scott said. "Witigo Alliance is gonna be huge in this city. They'll use the FF to get there."

"The Wit what?" Sadie asked, realizing she'd heard the name already from Jake the Snake.

"The Witigo Alliance." He put his hands on the table and leaned in. "They worship the power of darkness and I'm pretty sure they're recruiting the bikers for their power and muscle."

Sadie looked over one shoulder and then the other.

"Am I on some kind of prank show? Are you going to have a guy wearing devil horns pop up and scare the crap out of me?" But even as she joked, she recalled Penny Torrez and her bloodred eyes and heard Maeva's warnings. In spite of the heat, she felt chilled.

"I don't need you to believe, Sweets, although it would be nice. I just need you to help me get some more documentation to prove the connection between Satanism and bikers."

"What makes you think there *is* a connection?"

"My gut." He pointed to his flat, hard stomach.

"How could I possibly help you hook up with bikers and a satanic cult?"

"That is the million-dollar question." He slammed his palm on the table and made her jump.

"In another words you don't have a clue."

"Oh, I've got clues all right." He took an envelope from the back pocket of his jeans and pulled a photo from it.

He slid the picture across the table. Sadie glanced at it and paled. The image was grainy and slightly blurred, but there was no denying it was a goat, its carcass cut from neck to groin. It appeared to be on some kind of altar surrounded by candles.

"Hmm. Looks like a Seattle meat shop is messing with your head," Sadie said, offering him a crooked smile.

"Nope. I got the picture from someone on the inside of Witigo's Oregon chapter. Besides, I don't know many butchers who surround their product with black votive candles."

Okay, you've got me there.

"This is what you saw inside that shed." He watched her closely. "The goat was surrounded by candles and the baby was stuffed inside the goat, right?"

Obviously he'd gone to the same weird seminars as Maeva and her boyfriend.

Sadie forced a laugh. "A baby *inside* a goat? What kind of sick horror movies do you see in your spare time?" She lowered her tone. "Look, I'll confirm what you've already heard and what was already made public, thanks to Emerald Nine. Yes, there was a goat, and yes, there was a baby. If you go on air telling people the baby was *inside* the goat, you're going to make a fool of yourself."

He shrugged. "It doesn't matter. My sources already confirmed a ritual was performed there. The thing is, they keep moving locations. They don't want to get caught."

Sadie kept her face impassive and Scott was quiet a moment but was obviously thinking hard about the matter.

"This time, though, they were almost caught. You interrupted them." He waved a finger in her face. "That can't be good for you."

Then Scott flipped his wavy hair and switched topics hard and fast.

"The Kirkland house," he said. "The guy shot there. His name was on my list of Witigo associates."

"Jake the Snake," Sadie murmured before stopping herself.

"Right." He pointed his finger at her again and Sadie swatted it away. "You do your homework. Impressive. Anyway, word on the street said Snake was not so into it, but his girlfriend was."

Sadie felt his eyes on her as she struggled to keep her face impassive. She sipped her coffee quietly, waiting for him to continue.

"So what do you think of that?"

"Of what?" Sadie asked.

"That Torrez was a Satanist and now she's dead."

Sadie said nothing.

"You're playing it cool. Okay. Well, how cool can you keep it now that a shitload of bikers are pissed off at you for locking up their cash in an evidence locker?"

Sadie swallowed thickly at the thought of all the bikers who'd barricaded her and Jackie in the driveway of the Kirkland home.

"Look, Scott . . . bikers, Satanists . . . this all sounds like a bad B movie and I don't have time to—"

"The cops raided another FF meth lab. This one's in Bellevue. My connections told me that there was a satanic ritual held in that house just before it was shut down."

"So?"

"I want in. When you get the call to clean the place, I want to do the initial walk-through with you."

"Forget it."

"You always go through a place on your own first to take some pictures for your records and all that."

Sadie felt uneasy that he knew her work habits so well.

"So it'll be no big deal," he continued. "I'll come inside with you. I won't interfere with your actual clean and I'll wear a hazmat monkey suit too, so nobody will even recognize me."

"No."

"All I want is evidence that Witigo was there."

"What part of *no* don't you understand?" Sadie got to her feet.

"Fine." Scott sighed. He followed Sadie as she walked to the door. "Well, I need something to run with." He held the door to the coffee shop open and Sadie stepped outside. As she passed, he whispered to her back, "Guess my story will have to be an ex-cop's drug addiction that forced him to mop blood and meth labs for a living."

Sadie gave him a seething, furious look.

"Hey, I'm just doing my job."

"Go to hell," she snarled, and stomped across the lot to her car.

He walked just as quickly behind her.

"Who would you rather protect? Fierce Force, a biker gang that cooks meth and sells it to little kids; Witigo, the Satanists that stuff babies into dead animals; or your very own employee and lover?"

She whirled around to face him, glaring with murderous intent.

"Me!" she shouted, stabbing a finger at her chest. "My business and its integrity! That's what I'm protecting."

"Sure. I get that. But what about Zack?"

Sadie thought of the anguish and grief the publicity would cause Zack, and her heart thudded painfully. She closed her eyes and debated what to do.

"What if I don't get the call to clean that meth lab?" Sadie asked. "I'm only helping out Scour Power until Egan returns."

He shrugged. "If you don't get the call, you're off the hook. Then I'd just have to try and convince Egan."

Relief washed over her. The cops could be working that lab for evidence for another few days and Egan would surely be back by then.

"And you'll forget your attack on Zack if I'm not the one to get you inside?" Sadie asked.

"You have my word."

Sadie didn't think that meant a lot, but she conceded.

"Fine. If I get the call to clean that lab, you can do the initial walk-through with me, but under one condition."

"Name it."

"You'd have to agree not to touch or take anything that's inside the house." Not that she expected he'd make it inside that house. At least not with her.

"Absolutely."

She nodded stiffly and turned to walk the final couple of steps to her car. Pressing the button on her key chain, she unlocked the door. She didn't realize Scott was still behind her until he spoke.

"By the way, thanks for coming out for coffee with me," he said. "It may have been a short date, but it sure was sweet."

Sadie turned around, surprised to find him so close.

"Scott, you're crazy." She laughed in spite of herself. "This was so *not* a date."

"Sure it was. The two of us gazing into each other's eyes in a cozy little coffee shop late at night." He smiled warmly and took a step closer.

Sadie stepped back and found herself against her car. She planted her hands on her hips and glared.

"You coerced me into meeting with you and then threatened to hurt my employee and my business to get what you wanted. What part of that could possibly be considered a date?"

"This part."

Scott put his hands on her shoulders, leaned in, and brushed his lips lightly against hers. Sadie lifted her hands up quickly to push him away, but her fingers seemed to get lost along the way. She was surprised by the feathery gentleness of his lips on hers. The kiss deepened and grew hotter. As he drew her closer against him, Sadie was appalled to find that she was kissing him back. It was like her lips had a mind of their own. Just as the embrace loosened, Sadie pushed Scott so hard he stumbled.

"It was *not* a date," she said emphatically, but her voice cracked when she got the words out.

Scott chuckled softly and offered her a wave as he walked toward his own car, a sporty black Solstice convertible.

"What's wrong with me?" Sadie asked herself as she started up her car. "I can't believe I actually kissed him back."

She pulled out of the parking lot and gunned the accelerator. She barely remembered the drive back home, but when she turned the corner onto her street, she got a blast of cold reality. At least a dozen Harleys were idling loudly in her driveway.

6

"Are they still there?" Zack asked her over the phone.

"I don't know. The second I saw all those bikers, I made a U-turn and took off like a bat out of hell," Sadie admitted. She'd called him up babbling hysterically at first but had finally managed to relay the problem.

"Where are you now?"

"Parked behind a 7-Eleven two blocks away." She unwrapped a 3 Musketeers bar and took a bite.

"Let me guess, you panicked and headed for the nearest chocolate bar."

She could hear the laughter in his voice.

"It's probably the kind of logic only a terrified woman understands," Sadie said around a second bite of chocolate. "So are you going to come and rescue me or what?"

"By 'rescue,' do you mean stand up to a dozen angry biker dudes?"

She thought about it.

"Guess that's asking a bit much," she admitted. "How about if you just drive by and see if they're still there and call me if the coast is clear?"

"And if they are still there?"

"Then call the cops."

He sighed, then relented.

"Give me half an hour."

By the time Zack called her back, she'd made her way

through an Almond Joy and a bag of salt and vinegar Lay's, and was almost done sipping a Big Gulp.

"Not a biker in sight," he announced when he called her back.

"I'll be there in five minutes," she said, turning the key in her ignition. "Don't leave."

Sadie relaxed considerably when she turned the corner and spotted Zack's Mustang parked in her driveway instead of a bunch of long-haired thugs with attitude. She parked in the garage and then invited him in for a drink. After a brief hesitation he accepted. Once inside, Zack went through her place and made sure there weren't any bikers hiding in any of her closets or underneath her bed.

"All clear," he announced, walking into the living room.

"Thanks." Exhaling with relief, she handed him a cold beer.

"Now, about what you said over the phone," he began.

"You mean when you answered and I started screaming hysterically that Fierce Force was waiting in my driveway to kill me?" She smiled wryly as she sank into a chair.

"No, the part when you said that you figured Fierce Force was out for revenge because you turned in the money." Zack took the sofa and propped his feet up on the coffee table.

"It's true, isn't it?"

"I don't like the fact that they know where you live, but if they were really interested in making you afraid, they probably would've done more than just idle in your driveway."

Sadie chewed her lower lip. "I don't want to find bikers hanging out in front of my house. My neighbors will kill me. Already I'm not invited to any good parties."

"I've got a friend working the gang task force. I'll see if he can put the word on the street that you had nothing to do with it. Maybe he can spread a rumor that the cops got an anonymous tip about the money and were on their way already when you called."

"Think that'll work? Scott Reed said they're going to be hugely ticked off that all their cash will now be sitting in an evidence locker." She regretted the words the second they left her mouth.

"And when did you talk to Reed?" She could tell by the slight twitching in his jawline that Zack was clenching his teeth.

"I met him for coffee tonight. He made me think he had news about that poor baby. Really, he's just working on a news exposé about a satanic link to Fierce Force."

He paused with his beer halfway to his mouth.

"Satanic shit, huh? Hmm." He took a long pull from the bottle. He seemed to be turning the idea over in his mind.

Sadie didn't want to tell Zack about Scott's threat to expose his past. If he knew, Zack could fly off the handle and confront the reporter and that would only make matters worse.

"You know what I think?" Zack began, looking at her intently. "I think Reed asked you for coffee 'cause the guy has a thing for you and used the satanic stuff as an excuse. I bet he even asked you out, didn't he?"

"No. Not really."

"Not really?" He scooped up Hairy from the floor and petted him for a minute, covering himself with rabbit fur.

"He said my meeting him for coffee was considered a date." She could feel a blush creeping up her collar and laughed to cover it up.

"He's crazy. If meeting for coffee is a date, then one half of Seattle is dating the other half."

Zack put Hairy down and got to his feet. Sadie walked him to the door, thanking him along the way for coming to her rescue so quickly. Just before he left, he hesitated s if there was something pressing he had to say. Sadie looked up at him and waited. He leaned slightly forward and for a split second Sadie thought he was going to kiss her.

"Have a good night," he said roughly, and then left hurriedly, closing the door harder than necessary behind him.

Sadie dumped their beer bottles in the recycling bin on the back deck and then fed Hairy some alfalfa pellets and half a carrot. She was putting the bag of rabbit food back in the cupboard when she noticed the light was blinking on her answering machine. The call must've come in when she was out for coffee with Scott. Sadie pressed play and her mother's accusing voice filled the room.

"Since you don't seem to return my calls these days, I'm forced to do this over the machine." She was quiet a second in case Sadie would suddenly pick up, then sighed deeply and continued with her message. "Your aunt Lynn will be in town this weekend. I thought it would be nice to have Dawn's baby shower while she's staying with us, so I've decided to make the arrangements. It's going to be here at my house two o'clock Saturday. Chloe said the time works for her and she already called and invited all Dawn's friends. Since I've taken care of place and invitations, I expect you to take care of the food. And, Sadie, it had better be *good* food." There was a pause before she added, "Your father tells me you were on the news, but I didn't get to see it. Some kind of horrible business involving a goat and a baby?" She made *tsk*ing noises. "Let me know if you've decided to make a career change. I hear they're hiring at Safeway."

"Oh, double damn," Sadie grumbled.

For her mother to leave a message this late at night, she must be getting desperate. Sadie picked up the phone and dialed Maeva. It was after midnight, but Maeva and Terry were usually still up. Still, she only got her friend's voice mail.

"Look, my mom just told me the baby shower's to be Saturday. This Saturday. If Terry can't do the food on that short notice, I need to know right away because my mom will freak if I don't bring good food." Sadie paused. "Also, Scott Reed kissed me tonight and there were a dozen scary bikers in my driveway, but Zack took care of that. I guess that's all that's new in my life for this second."

She hung up and found Hairy had hopped over and was looking up at her curiously.

"I had to tell somebody about the kiss or I'd explode," she explained to the rabbit. She thought his look was judgmental, but he was probably just hoping for yogurt treats.

Sadie walked to her bedroom and stared hard at the boxes Dawn brought over, but didn't touch them. She went back to her computer and typed in "Witigo Alliance." Thousands of results came up. All the ones she found described basically the same thing. WA got their name from an Algonquian legend about windigo, also known as witigo, a creature so cannibalistic it had no lips because it ate them. When Sadie was done laughing, she checked around the net a bit more and discovered that some described the Witigo Alliance as a secret society, some called it a cult, and others referred to it as a club. Only a couple sites mentioned goat rituals and both of those contained links about paranormal workshops discussing those rituals.

Sadie gave up on the research and went back to her bedroom. She was just slipping out of her clothes and pulling an oversized T over her head when the phone rang.

"I feel like I'm the last to know! Since when are you dating that sexy reporter?" Maeva blurted in her ear.

"It wasn't a date."

"What was it? A drive-by kiss?"

"No, he convinced me to meet him for coffee and then afterward he ambushed me by my car and stuck his tongue down my throat." The tongue part was technically a lie, but Sadie figured tongue was a definite possibility if the kiss had lasted a second longer.

"Hmm. And I'll just add *yum-m-m*. Whenever I see him on the news with his hair blowing in the breeze, I almost wet myself."

Sadie heard Maeva's boyfriend, Terry, complain loudly in the background and Maeva added loudly as an aside, "Of course he's not as hot as Terry." Then she lowered her voice to Sadie. "Terry *is* hot, but Scott Reed is sizzling."

"Reed also brought up Witigo Alliance," Sadie said.

"Wow. Cute and informed. That makes him twice as sexy."

"He wants me to bring him through a meth lab where he thinks they had a ritual or meeting or something. He wants more stuff for his story."

"That might not be such a bad idea. Shining a spotlight on dark forces always makes them dissipate. Then again sometimes it just drives them further underground. If you don't want to help Scott with his research, I'm volunteering. I practically have to run and have a cold shower after every newscast."

"Speaking of showers . . ."

"Right. Dawn's baby shower. Terry already said no problemo about this Saturday. He's got a private party in the evening, so he'll just make up some extra trays of appies and throw together cutesy sandwiches with pink and blue umbrellas. Oh, and I also convinced him to make a divine cake in the shape of a stork."

"Terry is a saint. I owe him big-time."

"Before I ask about the bikers, tell me when you plan on seeing Scott again."

"Never," Sadie replied emphatically. She thought about Scott's desire to accompany her on a meth-lab walk-through and put in, "It had better be never."

"Hunh," Maeva grunted, sounding disappointed. "Now, what about this motorcycle gang? How did they find out where you live and why were they at your house? Did they threaten you?"

Sadie answered all her friend's questions, hoping that afterward Maeva would tell her she was silly to be worried. Instead, Maeva begged Sadie to come over and stay with her and Terry, but in the end, she was pacified by Sadie setting her house alarm and promising to sleep with her gun close at hand. Sadie lied about the gun.

She had no sooner disconnected from Maeva than her office phone rang again. It was too late. She should let it go to voice mail, but she knew too well that death cleanup had no time restraints, so she put on her business tone and answered.

"Scene-2-Clean, how may I help you?"

"You clean blood, right?"

"Yes. Who's calling?"

"Lou Montie. We've got a mess in our RV and the cops said you could help out."

"An RV? You mean, like a trailer?"

"This unit is a motor home. It ain't no trailer," he said, offended.

"Okay, um, may I ask what kind of incident brings you to needing my services?"

"We keep it on some farm property when we're not using it. Some homeless bums broke into the unit. They made themselves right at home but must've had some kind of a fight. They left a bloody mess. We called the cops and they came and did their thing, but it's not like they're breaking a sweat over it. They said it wasn't enough blood that someone could've died, and probably the creeps moved on after they bled all over the bedroom. Anyway, my wife sure as hell doesn't want to be cleaning the blood, what with all the diseases around, and I tried bringing it in to a local auto-detailing place, but they won't touch it. The insurance company said we needed to call in someone who did trauma clean and that would be you, right?"

"Right."

Sadie took down the approximate address and arranged to drive by the place in the morning.

"It's a little hard to find, so let me give you directions. We keep the unit on a driveway off a farmer's field when we're storing it."

Sadie jotted down the details.

"Usually I come to a scene first to take pictures for the insurance company," Sadie explained. "And then I return with supplies and my employees to—"

"But this is such a small job," Lou interrupted. "It's not like you'll need anyone else to help you out. Hell, it'll prolly only take you a half hour on your own to rip out the materials that got stained."

Everyone's an expert on trauma clean.

"Since it is such a small job, I'll just bring my supplies and I'll be able to start right away."

After the call Sadie climbed into bed, once again trying not to look directly at the boxes in the corner of the room. Her mind was filled with thoughts of her dead brother's belongings, Scott Reed's kiss, and bloody RVs when she dozed off.

In the morning Sadie opened her bedroom drapes and let in the sharp glare of the early-morning sun. She closed them again. When she turned and walked away, she bumped her shin against one of the boxes.

Sadie didn't have to go to look at the RV for a couple more hours. She frowned at the boxes and finally sighed, figuring she might as well look through them now. Well, maybe not *right* now. After a quick jog. That would give her more energy. Then she'd shower and have a coffee and bagel. Then Hairy's litter box hadn't been cleaned for a couple days.

Surprisingly, she managed to get all those tasks completed and still had time on her hands. She scowled at the cardboard containers and with a feeling of resignation sank to her knees and tore the packing tape from the top of the first one. After a couple of calming breaths and a quick prayer, she unfolded the lid and peered inside.

Paperwork. No heart-wrenching photos of Brian smiling into the camera as if he weren't going to kill himself at twenty-eight. Just paperwork.

"All right, then," Sadie murmured. "I can do this."

Hairy hopped over and nibbled at one of the cardboard flaps. Sadie pushed him aside with the back of her hand and reached for a stack of loose paper. She felt more at ease now.

I'll just toss most of this into the recycle bin, she thought.

The first few sheets were Brian's household bills. She ran across a membership-renewal notice for an indoor rock-climbing gym. That one stung a little. If Sadie closed her eyes, she could see her brother decked out in rock-climbing gear, ready to climb Mount Hood.

"Mom always figured he'd die falling off a mountain, not with a gun to his head," Sadie said sadly.

She tossed it onto the pile that she'd designated for recycling. Then she came across a couple of novels. Romances. Sadie frowned. Brian was definitely more of a Stephen King fan. Obviously the paperbacks must've belonged to Joy, Brian's fiancée.

After Brian's death, Joy hadn't stuck around to pack up Brian's stuff. Instead, she'd returned to the house only briefly to pack up her own belongings. Then she headed to Los Angeles to live with her mom and dad. Sadie didn't blame her. They all felt like running away after the tragedy.

Sadie started a second pile with the novels and mentally labeled the pile *stuff to be donated to charity*. She added to that pile a clock radio and some knickknacks.

Once she was three-quarters of the way through the first box, the recycling pile was much higher than the others. She'd started a third pile for things to be kept and the largest item in that stack was a photo album.

Sadie had expected a sharp jolt of pain when she'd opened it, but there was only a remote ache. She wasn't ready to buy into the old adage that time heals. Nobody ever fully recovered from burying a family member. It was bittersweet for Sadie to realize that six years had dulled the sharp edges of pain surrounding her brother's suicide.

She pushed the album aside and quickened her pace in going through the remnants at the bottom of the carton: a couple of glass paperweights carefully wrapped in newsprint and another folder of mixed receipts and various household bills.

When she tossed the last of those sheets into the recycling pile, a glossy pamphlet fluttered from the folder. Sadie reached for it and looked it over.

Onyx House: A Journey to Within blazed across the front in red glossy lettering. Curious, Sadie flipped open the brochure and scanned the description of services. At Onyx House you could get your chakras balanced and your energies unblocked. You could also attend workshops on shamanic divination, vibrational healings, and Ortho-Bionomy along with psychic readings. All the services were offered in a "relaxed bed-and-breakfast environment in the heart of Seattle's Capitol Hill." Huh. The photos showed a turn-of-the-century home with lush gardens and inside rooms that were warm and filled with comfortable antiques. Not exactly the kind of place she could see Brian frequenting on a regular basis.

Then Sadie closed the brochure and noticed a slip stapled to the back page. She looked at it and frowned. It was an invoice for a weekend at Onyx House with both Brian's and Joy's names listed on the reservation.

Okay, I guess it is *the kind of place Brian would go to,* Sadie thought.

The itemized bill showed the couple had spent three nights there partaking in a so-called "Psychic Retreat for Advanced Mediumship—Learn to Hone Your Skills for Contacting the Departed."

"What the hell?" Sadie cried.

Her jaw dropped and she slowly shook her head from side to side.

The fact that her brother, a very down-to-earth and outdoorsy kind of guy, had actually stayed at the place struck Sadie as odd. More than odd. Downright weird. Stranger still was the fact that he'd attended a workshop on contacting ghosts.

But what caused her hands to tremble was the date on the receipt. According to the itemized invoice, Brian and Joy would've been guests at the freaky B and B only days before Brian sat in his bathtub, put a gun in his mouth, and blew his brains out.

7

When the phone rang, Sadie had no idea how long she'd been sitting on the floor surrounded by paperwork. Absently, she got to her feet and reached for the bedside phone.

"Hello?"

"Finally," Sadie's mom said with exasperation. "I've been trying to get you for days. Did you get my messages?"

"Yes."

"Then why didn't you call me back?"

"Sorry, I've been busy," Sadie murmured. "Can we talk later?" She glanced down and realized she was still holding the Onyx House pamphlet.

"No," her mom said angrily. "We need to talk about the shower."

"Okay."

"Well?"

"Well, what?"

"Damn it, Sadie, the food!" she shouted. "Are you or are you not going to take care of the food for Dawn's shower? We've got only a few days to pull this together and I don't want you picking up a bag of potato chips on your way over. I want some real effort and—"

"It's done. I've already taken care of everything. Stop worrying."

"Really?" Mom's tone was laced with disbelief.

"Yes. Really. I've asked Maeva's boyfriend, Terry, to take care of the food. He's an excellent high-end caterer, and he's going to provide loads of appetizers, sandwiches, and a cake in the shape of a stork."

"Oh." She paused. "If he's an excellent high-end caterer why is he available at such short notice?"

"God, Mom!" Sadie blew out a breath. "He has a catering job Saturday night and that's why he's okay providing food for us Saturday afternoon. He's just making extra trays and the cake."

"Okay, then." She finally sounded satisfied. "That sounds good."

"It'll be great." Sadie looked again at the brochure. "Mom, have you ever heard of a place called Onyx House?"

"Onyx House?" she repeated. "No, I don't think so. Why?"

"I'm going through Brian's things and I happened to come across an invoice for a local B and B with that name. Brian and Joy stayed there."

"I've never heard of it, although I remember Joy saying they'd thought of using a local B and B for the wedding reception."

Her mother's voice had taken on the wounded and distant tone it always did when her brother's name came up.

"This place sounds kind of . . ." *Weird. Bizarre.* "New Agey. Not exactly like Brian's thing."

"Well, Joy really liked that kind of stuff," Mom replied. "She was into all kinds of off-the-wall things like tarot cards and such."

"Really?" Sadie said with surprise.

"Sure, I remember Brian teasing Joy about going to get her chakras aligned or some darn thing."

"Huh." Sadie was taken aback by this bit of news. Truthfully, she hadn't gotten to know her brother's fiancée nearly as well as she probably should have. Joy had always seemed standoffish around Brian's family and Sadie hadn't wanted to push. At the time, Sadie figured she'd have a lifetime to get to know Joy.

"I saw her the other day, you know," Mom said.

"Who?"

"Joy."

"Here? In Seattle?"

"Of course, here in Seattle! It's not like I've been out gallivanting across the country lately."

"Right. I just meant that last I heard, Joy was in Los Angeles living with her mom and dad."

"She did that for a while. When I ran into her at the grocery store, she told me that she'd moved back to Seattle just a few months afterward."

She didn't have to say after what.

"So she's been back here for years. Her mother and father retired and moved to Texas."

"So how is Joy?" Sadie asked for lack of anything else to say.

"Fine. She got married," Mom added, her voice thick.

Sadie knew what her mom was thinking. That the plan had been for Joy to be married to Brian. Of course she would've moved on. She was a young woman. It was only natural that after six years she would've found someone else. But it still hurt. Sadie quickly changed the subject.

"Terry will drop off the food early on Saturday," Sadie blurted. "So just make sure there's room in your fridge. Did you want me to pick up wine and mixers?"

"No, but you could help with decorating. Your aunt Lynn will help, but the woman is hopeless when it comes to crafts."

"If I have time, I'll drop by," Sadie said, thinking it was the last thing she'd find time to do.

They finalized the details and just as Sadie was saying good-bye, her mother quickly added, "Your aunt Lynn drove into town last night. Since she's got her car here, she plans to do some visiting and she asked for your number. If she calls, be polite and invite the woman over for tea."

"Yeah, sure," Sadie replied, but she inwardly cringed and not just because she hated tea. She hadn't seen her aunt since Brian's funeral.

When Sadie hung up, she grabbed her digital camera and headed out to her garage, pausing only to activate her house alarm. In the garage she spent a few moments making sure the Scene-2-Clean van was well stocked before she climbed behind the wheel.

While she traveled south on the I-5, Sadie called Lou Montie to let him know she was on her way. She made a quick stop at Starbucks for a triple latte and was taking the first sip when Zack called.

"Anything happening today?" he asked.

"I've got a small job a little bit out of town. I'm on my way there now."

"Need help?"

"I don't think so. It's an RV with some bloodstains inside."

"An RV? That's something new."

"Apparently people will bleed just about anywhere," Sadie said. "I'll call you when I'm done."

They ended the call and Sadie cranked up the radio and sang along with Sarah McLachlan. After a while she checked the directions Lou Montie had given her. Based on the directions, Sadie had estimated she'd arrive in less than half an hour, but she hadn't counted on traveling down an extremely narrow gravel road. Deep ditches lined either side and since her van was big, she straddled both lanes and slowed. Her tires kicked up clouds of dust as she drove the big Scene-2-Clean van past a tall line of cedars on her right. Mr. Montie had indicated she'd be able to see the RV on a driveway not far from this clump of trees.

The dirt road climbed a slight hill and when she reached the top, Sadie could see a large outbuilding with brown vinyl siding about a quarter mile down on the left side. Then, suddenly, there it was. A short driveway seemingly in the middle of nowhere with an impressive silver motor home with teal-striped detailing parked there gleaming in the sun.

The road she'd driven on was narrow, but the driveway appeared to be an even tighter fit. The RV was parked in a field, but the bumper protruded into the driveway, so there was barely enough space for Sadie to park. She carefully backed into the driveway until the back of the van was close to the RV. When she opened the door of her van, she had to climb out carefully so as not to step off the drive and into the deep gully on either side.

A hot breeze blew across the field, and dust swirled around Sadie's feet as she opened the rear of the van. She snagged her camera, slipped into a hazmat suit and went looking for the key to the RV. Mr. Montie said it would be in a magnetic key box under the metal stairs. Her fingers flicked away a large spiderweb and then found the box. She stuck the key into the door of the motor home and stepped inside.

The door opened onto a stylish living area with a beige leather-look sofa and soft mocha-colored blinds shading the windows. Beyond the sitting area was the cockpit driving area with comfy captain chairs in the same leather look. To Sadie's left was an impressive kitchen area with honey oak cabinetry and a booth dinette. Sadie couldn't believe the good-sized fridge, stove, and even microwave. The spacious luxury of the unit made Sadie think a cross-country vacation could actually be appealing.

On the left was a hall with a couple doors most likely leading to a bedroom and bath. Since Mr. Montie had told her the knife fight took place in the back bedroom, she headed down the hall.

Guessing the bedroom would be through the door right at the end of the hall, Sadie headed straight there.

She opened the door, squinted in the bright light, and frowned. The blinds had been pulled up, making the room unbearably hot. The sun also flooded the room with light, shining a spotlight on every corner. Sadie couldn't see a single drop of blood. She walked to the other side of the bed and looked around from that angle. She was beginning to think she was either in the wrong room or in the wrong recreational vehicle.

Deciding to check the other rooms off the hall, Sadie took a step toward the door and stopped short when movement outside caught her eye. The barn-sized outbuilding up the road had opened its doors. Sadie heard the low rumble of a motorcycle engine and watched as a lone rider in black slowly rolled out of the doorway and idled there. He wouldn't be able to see her from this distance, but Sadie felt like he was looking right at her.

"It's one motorcycle guy," she chastised herself. "Not every guy who rides a Harley is a member of Fierce Force."

She left the room and went down the hall. She flung open the next door and it opened onto the cramped quarters of the bathroom. There was an angled corner shower on one side and a toilet on the other. In the middle was a small counter with a stainless steel sink. Sadie gasped in startled surprise. Bent over the sink with stringy bleached hair hanging in her face and a nose pressed to that counter was a woman. She was extremely skinny and wore a hot pink miniskirt and matching tank top. The skirt was really more of a belt and as she bent over the sink, Sadie cringed at the realization she wore nothing underneath.

The woman (actually girl, because she couldn't have been more than twenty) looked up and casually wiped a dusting of white from under her nose.

"Wow. Can you, like, see me?" she asked. Her eyes were glassy with huge pupils, confirming she was stoned out of her gourd.

"Yes. Are you dead?" Sadie asked.

"I like to think of it as permanently just ha-a-anging around at the party," she drawled through a mouth smudged with crimson lipstick. She broke into a bark of laughter that led to a smoker's coughing jag, then winked at Sadie. "Wanna do a line?"

She pointed to the bathroom countertop and was obviously trying to indicate lines of cocaine that only she could see.

"I'll pass. I'm working."

"At what?" The girl giggled. "At being a spaceman? What's with the getup? You sure don't look like any of the usual party girls who hang here."

"I'm Sadie Novak and I'm here to clean a crime scene. Except I can't find one. Unless you bled out somewhere that I don't know about?"

"Nope. No blood." She closed her eyes and her lips formed a dreamy smile. "Just got some Grade A and drifted awa-a-ay."

"I'm so sorry," Sadie said sincerely.

"Oh, don't be sad about it. I'm not. Hell, things are easier now than they've ever been in my life. All the Grade A I want and I don't even have to put out for it. What more could a girl want?"

Um, to be alive?

"What's your name?"

"I'm Bambi."

Of course you are.

"How long have you been dead, Bambi?"

She screwed up her face in concentration. "Gee. I'm not sure." She shrugged. "My old man was pretty shook-up when it happened. He didn't mean for me to get hold of the good stuff. The stuff they give us workin' girls is usually cut. He felt bad I got into his pure stuff. I think he even cried. That's kinda good to see, ya know? The guy treated me like shit mosta the time, so it was good to see he really cared I was gone. He even told 'em to bury me under the monkey tree in Kenmore. Man, I really loved that tree." Her voice was sad and wistful. "Curly loved me a lot to see I was buried there."

Pretty pathetic when the measure of how much somebody loves you is where they hide your body.

"Was that the meth lab in Kenmore?" Sadie asked.

"Yeah. I spent some wicked fun time there. Even when the WA had their freaking meetings at night, the place was a fun place to hang out." She giggled, then grew serious. "Wait a second, did you say your name was Sadie?" She pointed a long hot pink fingernail in Sadie's face.

"Yes. Sadie Novak. Like I said, I clean crime—"

"I heard about you. You're the one who pocketed some of Curly's cash. Man, he's sure pissed at you." She slapped her hand over her mouth and her eyes grew even wider as she spoke from behind her hand. "Wow! You must got a big pair of balls under that jumpsuit to steal from the FF."

"Wait a second." Sadie held up a gloved hand. "I don't know what you're talking about. Who said I stole from Fierce Force?"

"Well, Curly was talking to some of the boys about it when they met here earlier." She sniffed and wiped at her nose. "Said some Sadie broad cost them a hundred g's to the cops and another hundred g's in her pocket." She looked at Sadie. "That's a lot to try and sneak off with. You're either brave or one stupid bitch." She tossed back her head and laughed throatily.

Sadie stepped forward, wanting to reach out and grab Bambi's thin shoulders and shake her.

"The money was in the walls of a house in Kirkland. I had to report it to the cops."

"Curly said you took a chunk first." She waggled a finger in Sadie's face and then shrugged. "Hey, I prolly woulda done the 'xact same thing. A girl's gotta take care of her future."

"I'm not a thief," Sadie said angrily.

"Makes no big diff to me." She shrugged. "Of course,

nobody steals from the FF and lives long anyway. That's why they asked you to come here. You and I will soon be roomies."

The heavy heat in the RV was suddenly suffocating.

"It's a setup," Sadie said. She let out a whoosh of breath at the realization and then she heard it. The rumble of a motorcycle a lot closer than she would've liked.

Sadie bolted down the hall, flung open the door to the RV, and leapt down the steps. She skidded to a stop behind her company van. In front of the Scene-2-Clean vehicle, blocking the only exit off the field, was a motorcycle. A black cherry Harley with flames on the tank. Straddling that bike was the same bearded caveman who'd run her and Jackie off the Kirkland property.

She thought of running, but there was no way a girl in a hazmat suit could outrun a dude on a Harley. The astringent burn in Sadie's gut gave way to a strident alarm in her head.

She was biker bait.

8

Sadie bolted for her van door, but for a big guy, the biker moved surprisingly fast. He quick-stepped down the narrow stretch of gravel between her van and the ditch and met Sadie at the rear. In one quick movement, he had her pinned with her back to the van and a knife to her throat.

"We meet again, huh?" The tight curls of his beard vibrated as he spoke.

He smelled of body odor, leather, and rotting teeth. Sadie almost gagged, but she was terrified to do so much as swallow with the long blade pressed against her larynx.

"I didn't do it, Curly!" Sadie squeaked. She knew she was taking a chance calling the guy by name.

He raised his eyebrows.

"Do what? Huh? How do you know who I am, and how can you know what I'm pissed about, bitch, if you didn't do it?"

He leaned one forearm on her throat and pressed his body weight against her, while his right hand, which held the knife blade, moved up to the side of her nose. "I want what's mine," he snarled, and the spray of his spit hit her face. "I can't help what the pigs took, but I can sure get back the other half. I didn't know it at the time, but we saw you load it into your van."

Sadie couldn't breathe. Her vision was blurring and she could only think of one word.

"Bambi," she said, the sound of her voice a choked gasp.

"What did you say?" He startled backward, releasing his arm from her throat.

Sadie nearly collapsed and she brought air into her lungs in huge gulps. Thinking quick, she started to talk.

"Bambi. She told me she knows you feel bad about what happened, Curly. She knows you love her."

"Bambi's dead." He narrowed his black eyes to slits and his fingers tightened on the knife.

Sadie took a chance.

"They just wanted you to think she was dead. Your boys thought she'd turned informant, so they fed her extrapure coke. They told you they buried her under the monkey puzzle tree on the Kenmore property, but she wasn't dead. She escaped and she's inside the trailer right now."

"You're lying!" he screamed

Sadie shrank away from the blow she thought was coming, but he didn't hit her. Yet.

"I saw her with my own two eyes and I know dead when I see it. Trust me."

She did trust him on that one, but she also knew bad guys themselves did not have a very high trust ratio. Sadie was betting Curly would've sold his own mother for a few bucks, so it was in his nature to believe everyone else was just as corrupt.

"I'm sure you *thought* she was dead. It was a close call."

She could just about smell rubber burning as he considered what she'd told him.

Sadie rushed on. "Come on, think about it. How else would I know anything about Bambi? Go inside and see for yourself."

"I will. If you're lying, you're dead," he hissed.

As if I was walking away before, Sadie thought.

"Hand over your keys," he said.

Without flinching, Sadie handed him the van keys that she was holding. He stuffed them in the front pocket of his jeans and turned on his heel, his boots kicking up dirt as he went. He walked up the steps of the RV and when he was at the top one, he called over to her.

"There's nothing but farmland for five miles in every direction. Don't even think you can run."

But the second he was inside the RV, she did just that. Sadie bolted around the side of her van, reached behind the front tire, and found the magnetic box that held her spare key. Her hands shook as she sprang the key from the box. Then in one fluid movement she hopped onto the driver's seat, closed the door, and managed to stab the key in the ignition. The engine sprang to life and in her rearview mirror Sadie saw Curly fling the door to the RV open and bolt down the steps. She punched the accelerator and heard the crunch of metal as her van winged the Harley in front of her and sent it flying into the ditch off to the side.

Cranking the wheel, she was out of the driveway, barreling down the gravel road. She was back careening down the highway before she let up on the gas.

When she pulled into the parking lot of Zack's apartment building, Sadie decided she'd better call first before just going straight to his apartment. When he didn't answer in his apartment, she called his cell. He picked up on the first ring and she didn't give him a chance to say more than hello before she told him everything.

"Jesus H. Christ, Sadie." He blew out a breath. "Don't go home."

"I'm not at home." She paused. "Actually, I'm in the parking lot of your apartment."

"I'll be there in a few minutes. I'm just out for coffee with a friend. I'll bring him along. Wait there."

When he showed up, Sadie was really glad to find out that his friend was a cop.

Nobody said too much until they were inside Zack's apartment, sitting down with beers in their hands. Zack introduced his cop friend as Nick. He was in his forties with the start of a beer gut and military hair with a bald spot.

"Zack told me you were lured out to the middle of nowhere for a job on a trailer, and it turned into a setup with a biker named Curly. Is that correct?"

Sadie nodded. She noticed her hands were trembling and she tightened her grip on her beer.

"And I'm to believe you had enough horseshoes up your ass that you were able to get away and you drove over his motorcycle?"

"Yes."

He let out a low whistle.

"First I'm going to need to know where this all happened."

Sadie gave him the precise directions she'd received from the man who gave his name as Lou Montie.

Nick the cop got up, made a phone call, and sat back down.

"We got a car going out to check," he said, and downed what remained of his beer. "Describe Curly."

"Ugly," Sadie said, and drank from her own bottle. "Curly beard that's kind of reddish. Fat head. Big belly. Mean eyes. About five ten."

Nick nodded. "Sure as hell sounds like Carl Boyle." He walked across the room to Zack's desk and punched the name into the computer there. A few clicks later and a picture filled the screen.

"That's him," Sadie said, her lower lip trembling.

"Carl Boyle," Nick said. "He was the very first president of Fierce Force when it started up in the early nineties. He ran the organization like a finely oiled machine and never hesitated to take out the competition. Carl goes by the name 'Curly the Cutter.'"

Sadie thought about the sharp knife pressed to her throat.

"I don't think I want to know why he goes by 'Cutter,' " she said, a hand to her throat.

"No. You don't," Nick said seriously.

"I remember hearing about him when I was on the force," Zack said. "But I thought he moved out of Seattle years ago."

"He moved a little north, but he kept his fingers in the FF pie. The feds have had their eye on him for ages. They suspect he's been laundering money through his business in Bellingham."

"What business is that?" Zack asked.

"He runs an RV lot selling used and new motor homes," Nick said matter-of-factly.

"He thinks I stole from the FF. Half the money in the walls was taken as evidence. There was a hundred thousand, right?"

Nick nodded in confirmation.

"There was supposed to be double that. Curly thinks I took it. Loaded it into my van in the waste bins." She took a deep breath. "If I could write him a check, I would. I've got a feeling this isn't going away."

"Especially after you drove over his baby. His black cherry Road King Classic Harley," Nick said, and offered her a wry smile.

Zack smiled too, but it was more of a way to break the tension, because nobody really found any of this funny.

Sadie gave Nick the contact phone number she had for Lou Montie, now Curly the Cutter.

"We'll look into it, but—," Nick said.

"It's most likely an untraceable cell phone that has already been tossed into the ocean," Zack finished.

"Yup," Nick agreed, getting up to leave.

"There's more," Sadie said quietly.

Zack's gaze cut quickly to her face, trying to read what she was going to say. Sadie had been attempting to figure out a way to say it without revealing her secret talent. She had a choice to lie or tell the truth. Today, lying won.

"Curly said something about the body of a woman buried under the monkey tree on the Kenmore property."

"You mean Penny Torrez, the woman who had the baby cut out of her?" Nick asked.

"No. It's a different one. Someone named Bambi. She may have been a prostitute."

"Hot damn." Nick rubbed his hands together. "The feds may be trying to put Curly away for money laundering, but murder's even better."

Not for Penny or Bambi, Sadie thought.

"I'm pretty sure it was an accidental OD," Sadie said.

"If there's a body, we'll let the coroner decide cause of death," Nick said.

Sadie couldn't argue with that.

"I need to get home," she said.

"You're not going anywhere," Zack said.

"He's right." Nick nodded. "Sounds like Curly's got a big hard-on for making sure you end up dead. You need to stay safe."

Sadie thought about the tip of the razor-sharp blade as it pressed against her throat, and felt her legs go weak. She sat down on the sofa.

"So it's settled. You'll stay here," Zack said firmly.

"Over my dead body," Sadie grumbled.

Zack strode angrily toward her and stabbed a finger in her face.

"You *will* end up dead if you think you can go toe-to-toe with bikers." He turned to Nick. "Tell her how stupid she's being."

"Stupid?" Sadie narrowed her eyes and let anger propel her to her feet. "Don't call me stupid."

"Then don't act stupid," Zack said.

Sadie knew she was in danger from Curly the Cutter if she didn't go into hiding, but she wasn't all that sure that staying with Zack would be less dangerous for her heart.

9

"It's just a bad idea," Sadie said.

"It's the only idea," Zack countered.

"I'm not staying with you, and that's final."

"You'd rather be dead?"

"You're not exactly the only person I know with a sofa!" Sadie shot back.

"Well, I'll let you kids work out the details," Nick said. "I'm going up to Kenmore to watch 'em dig for a body. Given that you two are the ones who called it in, I could pull some strings to allow you to be on the sidelines. You game?"

"Yes," Zack said.

"Whatever," Sadie replied.

Nick took his own vehicle. Sadie and Zack drove in Zack's Mustang. They didn't talk and Sadie was relieved. She was petrified of Curly finding her and dissecting her with his knife. But she was also scared to death of sleeping in Zack's apartment and making an already stressed-out situation more difficult.

They were almost in Kenmore when Sadie's phone rang. It was Dawn, and Sadie was never more relieved to hear her sister's voice.

"What are you doing?" Dawn asked.

"Oh, you know . . . same old, same old," Sadie replied drily. "A body here, a ghost or two there."

She saw Zack's fingers tighten on the steering wheel. His own cell phone rang and he answered.

"If you have the time, I'd appreciate it if you'd come over and save me," Dawn whispered. "Auntie Lynn's been camped out at my kitchen table all morning. She's driving me nuts!"

Sadie heard Zack talking into his own phone and relaying what he was up to. By the way he talked, Sadie figured he was talking to Jackie.

"I thought you liked Aunt Lynn," Sadie said into her phone while she tried to listen to Zack's conversation.

"We haven't really seen the woman much since Brian died. Apparently in six short years a woman on her own can totally lose the ability to tell when people want her to stop talking," Dawn hissed.

Sadie laughed.

"Okay, well, if Auntie Lynn's at the kitchen table, where are you?"

"I'm in the bathroom. This baby is sitting on my bladder and I have to pee every fifteen minutes."

Sadie heard the toilet flush.

"As much as I'd love to save you, I'm kinda in the middle of something right now." Then Sadie thought about her own situation and how she needed saving herself. "But I could use a place to stay. Would you consider putting me and Hairy up for a couple days?" Sadie carefully ignored Zack's big sigh.

"Any particular reason why you need a place to stay?"

"Um. I got a rat problem." Big hairy tattooed rats.

"It's good timing. John's going to L.A. for a conference and he'll be gone for a few days. It would be nice to have company. I'll roll out the welcome mat if you get your ass over here before Aunt Lynn tells any more stories about how I used to run around without panties."

"You were quite the exhibitionist."

"I was three years old!" Dawn shrieked. Then off to

the side she added, "I'm fine, Auntie Lynn. I saw a spider in the tub, that's all. I'll be right out." To Sadie she hissed, "Hurry up. You owe me for doing such a half-assed job on arranging my baby shower."

Dawn hung up before Sadie could argue. By then Zack was just pulling onto the street at the Kenmore house. No sooner were they climbing out of Zack's Mustang and onto the sizzling hot pavement than they saw an Emerald Nine News van pull up behind them.

"Oh, great," Zack growled as Scott Reed hopped out of the van followed by his cameraman. "The wolf has sniffed out a fresh kill."

"Hey, Sweets," Scott Reed called out.

The journalist sauntered over to them, wearing freshly ironed khakis and a royal blue shirt that made his eyes look almost impossibly blue. Zack cursed under his breath as Reed strolled over until he was scant inches from Sadie. She took a step back to protect her personal space.

"We're busy," Sadie said, feeling sweat already pooling beneath her breasts.

"Hey, I'm working too," Scott said. "This isn't all fun and games, but I gotta say it's a nice surprise to see you so soon after our date." He made a comical clucking noise and punctuated it with a wink.

"It wasn't a date," Sadie said curtly.

"Ignore him," Zack said, putting a hand on Sadie's elbow.

"Oh, it was a date, Sweets." Scott leaned in close to Sadie but spoke loud enough for Zack to hear. "My favorite part was the good-night kiss."

"You kissed him?" Zack demanded roughly, releasing Sadie's arm. A look of hot fury fled across his face.

"He kissed *me*," Sadie said. *Not that it's any of your goddamn business.*

"Yes," Scott admitted. "But you definitely kissed me back."

"You kissed him back?!" Zack demanded.

"Oh, for God's sake." Sadie threw her hands up in exasperation. She noticed more investigators had arrived on scene and the Emerald Nine van was blocking access to parking. "Look, Reed, you're going to have to move your vehicle before the cops get pissed and throw you out of here."

"About that, my sources tell me you've encountered yet another Fierce Force crime scene. How about some details, Sweets, and I'll not only move my vehicle—I'll take you in the back and rock your world."

"Argh!" Sadie shouted. She stormed off in the direction of Nick, who was talking with Detective Carr in the driveway of the house.

"Well, if it ain't Typhoid Mary," Carr quipped under his breath.

"I don't kill people," Sadie shot back.

"No, but every time I hear your name, it seems to be surrounded by death," Carr countered.

Sadie couldn't deny that.

"They found a woman's body," Nick said to her.

"Buried under the tree?" Sadie asked, looking from Detective Carr to Officer Nick.

The detective gave a sharp nod.

"But that's not all. There was another body buried beside her."

"Another body?"

"Yeah, but it'll take a while to identify this one. It's burned beyond recognition."

"Oh my God," Sadie gasped, rubbing the back of her neck.

"What I don't get is why the hell Curly the Cutter would confess murder to you."

"I guess because he was about to kill me too," Sadie said, forcing herself to look him in the eye. "He was trying to scare me into telling him where I put the money I took from him."

"Don't get that either," Carr said. "Why does he think you took money if he knows it's in evidence?"

Sadie was getting hot under the collar and not just because the sun was blazing ninety degrees of concentrated heat on her head.

"Because he claims money went missing before the cops showed up and took the rest into evidence." Sadie threw her hands up in the air. "Look, I'd like to know all the answers too. Hey, I've got an idea, why don't you guys get in your little cars and go driving around to find the asshole so we can ask him?" Sadie screeched.

"Cool it," Zack said, his gaze sliding over to Scott Reed, who was obviously pointing out their loud discussion to his cameraman.

Sadie hadn't noticed Zack come up behind her, but she turned on him now.

"Don't tell me to cool it!" She squared her shoulders and pinged her sharp gaze off each of the three men. "I was the one that was almost carved into itty-bitty pieces by some crazed lunatic just a couple hours ago! And let's not forget that I just helped you get evidence to lock this guy away."

"Not that we don't all appreciate finding the body, but it's a long shot from proving the guy's guilty," Carr pointed out.

"Oh, and the fact that Curly told me where the body was doesn't help?" Sadie asked. "Did you expect me to get him to write it out in my blood for you too? He tried to kill me! Isn't attempted murder still a crime?" She squeezed her eyes shut against a powerful headache rolling up her shoulders and into her neck. "You don't need me here, do you?"

"No. I can get your statement later," Carr said. To Zack he said, "You shouldn't be on this scene anyway. Guess you can take her back to your place for safe-keeping."

"Why the hell does everyone assume I'm staying with Zack?" Sadie asked. "I do know other people."

Nobody said a word. Sadie whirled on her heel and

walked away, realizing she had no vehicle to hop into. She saw a couple of uniformed officers shooing Scott Reed away from the street. Sadie elbowed her way past the officers and right up to Reed.

"Can you give me a ride to my sister's house?" she demanded.

Scott Reed raised his eyebrows in surprise. "I'd rather bring you back to my place and—"

"Cut the crap. Can you or can you not drop me off at my sister's place? She lives in Green Lake on Sixty-sixth Avenue."

"Sure." He nodded, his face serious. "I can do that."

The cameraman was not at all happy about riding in the back while Reed drove and Sadie rode shotgun.

Sadie was surprised Scott waited an entire ten minutes before his first question.

"How did the woman die?"

"What woman?" Sadie asked.

"The woman whose body they dug up today."

"How did you find out it was a woman and that she was buried?" Sadie asked him.

"I didn't know for sure, but thanks for confirming it." He smiled. "My source only told me there was more action going on at that location and when I got there, Jacob"—Scott nodded to the cameraman in the back—"used his telephoto lens to get a look at the fact they were digging up something in the yard under a tree."

"Don't do that," Sadie said, her voice tired.

"Do what?"

"Trick me into giving you answers that you'll use to destroy my reputation."

"Hey, Sweets, I'm not going to do that," he said with a reproachful tone. "I can just say a source that wishes to remain anonymous told this reporter that information."

"You don't get it. I saw you guys filming while I had

words with the cops. If you show that footage and then say a source told you, you and I both know people will think I was your source."

"I don't think Jack and Jill Q. Public are bright enough to put that together, darling."

"You have a pretty low opinion of Seattleites, then," Sadie said.

She blew out a breath and folded her arms over her chest and refused to say anything more except to give him directions to Dawn's house in Green Lake. When he pulled his van in front of the split-level, Sadie thanked him politely for the ride and hopped out.

"Hello!" Sadie shouted as she used her key to let herself into Dawn's house.

"We're in here," Dawn shouted back.

Sadie kicked off her shoes. She took a deep calming breath and pasted a big smile on her face before crossing the living room and entering into the kitchen at the back of the house.

"Sadie!" Auntie Lynn exclaimed. She jumped to her feet and tugged Sadie into a bear hug far greater than should've been possible for a four-foot-eleven white-haired lady in her seventies. The woman released her niece and smiled. "I can no longer say, 'My, how you've grown,' but I can sure say, 'My, how lovely you look.' You're too skinny, but you're beautiful!"

"Thanks," Sadie said, noticing that Dawn, on the other hand, looked mighty relieved. "You look wonderful too, Auntie Lynn. You haven't aged at all since we last saw you, has she, Dawn?"

"Nope," Dawn said, chugging down a glass of water and looking like she wished it could be whiskey. She got to her feet with some effort, covered her mouth in a yawn. "I'm sorry, Auntie Lynn, but I'm just beat." Dawn put a hand to her belly. "This little person seems to suck up all of my energy. Now that Sadie's here, would you mind if I disappear for a short nap?"

"Not at all," Auntie Lynn assured her. "It'll give Sadie and I a chance to catch up on the last six years."

Sadie was pretty sure the look she got from Dawn as she passed said *nya nya nya* instead of *I'm tired*.

"Sit, dear, sit," Aunt Lynn encouraged. "I'll pour you some of the wonderful coffee Dawn was kind enough to make me."

"I'll pour the coffee," Sadie insisted.

Sadie brought the pot over and filled their cups. Then they sat down together and smiled at each other. Sadie wondered what on earth Dawn was complaining about. Aunt Lynn wasn't so bad.

After they were halfway through their first cup of coffee, though, Auntie Lynn took a deep breath and began a long dissertation listing absolutely every item she planted in her large vegetable garden that was surely going to dry up to nothing in this heat wave.

"How was your drive up from Redmond, Oregon?" Sadie asked to get her off the topic of dehydrated radishes and desiccated strawberries.

"The drive was fine. Peggy acts as if I'm a total fool to hit the road by myself, but then your mother was always directionally challenged. She once got lost in a mall parking lot." She rolled her eyes. "But the drive is really no big deal. I just took the Ninth Street north until I got to Highway 26, and then took the I-84 toward Portland, and by the time I was on the I-5, the traffic was busy but, you know, I'm not afraid to drive in traffic and—"

"So you're still in the same house?" Sadie interrupted.

"Yes, I know Peggy suggested I move here after Glen died, but I'd been living on my own for ten years before that, so I was used to it." The woman closed her eyes and sighed. "Those were the really hard years."

"The ten years Uncle Glen was, um . . ." In the loony bin?

"When he was in the institution." She sighed again and this time dabbed at her eyes a little. "Sometimes I wondered if I did the right thing letting the doctors put him in there. Seemed like once he got locked up, things only got a lot worse. He heard voices all the time."

"Schizophrenia is a terrible disease, Aunt Lynn, but I'm sure Uncle Glen knew you loved him." When he wasn't hearing voices from outer space.

"Brian came to visit Glen at the end. It was so sweet of him and I hoped just for one day he could see the old Glen. He was a lot like Brian when he was younger, you know."

"I forgot Brian used to drive up to visit you," Sadie said thoughtfully.

"Well, truthfully he wasn't there to see us nearly as much as he was there to climb Smith Rock." She chuckled. "Why on earth rock climbers come from all over to climb that damn sheet of rock is beyond me."

"I'm sure he enjoyed visiting you too."

"Well, his timing was something else. You know Brian was actually there in the room with me when Glen passed on. Of course the stroke really killed him the week before, but he took his last breath with just Brian and myself standing there."

Sadie shook her head. "I didn't know that."

And then Brian shot himself only a week later.

Aunt Lynn must've been thinking the same thing.

"I never thought your brother was unhappy in any way. He was so patient with Glen," she added wistfully. Then, as if she was determined to keep the conversation more upbeat, she clapped her hands and announced, "I need more coffee. How about you?"

Sadie declined a second cup and when her aunt returned to the table, she was smiling brightly.

"By the way, I know all about you." She leaned in and whispered, "I've seen you on the news."

Oh, great. Just great. Even her aunt saw her flirting with Zack.

"Actually, we're just coworkers."

"Huh?" She looked puzzled. "I mean I know what

you do for a living. Your mom kept telling me how you ran some kind of fancy cleaning company as if I'm an utter buffoon that can't see for myself from the TV and newspapers that you clean crime scenes."

"Oh. Well, I think Mom tells herself those things so she can sleep at night. I don't think she can deal with the reality of my job. It makes her uncomfortable."

"She doesn't see that you started it all for her?" Auntie Lynn asked, shaking her head slowly from side to side so that her tight white curls shook. "Doesn't she know that cleaning up after Brian killed himself made you want to do it to help other families too?"

Tears clogged Sadie's throat with emotion and she didn't answer. Picking up her coffee cup, she blinked them away while she sipped her drink.

"You're like a modern-day heroine. That's what you are." Auntie Lynn reached and patted Sadie's hand.

Sadie put down her coffee. "I'm not a hero. Most of the time, when I'm working, I'm just trying not to think about what I'm doing."

"Exactly, and that's why I was going to also say, don't you think it's time you went back to teaching second grade?"

Sadie stiffened. "What do you mean? Why would I go back to teaching?"

"I imagine your work is hard on you emotionally. Nobody could possibly do what you do . . . see the *things* that you do, day after day without becoming, well, hardened to the world, I guess." She looked at her watch. "Oh, Lord, look at the time." She guzzled the remains of her coffee. "Be sure to say good-bye to Dawn for me, but I've got to run off and visit your cousin Tina before she goes in to work the night shift at the hospital." She leaned in to hug Sadie and whispered in her ear, "You don't have to worry. Dawn knows nothing about the shower. It's going to be a wonderful surprise."

Aunt Lynn had been gone for less than a minute when Dawn poked her head into the kitchen.

"Is she gone?"

"Yes," Sadie said drily. "Nice escape trick. I'll have to remember to use napping as my own excuse next time."

"It only works for pregnant women," Dawn said, sitting down at the kitchen table across from her sister.

After a moment of quiet Sadie asked her, "Do you think I've become hardened because of what I do?"

Dawn was contemplative.

"I'd like to say no, but the truth is, you've changed since you've been doing this job," she whispered. "It's like you're scarred on the inside."

"Last month I cleaned the scene of a home invasion where a single mom and her baby were shot to death by a drugged-out lunatic."

"I remember hearing about that one. That must've been awful."

"It was. While I'm cleaning the living room, I can see and hear the ghost of the baby. He's crying and crying, but I can't help him. When I went to clean the corner of the room, I found the mom's eyeball. I guess the ME missed it when he was picking up the rest of the body parts. The whole time I'm dealing with the mess, I've got the ghost baby bawling for his mom." Sadie looked at her sister. "How can anyone experience that kind of thing and *not* be scarred?"

10

Dawn returned from throwing up in the bathroom and sat back down at the kitchen table.

"Sorry. I didn't mean to make you sick," Sadie said.

"That's all right. I should know better than to discuss your job. How about we talk about something else? Like the fact that you don't have rats, so why will you be sleeping on my futon?"

Sadie gave Dawn a rundown on the Curly the Cutter situation.

"You're a magnet for trouble," Dawn said. "Can't they put you into police protection?"

"They've recommended I stay with Zack for protection."

"And you chose to stay with me instead? Are you insane?"

"Things with Zack are complicated."

"Huh. Well, then let's concentrate on thinking up fun things to do to take your mind off a crazy biker and my mind off the fact that a large object will try and leave my vagina soon." She sipped a glass of water. "Do you want to watch me fold and refold the baby's clothes?"

"Is that supposed to be fun?"

"I can't help it. I've got this nesting thing going on." Dawn sighed. "I know! Let's go to Macrina for a bite. I've been dying for an avocado and peppers sandwich. Oh, and that great dessert with the apricots and toasted hazelnuts." She closed her eyes and licked her lips. "Puleeese?"

"Hey, I think I even have a coupon for that place," Sadie replied, digging into her purse. But what she pulled out was the B and B pamphlet she'd found with Brian's things. *Onyx House: A Journey to Within*. It didn't sound any less strange the second time she looked it over.

"What's that?" Dawn asked, snatching the brochure from Sadie's hands. "I didn't know you were into this kind of stuff. Shamanic divination and vibrational healings?" She wrinkled her nose at the grocery list of services. "What kind of bed-and-breakfast is this place?"

"The kind Brian would go to," Sadie responded drily.

"Brian? No way."

"Way."

Sadie flipped to the back of the brochure and showed her sister the invoice, complete with names and dates. "Apparently Brian and Joy checked out just days before Brian killed himself."

"Really?" Dawn shook her head. "Weird. I never knew he was into this kind of thing."

"I don't think he was. I think it was Joy's thing."

"Really?"

"That's what Mom said."

"Huh. Do you get the feeling we didn't get to know our future sister-in-law as much as we should have?" Dawn asked, handing the brochure back to Sadie. "I've changed my mind. I think we need to go and check out a certain B and B before we go eat."

"It's been six years since Brian and Joy spent a weekend there participating in wacky workshops. The place has probably closed."

"Let's see."

Dawn picked up her phone and punched in the phone number on the front of the pamphlet. She put it on speaker and it rang twice before the call was answered.

A woman's melodic voice answered the phone.

"Onyx House, how may I be of s-s-service?"

Dawn dropped the phone to the table as if it were a live snake. Sadie could only stare at it.

"Hello?" the voice came across the speaker again.

Sadie reached out and pressed the off button.

"Holy shit," Dawn whispered.

"Yeah," Sadie agreed. "Maybe we're wrong."

"Both of us?" Dawn rolled her eyes. "Have you ever met anyone other than Joy with an *s* stutter?"

"No," Sadie reluctantly agreed.

It sure sounded like Brian's fiancée but it had been years, so Sadie couldn't be sure.

"There's only one way to find out," Dawn said, getting to her feet.

It didn't take long for Dawn to drive her car into the upscale area of Capitol Hill. They entered a cul-de-sac lined with mature trees and Sadie spotted a small sign for Onyx House almost immediately.

"It's at the far end," Sadie said.

Dawn slowed and as they got closer, Sadie made out the curved barnlike roofline above a hedge of tall cedars. They could see beyond the wrought-iron arbor entrance from the sidewalk to a turn-of-the-century two-story tucked far back onto the pie-shaped lot.

Three young girls played on the street in front of the driveway. Two of them skipped rope as fast as they could, while the other sat cross-legged on the sidewalk and watched.

"Just park in front of the next house," Sadie suggested so as not to interrupt their play.

Once they were parked and Dawn had removed her keys from the ignition, they sat for a moment.

"So if it is Joy, what do we say?" Sadie asked.

Dawn cracked her knuckles as she contemplated her answer.

"Let's just be honest."

"What? And tell her that we found the brochure for

this place in her dead fiancé's belongings and we're coming to see what kind of voodoo happens here to make a normal guy want to kill himself?"

"Maybe not that honest. How about we stick with 'We found the brochure in Brian's stuff and were curious'?" Dawn turned to Sadie and shook her head in wry disbelief. "You don't really think Brian committed suicide because of something that happened at a B and B, do you?"

Sadie didn't reply. She opened her car door and waited while Dawn unfolded her legs and then heaved herself, belly first, from the driver's seat.

They stepped up on the curb and each took a deep breath as they stood next to the sign for Onyx House. To their left, the little girl who'd been sitting watching her friends jumped to her feet. She eyed Sadie and Dawn curiously, but the other two merely sped up the spin of their ropes to a loud rhyme.

> *Never laugh when a hearse goes by*
> *'cause you might be the next to die.*
> *They'll wrap you up in a great big sheet*
> *and send you down fifteen feet.*
> *One . . . two . . . three . . . four . . . five . . .*

The girls madly sped their skipping ropes until *fifteen,* then fell together in a squealing, giggling hug.

Sadie and Dawn looked from the girls to each other and chuckled.

"Seems like just yesterday that was us," Dawn said.

"Yeah."

They paused for a moment before stepping through the vine-covered trellis. An interlocking-brick path led toward an older two-story home. The exterior wood was stained dark green and the trim around the windows was painted white, giving the large house the appearance of a cozy cottage. The grass in the yard was almost impossibly green in this heat. In the far corner of the yard half a dozen Adirondack chairs were arranged in a cozy circle around a small copper *chimenea* fire pit. It looked like a perfect getaway spot. Sadie found it hard to believe that she was less then a half hour from her own home instead of in the backwoods.

"Man, I could get used to this," Dawn said dreamily, echoing Sadie's thoughts. "I'll have to tell John about this place."

In the shade of the house lush flower beds boasted rotund rhododendron bushes covered in globes of blood-red blossoms. As they got closer, Sadie could hear the soft hum of bees buried deep into the flowers. They walked up the wood stairs to a large wraparound deck that had more deck chairs and a porch swing that begged dreamy days with a glass of lemonade in one hand and a romance novel in the other.

To the right of the front door, dangling on a chain was an oval wood plank that had ONYX HOUSE branded into the wood. It was old and faded from the sun, but the *O* in ONYX had red spokes that reminded Sadie eerily of the Fierce Force flaming *O*.

You've got bike gangs on the brain, she chastised herself.

Dawn lifted her fist to knock when the door flew open. A surprised look creased the face of a middle-aged man with a clean-shaven head and a blond goatee.

"Hi!" he said, smiling broadly as he stopped short. "I just about ran you two over. Sorry, I didn't hear anyone at the door and I was just on my way out."

"We hadn't knocked yet," Sadie said, smiling back.

"You're early, but no worries, the rooms are ready and we're just about to put out some coffee and fresh baked goods." He stepped to the side and held the door open for them. "Let me help you with your bags. Are they in the car?"

"We're not checking in." Because some explanation

seemed necessary, Sadie continued. "We just heard about your place and thought we'd come by for more information."

"It looks lovely," Dawn added.

"Come on in, then. I'm Tim and Onyx is my baby." He smiled, flashing a spark of silver from a cap on his eyetooth. "There are pamphlets about our rates and services on the side table to your left. My gal is in the kitchen setting the table. I'll just go get her for you. She can give you a quick tour and answer any questions you have about our little B and B."

Sadie took a few steps inside the wood-paneled foyer and Dawn followed. The floors were dark hardwood covered in faded area rugs that led up a staircase in front of them as well as into a bright room to their left and down a long hall straight ahead. Dawn took the left into the sitting room.

Tim retreated down the hall, then returned.

He nodded to a nearby matching console table. "Help yourself to the brochures. I have to make a run to the store, but Joy will be out in a moment and she'd be happy to give you a tour."

When Tim left, Dawn and Sadie simultaneously mouthed the name "Joy."

"Now what?" Sadie hissed.

"I guess we talk to her."

Dawn picked up some advertisements and brochures from the console table and took them across to an overstuffed chair by the window. She lowered herself onto it and looked perfectly relaxed. Sadie sat down on one of the straight-backed chairs, feeling suddenly even more awkward and uncertain. What could she possibly say to her dead brother's fiancée after not speaking a word to the woman in six years?

"This is too weird. Let's just leave." Sadie got to her feet and took a step toward the door.

"Sit down," Dawn whispered. "You worry too much."

Sadie turned around to plead with Dawn. Her back was turned, but she heard someone step around the corner.

"Hello? My husband s-s-said you had questions regarding our little place here?"

Sadie turned and smiled sheepishly. She remembered Joy as a timid, wide-eyed young woman with a sheet of flaxen hair. Gone was the shy nature—this woman carried herself with an air of self-confidence, and her previously long blond hair was cut severely short and spiked on top. She wore a sheer black blouse, chocolate Capri pants, and shockingly high black heels.

Suddenly recognition hit Joy's fine features, and the wide eyes Sadie remembered grew huge.

"Wow! S-S-Sadie, is it you?" Joy asked. Then her gaze whipped across the room. "And Dawn too?"

"Hi," Sadie and Dawn greeted simultaneously.

Unsure of what the proper form of greeting was for someone who used to be almost family, Sadie erred on the side of familiarity. She stepped forward and embraced Joy in an upper-body-only awkward hug.

"I'd get up but it's not as easy as it looks these days," Dawn quipped.

"Well, just look at you," Joy gushed, walking over to place a hand on Dawn's stomach in a move that Sadie knew would annoy her sister. "Is this your first?"

Dawn nodded.

"When are you due?"

"A couple weeks," Dawn replied.

"Sorry to just pop in on you like this. We were just curious and wanted to get more information about this place," Sadie blurted, trying to assure her that they weren't spying on the place, or on Joy. Even if they actually were. "So this is a surprise that you work here."

"Tim, my husband, and I own the place," Joy said. "Wow. It's good to s-s-see both of you!" Joy said, but her big smile looked unsure and her face was pinched.

It was obvious Joy felt even more uncomfortable then they did. "Well, I'm sure I can answer any questions you have about Onyx House, s-s-so ask away."

She bustled past, towering over Sadie in her heels, to choose one of the chairs around the coffee table and perched herself on the edge expectantly. Smiling stiffly, Sadie walked over and sat down on the other side where she could face Joy.

"My mom said you were back in Seattle," Sadie said. "She mentioned that she ran into you at the store. I thought you were still in Los Angeles with your parents."

"No," Joy said quickly. "I was only there for a few months. It was nice to be with my family after . . . well, you know. . . ."

"Yes."

"But," she quickly rushed on, "living with my parents wasn't exactly easy after being on my own for s-s-so many years and I missed Seattle. Even the rain."

"And I guess you knew about Onyx House from when you were here with Brian for the weekend," Sadie said matter-of-factly.

Joy looked momentarily startled. Her color deepened.

"Sadie just now got around to going through some of Brian's things," Dawn explained. "So she found the brochure and invoice showing you two had stayed here and, of course, we got curious, so here we are."

"We had no idea you worked here, though," Sadie said, "or we would've called first."

Joy nodded, her face growing less red.

"But finding the brochure made me think back, because I remember that you and Brian were supposed to go on a holiday . . ." Sadie prompted.

"Yes, of course you all knew we were going away and thought we were camping for two weeks and that's why—"

She seemed unable to find the right way to finish. Sadie helped Joy out without sugarcoating the anger that had built up inside.

"That's why Brian's body was rotting in his bathtub for a couple weeks before we discovered it?"

It was a low blow, Sadie realized, but she didn't care. Even when Dawn gave her a scolding look. After all, Sadie's very first trauma-cleaning job had been wiping up the remains of her own brother. Sadie felt entitled to the heat behind her words, even though six years had passed.

"I'm s-s-so s-s-sorry," Joy said, her stutter becoming more pronounced with her nervousness, but the sincere look on her face made Sadie feel guilty.

"What Sadie means is—," Dawn began, but Sadie cut her off.

"What I meant to ask is, what happened, Joy?" Sadie softened her tone, but her words were still firm. "I'm guessing you two came here for the weekend instead of going on a two-week camping holiday like we thought, right? But then what? You never even went to see Brian afterward, or tried to call and wondered why he wasn't answering the phone?"

Because I wondered why he didn't phone when he got back from his trip. I wondered about it enough to go to his house. Enough to use my spare key and let myself into his place. Enough to be blindsided by the stench inside his house and still push forward to find his bloated body in the tub and his brains spattered all over his bathroom walls.

Sadie closed her eyes and put a hand to her stomach to ward off nausea that threatened to overpower her.

"I wanted to explain what happened at the time. really, I did," Joy exclaimed. "But, well, I didn't think Brian would hurt himself, and when he did, I was in just as much shock and pain as the rest of you." Joy drew in a deep breath and exhaled slowly. "Our original plan was to camp on Mount Rainier for two weeks. Brian loved camping. You know that. But, well, I didn't exactly love it as much as he did and we both only had two weeks' vacation." She looked from Sadie to Dawn.

"Well, I suggested we come here to Onyx House for part of the time and go camping afterward. I'd been here before and I loved it. I thought Brian would enjoy it too."

"Sounds like a good compromise," Dawn said.

She'd positioned herself so that she was leaning forward to listen, but she wasn't the only one. Sadie realized they were both hanging on Joy's every word. It was the first time they'd been able to hear about their brother's last days and it was as if both sisters were afraid to breathe in case they missed any of it.

"Go on." Sadie's throat burned as she swallowed the emotion that accompanied questions that had been a stone in her heart. "Why didn't you and Brian go camping afterward?"

Joy lowered her gaze to hands clasped tightly in her lap and a fat tear rolled out from under the fringe of her lashes.

"We had a fight when we were here. A big one," she said, her voice barely above a whisper. "I'd thought being here would bring us closer. The first couple days I just hoped he'd relax and enjoy himself, but he had, um, things going on. Problems. I guess coming here just brought them to a head."

"Problems?" Sadie repeated

She nodded and looked up to meet Sadie's intent gaze.

"Brian hadn't been himself. After our weekend was over, I thought we were still okay. I thought the fight would blow over and we'd just keep on. But Brian said he didn't want to get married anymore. I was shocked and, well, I was pretty pissed off." She smiled sadly and looked over at Dawn. "I'd already bought my dress. My parents were busy planning the wedding. I freaked out and told him to leave and never call me again." She drew in a deep breath to finish her story. "Brian left Onyx House." She looked up. "You can see why I didn't want to explain all that to his grieving family?"

Sadie and Dawn nodded.

"So after Brian was gone, I signed on to stay a few more days on my own to, well, clear my head. I think part of me expected Brian to call or come back and tell me he'd changed his mind. He never did. I was so mad at him, I never tried to call him either. After Brian's funeral, Tim offered me a part-time job here, but of course, I was too devastated to think about anything. All I wanted was to go home to my folks."

Even though Joy's tone was quiet and sincere, Sadie got the distinct feeling she wasn't telling them everything. Maybe not quite a lie, but not the whole truth. Sadie wanted to confront her about it. At least ask her a few more questions, but Dawn was already on her feet.

"I'm really sorry we just showed up like this," Dawn said. "But it was nice to see you again and thanks for telling us what happened and putting our minds to rest."

Put our minds to rest? Sadie thought. *My mind isn't resting. My mind is wide-awake.*

Dawn was walking to the door and Joy was following, so Sadie felt obligated to go along. She considered asking a couple more questions about Brian's stay at the B and B but right when they reached the front door, a young woman in preppy designer clothes walked through the front door.

Joy greeted her warmly and then made brief introductions, informing Sadie and Dawn that the woman would be giving a class on cleansing auras that afternoon.

"It's one of our most popular s-s-sessions," Joy said.

"You're welcome to stay for the session," the woman, a bubbly redhead named Louise, gushed. "Any friend of Onyx House is welcome."

"Of course," Joy said politely. "You should s-s-stay. Both of you. You might find it very interesting."

But even as she said the words, Joy had her hand on the door and was opening it to usher them out.

Dawn thanked her politely for her offer and before Sadie could say anything, they were out the front door.

"Let's stay in touch," Joy called after them in that we'll-do-lunch tone people use when they don't really mean it. "I'll call you."

Back in the car, Sadie realized she was fighting tears. She looked away so Dawn wouldn't notice, and found herself looking into the grinning round face of a brown-eyed girl with lopsided pigtails. It was the same little girl who'd sat on the sidelines while the other two skipped. She was maybe five years old and smiling brightly at Sadie.

Sadie lowered the window and smiled back.

"Yes?"

"Are you visiting my mom?" she asked.

"We were just getting information on the B and B," Sadie replied as Dawn started the car.

"Yeah, from my mom," the little girl said, pointing to Onyx House. "Joy."

"Joy's your mom?" Sadie asked.

"Yup." She nodded and a wavy lock of brown hair fell loose from a pigtail. "My name is Rhea. I'm almost six. What's your name?"

"Who are you talking to?" Dawn asked.

"This is Rhea, Joy's daughter," Sadie told Dawn, then turned back to the little girl. "I'm Sadie. Nice to meet you."

"Sadie," Rhea repeated slowly as if trying the name on her tongue. She smiled and nodded. "Come back soon."

The little girl took a step back from the car. She waved as she turned to go and Sadie saw a wink of silver on the girl's wrist.

"Wait a second, can I see your bracelet?" Sadie asked, reaching out the window toward the girl.

"It's mine." She tugged her arm quickly against her body.

"It's very pretty," Sadie said quickly. "I knew some-one who had one just like it. Could you just hold it up so I can take a look at it?"

Rhea reluctantly held up her hand. The man's thick-linked ID bracelet slid up her forearm as she held up her hand. Sadie's throat went dry. The name engraved on the bracelet was BRIAN.

Then the girl turned and bolted under the vine-covered arbor into the yard of Onyx House and disappeared behind the tall hedge.

"Did you see that?" Sadie said excitedly to Dawn.

"See what?" Dawn said, looking worriedly at her sister.

"The bracelet Rhea was wearing. It had Brian's name on it!"

"Sadie, I don't know what you're talking about. You were talking to air. There was no little girl."

11

"So Joy had a daughter named Rhea, who died," Dawn said. "How sad."

"I guess . . . ," Sadie said, sounding skeptical.

Dawn pulled her car away from the curb and circled the cul-de-sac to pull off the street. Just as she turned the wheel, a small white dog darted out of a yard right in front of them. Dawn hit the brakes. The little pooch sat down on the pavement and barked loudly at them but didn't move.

"Sheesh. That was close," Dawn muttered. "Stupid dog."

Sadie got out of the car and walked around to the front. She picked up the small Chihuahua mix, scooped it under her arm, and walked up the sidewalk to the small corner home. Sadie knocked on the screen door and soon an older woman with her head in curlers came to the door.

"Peanut!" she exclaimed, flinging the door open. "How did you get out?"

Sadie handed her the dog.

"He ran in front of our car," Sadie said, thinking that Peanut was almost peanut butter.

"Oh my God. Well, thanks for stopping." To the dog she said, "You're a very bad boy, Peanut."

Sadie smiled and turned to leave, but then she turned back.

"By the way, the place across the street . . . Onyx House . . . what is it like?"

The woman frowned. "Well, Tim and Joy are nice enough. Are you thinking of staying there?"

"Maybe."

"I hear it's quaint and relaxing. Although I could do without all the weirdos coming and going."

"The guests?"

She nodded.

"Lots of people show up for their seminars and workshops. Sometimes our street is clogged with vehicles. I don't complain because they had a tough year." She leaned forward and whispered, "Their little daughter died last year."

"How sad," Sadie said. "Did she have a terrible disease?"

"No, a terrible accident. It was a hot day like this one. The bedroom window was open and Joy was working in the garden beneath. I guess the poor little thing leaned out the window to say something to her mom and she fell. Landed only a few feet from Joy."

"Oh my God!" Sadie exclaimed, genuinely appalled. "That's awful."

"Yes. I heard Joy's scream all the way over here, so I rushed over. I was the one who called nine-one-one," she said proudly. "But of course there was nothing that could be done."

Peanut was squirming in her arms, so she stepped back inside the house and set him down.

"Thanks again for stopping your car," the woman said, and walked back inside her house.

Sadie returned to the car and as they drove out of the area, she told Dawn what the neighbor said about Rhea.

"That's the saddest thing I ever heard," Dawn replied.

Sadie agreed that it was tragic.

They headed to Macrina Bakery to eat, but there were no tables available, so Dawn took advantage of the bathroom and then they took their lunch to go. Sadie drove

Dawn's car and ate a Morning Glory Muffin, washing it down with coffee. Dawn devoured some kind of a sandwich made out of ciabatta bread and stuffed with vegetables.

"You have something green on your chin," Sadie said, smiling at her sister's exuberant eating.

Dawn dabbed at her face with a napkin. "It's avocado." She took another bite. "Man, I was starved."

"Are you sure it's all baby in your belly? I'm beginning to think it's all food," Sadie joked.

"Oh, it's all baby," Dawn said, lovingly brushing crumbs from her stomach.

Sadie steered around a slow-moving driver and they drove for a few minutes in complete silence.

"Do you mind if we stop at my place first? I'd like to get my car, pack an overnight bag, and pick up Hairy."

"Sure, but only if you tell me what thought has given you that serious, grim look on your face."

"You won't want to hear it."

"Is it about eyeballs and maggots?"

"No."

"Then tell me."

"The little girl, Rhea, said she was almost six." Sadie looked pointedly at her sister.

"Yeah, so?"

"So . . ." Sadie waited for her sister to get it. Apparently pregnancy hormones had slowed her ability to count.

"Oh, shit."

"Yeah," Sadie agreed. "If she's almost six and Brian died six years ago, she's either Brian's kid, and our niece, or Joy was screwing around."

"Or she just hooked up with Tim right after," Dawn said.

They drove the rest of the way in silence. At least until they pulled onto Sadie's street and realized a vociferous sound was the earsplitting shriek of Sadie's house alarm.

"Great. Just great," Sadie muttered as she pulled up in her driveway, alongside a Seattle PD cruiser.

"Do you think someone broke in?" Dawn asked.

Sadie didn't reply. An uneasy feeling caused her nerves to ping and her heart to pound in her chest.

"Maybe you should wait here," Sadie told Dawn. Before her sister could respond, Sadie was out of the car.

Two officers were just walking up her driveway toward her open front door.

"Hey!" she shouted over the wail of the alarm. "I'm Sadie Novak. I live here." Because she knew the drill, Sadie produced her driver's license as proof.

A middle-aged female officer with a sour look on her face nodded. Her partner, a young recruit with a quick smile, spoke first.

"We'll check things out inside. Wait here," he shouted back.

"Don't suppose you left your front door wide open when you went out?" the female officer asked.

Sadie could only shake her head.

"Maybe the siren scared 'em off before they could take much," the young recruit said over his shoulder.

The officers unholstered their weapons. The guy went around back, while the woman cautiously stepped through the front door and disappeared down the hall.

Seconds felt like hours while Sadie stood on her front lawn wringing her hands and watching lights flick on inside her house one by one. Her next-door neighbor peered at her from between parted drapes and offered Sadie a look of pure disgust. This wasn't the first time her alarm had gone off and it wasn't the first time the police had come by her house either. She wasn't exactly going to win neighbor of the year.

"It's clear," the woman officer shouted to Sadie. "Can you deactivate your alarm?"

Sadie hurried inside and froze. Her house was a chaotic disaster of overturned furniture and emptied closets. She blinked back tears as she stepped over a pile of jackets that had been yanked from her front closet. Her fingers trembled and felt clumsy as she punched in the code on the alarm keypad to disable the siren.

"I'm Officer Shultz," said the woman. "My partner is Officer Reagan."

"You want I should call for fingerprints?" Reagan asked.

He received a nod from Shultz, who then put a hand on Sadie's arm.

"You said your name was Sadie Novak. You're that entrails-cleanup gal I've heard about?" She had a look of revulsion on her face that she quickly shook away.

"Yes," Sadie admitted. "That's me."

"Then I guess you can handle seeing a mess. You've certainly seen worse on the job."

Officer Shultz led Sadie out of the living room, where sofa cushions were tossed to the floor and drawers were emptied from the end tables. Sadie followed the officer into the kitchen.

Sadie's gaze went to the wall across the room and a scream burned her throat. A black-and-white ball of fluff covered in blood was nailed to the center of her kitchen wall.

"Hairy!" she gulped. She would've dropped to her knees if Officer Shultz hadn't caught her under the arms.

"It's not real!" the officer hurriedly shouted. She yanked Sadie upright. "It's stuffed. Sorry, I kinda thought it was obvious. I shoulda warned you."

Ya think?!

Sadie blinked back tears and took a step closer. She tentatively reached out her fingers. Even though it was now obvious it was a stuffed bunny and the smell was definitely ketchup, not blood, Sadie still needed to touch it, just to be sure. She exhaled slowly, but her panic did not subside.

"Hairy," Sadie said, whirling around and looking anxious. "Have you seen him? My rabbit should be around here somewhere."

"I take it he looks like this one?" Officer Shultz asked drily.

"Except for the ketchup."

Officer Reagan returned and the three of them started the search. Sadie paused only a few seconds to take in the mass of upturned files in her office and the smashed computer monitor. Her bedroom was just as bad, with every drawer dumped out and the mattress ripped to shreds.

"Are you okay?" Dawn called out from the other room.

Sadie left the bedroom to meet her. Dawn was standing in the living room. Her gaze took in the disaster that was Sadie's house and she burst into tears. Dawn cried over just about anything these days, but Sadie felt like bawling along with her.

"It's a break-in. Stuff can be replaced," Sadie said, giving Dawn a hug. "Just wait for me in the car, okay? I'll just gather up Hairy." She swallowed thickly. "And I'll be right out."

"Probably best we don't add any more fingerprints to the mixture," Officer Shultz pointed out.

"Okay." Dawn nodded reluctantly and left the house.

"Last thing I need is for her upsetting herself and going into premature labor because some assholes tossed my place," Sadie grumbled.

"So did they find what they were looking for?" Officer Shultz asked.

"I don't know *what* they were looking for," Sadie said quietly. She called Hairy's name. Not that she expected Hairy to answer or come hopping along. He was kind of independent that way.

It wasn't long before they'd checked every room.

Oh God. What if they took him? she thought worriedly. *What if they took him for . . . oh, God!* She closed her eyes as the thought completed. . . . He could be rabbit stew in a biker's pot.

"In here," she heard Officer Reagan call from down

the hall from the combination mudroom and spare shower that was between the house and the garage.

Sadie rushed in to see the officer kneeling in front of the opened dryer door and holding Hairy in his arms.

"What kind of a sick puppy puts a cute little guy like this in the dryer?" Reagan asked, handing Hairy to Sadie. "Good thing the dryer wasn't turned on."

"He seems okay," Officer Shultz said

Sadie held Hairy's fuzzy body up to her face. She pressed her cheek against the warm feathery softness of his back, and his fur came away damp from her tears. She stifled a sob with the back of one hand. She did not want to think of what would've happened had the dryer been turned on.

"Hey, there's a note," Officer Reagan announced. He pulled a tissue from his pocket and used it to pull a white piece of paper from the dryer. He got to his feet and placed the sheet on top of the dryer so they could all read it.

" 'Give back what's ours or we'll take what's yours.' " Officer Shultz raised her eyebrows at Sadie. "Care to fill us in?"

"You need to call Detective Carr. This probably has to do with a meth-lab scene I cleaned. The one where all that money was found."

"That place over in Kirkland? I heard about that. Why would this have any connection?"

"You heard about the money?"

"Walls were full of it." She nodded.

"Apparently the bikers don't appreciate losing all their money to police evidence and I guess they blame me for that." Sadie paused and blew out a breath. "They might also believe I helped myself to a chunk of it." She met the officer's face. "I didn't."

"Of course you didn't," she said, but her face said she'd seen more-honest-looking people do even worse things. "That would be stupid."

"Yeah," Sadie agreed.

"Because even if you were stupid enough to steal money from a Fierce Force gang house, that doesn't mean you'd be so retarded you'd hide it in your own house."

"Um. Ri-i-ight," Sadie said. "Isn't there anything else you could be doing here? Like searching the neighborhood for a passel of bikers or canvassing my neighbors for witnesses?"

"Yeah, we'll go ask around to see if anyone saw or heard anything suspicious. But I'm guessing whoever did this didn't hang around for us to come looking for them."

"It took more than a few minutes to create this kind of disaster," Sadie remarked, tiredly looking around.

"The fingerprint guy'll be here and we'll take pictures and stuff, so, yeah, you might just want to go and stay somewhere else tonight."

"Yeah, I was planning on it. That's why I was here," Sadie said weakly.

She looked up and saw Dawn in the doorway.

"Sorry for making you wait so long. I'm . . . I'm just looking for Hairy's carrier."

"I heard the officer outside say this was gang related." Dawn's voice cracked. "God, Sadie, what if they come back?"

"They won't. They just wanted to scare me. Why don't you go back home? I'm just going to pack a bag and get Hairy's litter box and stuff and then I'm out of here. You look tired."

"I can't leave you in this mess. I'll help you clean up."

"I'm not going to get any cleaning done today because they still have to wait for the fingerprint guy to come and make an even bigger mess. Plus, Maeva called and invited me over to talk about the food for your shower."

"My surprise shower?" Dawn asked with a smirk.

"Right. It'll be great food and that alone will be a surprise, right?" Sadie smiled. "So I'm going to visit Maeva for a while before I go to your place for the night." Sadie felt she needed some time to digest what had happened and she didn't want Dawn to worry about her every second she was gone.

"Are you sure?" Dawn sniffed.

"Yes." Sadie waved an arm around. "Trust me, this looks worse than it actually is."

Thank God she didn't see the note or hear about Hairy.

After shooing her sister out the door, Sadie did pack a couple changes of clothes, toiletries, and Hairy's litter box and food. Then she piled everything, including her rabbit in his animal carrier, into her Honda. She was backing out of her driveway when Zack's Mustang pulled up and parked at the curb in front of her house.

Sadie rolled down her window as he walked over. His hands were in fists and his stride was angry.

"Why didn't you call me?" he growled.

"There's nothing you could do," she said, her voice extra calm. "I would've called and told you about it. I just wanted to get out of here and clear my head first."

"So I got to hear about it from my cop friends instead of you."

"Yeah, well, sometimes it's not great having a friend who's an ex-cop with connections."

"Friend. Right." He spit the words out like they were bitter.

She saw his fists unfurl and the hard edges of his face soften as he leaned into her window.

"So you're okay?"

"As okay as anyone can be after finding their pet stuffed in a dryer and receiving death threats from a crazy biker."

He glanced into her backseat where Hairy thumped his feet angrily in his cat carrier.

"Where are you staying?"

"With Dawn. John's out of town and it's probably good that I spend time with her before the baby comes."

He looked like he wanted to protest but didn't know how, so he just nodded sharply.

"I'll see if I can find out anything more," he said.

Without waiting for her to answer, Zack turned and started to walk away back toward his own car. Then suddenly he came back. He opened Sadie's door, reached in, unbuckled her belt, and tugged her to her feet. All the while Sadie was thinking, *What the hell?* but before she could ask what he was doing, Zack pulled her body up against his and kissed her.

His mouth was hard and fierce but then melted to soft. Sadie felt her insides dissolve to liquid. The second her mind began calculating whether her Honda had a big enough backseat, a cold splash of reality hit her and Sadie pushed him roughly away.

"You don't get to do that!" she shouted, and her voice was thick with emotion. "You don't get to treat me like a stranger for a year since we slept together and then just kiss me out of the blue! It's not fair."

She climbed back into her vehicle and slammed the door. Anger propelled her as Sadie whipped down her driveway and burned rubber up the street before the first tears came.

Sadie drove around aimlessly but wasn't surprised when her Honda parked at Seven Coffee Roasters, a small independent coffee shop. As for most Seattleites, coffee was Sadie's comfort food. The smell of fresh-ground beans was as soothing as a warm blanket on a cold night. Sadie got a four-shot Americano to go. She would've liked to curl up with it on the coffee shop sofa, but she knew Hairy was already pissed about being stuffed in the cat carrier.

When she got back to her car, Sadie slipped Hairy one of his yogurt treats, then found herself driving toward Maeva's place. When she told Dawn she was going to hook up with her friend to discuss shower stuff, she hadn't really planned on visiting the psychic, but it would be good to see her friend.

Sadie tucked her car into a visitor stall next to Maeva

and Terry's townhome. She hadn't bothered to call first and regretted that decision as she shifted Hairy's cat carrier from one hand to the other and rang the doorbell. She could hear voices inside. Happy, cocktail-type voices.

Terry answered the door.

"Hi!" A wide grin split his narrow face, and his spindly arms circled her in a bear hug. "Sadie's here," he called over his shoulder, then glanced down. "And she's brought Hairy."

"Sounds like you've got company. Maybe I should just go," Sadie said, still standing at the front door.

"Nonsense!"

Terry ushered Sadie through the small foyer and into their comfortable living room. Maeva was already on her feet and greeting Sadie at the door.

"This is kind of a surprise," Maeva said with a smile.

"Kind of?" Sadie asked.

Maeva just winked.

"Let me introduce you to another friend of ours," Maeva said. "This is Louise."

"Oh." Sadie blinked in surprise. "We've met."

The petite redhead with the pointy nose clapped her hands in delight. It was the same woman Sadie had met at Onyx House.

"How wonderful to see you twice in the same day. The stars must be aligned in our favor."

Great. I've come on weirdo night, Sadie thought.

"Right," Sadie said. "Um. Nice to see you again."

"Have a seat," Terry insisted. "You prefer white, right? I've just opened a nice sauvignon blanc."

"Thanks. Are you sure I'm not interrupting?" she asked Maeva.

"Of course not," Maeva said with a wave of her hand. "You're always welcome here. You know that." She took the pet carrier from Sadie's hand. "And for God's sake, let Hairy out of his jail and then tell us where you met Louise."

Sadie sat on a nearby chair while Maeva released Hairy. The rabbit scurried off in a big hurry, probably worried he'd be locked up again.

"I've never met anyone who has a rabbit as a pet," Louise said, sipping from her own glass of wine as she sat down on the love seat. "At least not someone who carries the thing around."

"Usually Hairy doesn't leave the house," Sadie said.

Terry returned with Sadie's wine and then took a seat on the sofa. Maeva scooted over so that she was close to her beau, and Terry placed his arm around her shoulders. They were both roughly the same height of five eight, but Maeva's pale complexion and wild curly hair stood in sharp contrast to Terry's Jamaican skin tone and shaved head. They looked impossibly happy together and it made Sadie's heart ache.

"I met Sadie today at Onyx House," Louise gushed.

"Really?" Maeva's eyebrows rose. "The reason I said your visit was only kind of a surprise was because Louise was just saying seconds before the doorbell rang that we'd be getting a guest," Maeva explained. "Now I hear that you, Sadie Novak, the ultimate skeptic of everyone's talents but your own, were hanging out at Onyx House? I'm shocked." She smirked.

"It's a long story. It's not like I was taking any of their weird courses or anything—" Sadie realized her mistake and her hand flew to cover her mouth as she looked apologetically at Louise. "I am so sorry. I didn't mean to imply that your aura-washing thing was weird."

Louise and Maeva laughed.

"So, is Louise part of your, um . . . ?" *Weirdos.* "Your group that meet every month at the Psychic Café?" Sadie asked, trying to keep her question innocent.

"No, but we've met at conferences occasionally." To Louise she added, "Sadie's the one I was telling you about. The one who talks to the dead and convinces them to go over to the other side," Maeva explained. "And she thinks that *we're* the weird ones."

This brought another round of giggles. Sadie tried to join in but could only offer a tight smile.

"What's up?" Maeva asked. "You're looking a little stressed?"

"Well, let's see. . . . Curly the Cutter almost dissected me, my house has been trashed by scary bikers who stuffed Hairy in a dryer because they think I took their money, and a little dead girl is wearing Brian's ID bracelet. Other than that, I'm just peachy."

The room quieted and Sadie sipped her wine.

"Nice wine," she said to Terry. "I may have to get some of this for the baby shower."

"I think we need details," Maeva said.

"I'm fine. I didn't mean to ruin your evening. I'm staying with Dawn, so maybe I should just head over there now before your night is a total loss." Sadie looked around for her bunny, who was no doubt noshing on designer arugula in the kitchen.

"You can't leave us hanging after you blurt out part of a story about bikers, ghosts, and bracelets," Maeva said.

"Wait a second." Louise held up a hand. "I'm getting a name." She tapped her temple with a long fingernail and muttered. "Z-Z-Zamir? No!" She tapped some more. "Zedekiah? No, that's not it." More tapping. "Zack! That's it. Maeva, you're thinking about someone named Zack." She pointed to Maeva, and Maeva in turn stared at Sadie.

"If anyone's thinking of Zack, it would be Sadie here. She's got the hots for one of her employees, an ex-cop named Zack Bowman. He has a gorgeous olive complexion, thick dark hair, and an ass that you just want to take a bite out of."

Sadie rolled her eyes. She should be used to Maeva's psychic friends by now, but truthfully, she had a hard time separating those to be taken seriously from those you'd hire for party tricks.

Shock and amaze your friends with a clairvoyant séance, on sale this week for only ninety-nine dollars!

"Actually, I wasn't thinking of Zack," Sadie said mildly.

"Oh, come on." Maeva rolled her eyes. "You're always thinking about Zack. Well, I guess except for those times you have your tongue down Scott Reed's throat."

"I'd rather not talk about the love life you imagine that I have," Sadie said.

Maeva shrugged and downed what remained of her wine.

"How well do you know Tim and Joy?" Sadie asked Louise.

"They've had me do sessions at Onyx House a couple times. They seem nice enough, why?"

"Joy used to be engaged to my brother. Before he died," Sadie explained. "I discovered a brochure for Onyx House in Brian's things and went to check the place out because I was curious."

"You're finally going through some of his stuff?" Maeva asked. "Good for you. It's about time." She rubbed her hands together. "I think we should move our conversation in another direction. We've got bigger fish—or should I say goats?—to fry." She put her empty glass on the coffee table and leaned toward Sadie. "Spill, my friend," Maeva said to Sadie. "Why did bikers trash your place and give your brother's ID bracelet to some kid?"

"Um, those are two separate incidents. Maybe we should talk about this later," Sadie said. "I'm sure Louise doesn't want to sit here and hear all about my problems."

"On the contrary," Louise said, wagging a finger at Sadie. "I sense you are the friend whose identity Maeva has kept carefully hidden this evening during our discussions."

"What?" Sadie asked with a frown.

"Maeva called me over to pick my brain about satanic rituals involving babies and goats, because she was concerned about a friend who'd interrupted a ritual. Given all that you've said so far, I can't help but assume that friend was you?"

"You're a regular Nancy Drew," Maeva said to Louise. "Thank you."

Sadie glared at Maeva. "So if I tell you something in private, you call up the psychic hotline to discuss it?"

Maeva shrugged. "Don't get your Victoria's Secrets all in a knot. I didn't use your real name, so it wasn't an invasion of your privacy. There's no way Louise would've known you were the subject of our discussions if you hadn't shown up out of blue."

"Yeah, don't be angry with Maeva," Louise said. "She only talked to me about it because she was worried and thought I could help. This situation you're in with Satanists could be quite serious."

"There *is* no situation," Sadie said seriously. "It was a biker dude who ended up killing a couple women who he probably first got hooked on crack. Come to think of it, he'd probably have to be on drugs himself to cut the baby from the woman's stomach, and it's a good thing Zack and I showed up when we did, because he's obviously a few fries short of a meal if he was planning on putting a baby in a goat. I was lucky we got there when we did." Sadie blew out a breath.

"Oh, stop feeding us such a line of bullshit," Maeva said, but her voice held no anger, only concern. "You act like it was no big deal a satanic force nearly burned you to death at that scene."

"It only *felt* like I was being burned," Sadie said.

"But Zack had to pull you away. You couldn't move," Maeva pointed out.

Louise got up and walked over to sit on an ottoman near Sadie's feet. She reached out and tenderly put a hand on Sadie's arm.

"Ewww!" Louise cried out. She shuddered violently, shrank away from Sadie, and wiped her hand on her pants as if it were covered with something vile. "I'm sorry, but you are just disgusting."

Startled and embarrassed, Sadie shrank back against the sofa.

"Sorry, I should've warned you not to touch her," Maeva said with a bark of laughter. "Since your psychic skills are touch sensitive like mine, you'll want to keep your hands away from Sadie. The first time we ever touched, she came in for a reading with her sister."

"It wasn't pretty," Sadie said drily. "She puked her guts out. Said it was because I walk with the dead." Sadie said the last with a small forced laugh. "Look, I don't mind hearing your opinion about . . ." *Weirdos and freaks.* ". . . Satanists who get off on baptizing babies by putting them inside dead goats, but I don't see what difference any of this makes. The baby is fine."

"Knowledge is power," Louise said. "You talk like this encounter with evil was a onetime thing. Of course, you could be right. But there's also a very real possibility that was just the beginning."

"I don't know that the spirit was evil . . . ," Sadie said, but remembered the glowing red eyes. "Then again she did donate her baby 'willingly.' " Sadie drew quotes in the air around the words and rolled her eyes. "Still, she was Jake the Snake's woman and most likely a crack-head whore."

"Drugs weren't necessarily involved," Maeva said.

"I'm sure it was coincidence all this happened in a shed behind a clandestine meth lab," Sadie said sarcastically.

"The meth could've been a cover-up for what was really happening on the property," Louise said. She got to her feet with her glass in hand and began pacing.

"But wouldn't that just bring more people around?" Sadie said. "I mean, if we're talking about some kind of woo-woo secret society of Satanists holding freaky meetings and sacrificing goats, you'd think they wouldn't want every drug addict in town traipsing through their location."

"She's got a point," Maeva agreed.

"Unless . . ." Louise tapped a long fingernail on her chin.

"Unless what?" Sadie asked.

"Who better to recruit to the dark side than those you already have some kind of power over?" Louise asked.

"I don't know. Sounds to me like this whole Witigo thing is nonsense."

"Witigo?" Louise asked sharply.

Her glass of wine slipped from her fingers and crashed to the floor.

12

At Louise's insistence, Sadie repeated numerous times what happened to her inside the garden shed and everything she both saw and felt. Terry had given up on the women and gone off to bed after helping to clean up Louise's broken wineglass and pouring everyone a refill. Sadie's wine remained untouched.

"How much longer do we have to go over this?" Sadie asked, stifling a yawn. "It's nearly midnight."

"Good thing you called Dawn a couple hours ago and told her not to wait up or she'd've called the cavalry out for you," Maeva said.

"I'm sorry, but I just need a couple more things," Louise said. She downed a gulp from her new glass of wine and leaned forward to focus her bleary eyes on Sadie. "After you 'fell through' "—she drew air quotes around *fell through* and continued—"and you experienced the 'burning' sensation"—air quotes around *burning*—"did you do a protection ritual in the area and cleanse yourself spiritually?"

"Did I what on my what?" Sadie asked.

Louise sat back.

"Oh my God, Maeva, she doesn't know a thing about the dark forces? Have you taught her nothing?"

"Lay off," Sadie warned, feeling a prickle of annoyance at the way Louise talked to her friend. "I haven't wanted Maeva to teach me any of that metaphysical mumbo jumbo."

"Our relationship has not been one of teacher and student," Maeva explained. "We're only friends that share a basic understanding of each other's ability."

"Still, to leave your friend so ill prepared . . . especially knowing her occupation. Surely you must've understood that in her dealings with the other side it was just a matter of time before she could be in over her head and accosted by a dark force?"

Sadie snorted and Maeva shot her a warning look.

"It's true that Sadie's work puts her in the position of helping wayward souls find their way over to the other side, but from everything Sadie tells me, it seems she is only called to help those who truly want to go over. That has been her place in the spiritual plane and I respect it."

"Thanks," Sadie said.

"You're welcome." Maeva smiled at Sadie, but then she sighed deeply and spoke to Louise. "But you're right. By not educating her even a little on the dangers that are out there, I've left her vulnerable. She had no skills to deal with the spirit of Penny Torrez, so she couldn't deflect the spirit's malevolent powers." She turned to Sadie. "Sorry. You could've done more in that situation if you knew in advance it might happen."

"I don't know what the hell you're talking about," Sadie said with exasperation. "I walked away from Penny Torrez's ghost. There was nothing else I could do."

"Not true," Louise said. "At the very least, you should've left a form of protection banishing the darker side from that area. Now Penny Torrez's spirit is hanging out there. Probably up to no good and—"

"Are you thinking what I'm thinking?" Maeva asked, a small smirk playing on her lips.

"Field trip?" Louise asked.

"Field trip," Maeva confirmed.

Both women simultaneously turned mischievous grins on Sadie.

"Oh, this can't be good," Sadie mumbled, feeling a quick flood of dread.

Since Maeva and Louise had consumed a couple drinks, Sadie was chosen designated driver for their little escapade. Louise rode in the back of Sadie's Honda, while Maeva rode shotgun. They left Hairy with Terry at Maeva's house. It was with trepidation that Sadie steered her Honda into the Kenmore area. She slowed down and took the gravel road that led them behind the acreage where the meth lab was located. She opted to take the road behind the tree line and not park near the house.

"Don't know why we have to go stomping around a crime scene in the middle of the night," Sadie grumbled as she made a hard left turn onto the back road.

"I've already explained it twice," Maeva said simply. "You can't just bring a spirit like Penny Torrez out into the open and leave her. She has to be dealt with and, hopefully, driven back."

"You make it sound like I sent out engraved invitations and asked her to pay me a visit," Sadie said, barely keeping the whine from her voice. "She just showed up when we found her baby. I wasn't looking for, or expecting, a ghost of any kind that day. Even the dog was a surprise."

"You summoned her when you interrupted the ritual," Louise pointed out, sounding sober after the drive. "Most likely her spirit would've moved on after the baby's baptism and whoever killed her would've made sure of that. But when you scared off the perpetrator and the ritual was left incomplete, well, Penny Torrez was left in a kind of limbo."

"Don't forget," Maeva pointed out, "that she willingly gave her life and her own baby for this cause. She believed that baby was going on to be something great because of her sacrifice. You took that away from her."

"Couldn't all of this just be about a really crazy thing that happened because of drugs?" Sadie asked.

"No," came the reply from Maeva and Louise simultaneously.

Sadie drove a few more feet before veering the car onto the shoulder. She cut the ignition and turned off the headlights, plunging them into complete darkness.

"So we're just going to confront a supposedly evil force in the dead of night and tell her to go to hell. Literally." Sadie shook her head. "Why am I the only one who thinks this is a very bad idea?"

"Because you don't know what I've got in my little bag," Louise said, holding up an oversized purse.

"Appetizers?" Sadie joked.

"No. My smudging supplies."

Sadie looked over at Maeva questioningly.

"Smudging is the burning of herbs. It's a cleansing ritual that helps to spiritually cleanse an area and it's been used for centuries to drive away evil spirits."

"So Louise is really a ghost buster with an oversized purse?" Sadie asked Maeva.

"Yes." Maeva wiggled her eyebrows. "Isn't this exciting?"

"Oh, it's great. Just great," Sadie mumbled. "Please remember that this is a crime scene, ladies. And not just the spot where Penny Torrez was killed. Remember, they dug up Bambi today after she was buried under a tree on the other side of the yard. Let's try not to do anything that'll destroy evidence or get our asses thrown in jail, okay?"

They agreed and climbed out of the car. Sadie felt immediately vulnerable as the inky blackness surrounded them in a thick, warm blanket. She felt her way around to the back of her car, opened the trunk, and snagged a couple of flashlights.

Sadie flicked hers on under her chin.

"Be afraid. Be very, very afraid," she joked as the beam eerily lit her face.

"Knock it off," Maeva hissed. She snagged the second

flashlight and shone it back in the car. "Hang on. I'm getting the holy water."

Maeva retrieved a small clear vial from her purse and stuffed it in her pocket. Then she pointed the light across the field beside them. "Show us which direction to go in."

Sadie used her light to point to a path between the tall cedars a few feet away and across the field of tall grass beyond to the shed.

"That's the shed where the baby and goat were found," Sadie said as they walked, her voice low. When they got to the cedar tree line, Sadie shone her light over to the left. "Penny Torrez's body was found over there."

Sadie swung the beam of light to the left, illuminating shrubs and blackberry bramble, to stop at a ribbon of yellow a dozen yards away. "The crime-scene tape is still up." Sadie swallowed thickly. "We shouldn't be here."

"We aren't going to do anything that'll disturb the crime scene," Louise said, sounding confident and strangely enthusiastic about their venture. "We'll burn some sage and a little bay leaf while I mumble a few chosen words and then we're out of here."

"All rightie, then," Sadie said. "You two go ahead and I'll be right behind you."

"Like hell," Maeva grumbled. "Stand next to us. We're a united front, remember?"

"Sure, but you two had a couple cups of wine for courage."

The tall grass rasped against the legs of Sadie's jeans as she walked shoulder to shoulder with Maeva and Louise. Beyond their own rustling movement through the field, the only other sound was a chorus of crickets.

"This is far enough," Louise said once they were a few feet from the crime-scene tape. "I'll just get my smudging supplies ready."

She slipped her bag off her shoulder and Maeva shone her flashlight inside the tote so that Louise could see what she was doing. She removed a couple of clear Ziploc bags.

"Huh. Look at all those little Baggies of green stuff. Don't suppose you brought rolling papers too?" Sadie asked.

But nobody responded to her nervous humor.

"I've got the herbs and my bowl, but I seem to be missing . . . ," Louise murmured. "Could you keep the light shining straight inside my bag? You keep shaking the flashlight and I can't find what I need."

"Sorry," Maeva replied, her voice trembling.

Sadie realized she wasn't the only one who was nervous.

"Could you tell me again what we're going to do?" Sadie asked.

"It's really simple. We'll be out of here in five minutes. Ten tops," Louise said, still routing around in the bottom of her bag. "I'll mix the sage and bay leaves and set them on fire. The smoke will billow around and—" She blew out an exasperated breath and stomped her foot. "Damn!"

"What?" Maeva and Sadie asked.

"Matches."

"Oh, c'mon, you mean we came all the way out here to have your minibonfire and you don't have anything to light it with?" Sadie said, feeling at once annoyed and relieved.

"Well, don't look at me," Maeva said. "Since I quit smoking a couple months ago, I've stopped carrying a lighter."

"A lighter!" Louise exclaimed. "That's it. I'll just run back to the car and use the cigarette lighter."

She snatched Maeva's flashlight from her hands, took Sadie's keys, and hustled back across the field toward the car.

"And then there were two," Sadie whispered. "It's like one of those bad slasher flicks where—"

"Don't you dare start telling scary stories!" Maeva hissed.

"You're scared," Sadie said. A smile played on her lips. "You act like you're the big mighty clairvoyant who'll solve all my ghostie problems, but you're really just as shit scared as I am."

Sadie lifted her flashlight a little. The beam of light played on something behind Maeva, and Sadie's blood ran cold.

"*I'm* scared?" Maeva chuckled. "You should see your own face. You're ten shades of pale and your hands are shaking like crazy."

"Maeva . . . ," Sadie whimpered. "Behind you . . ."

Maeva turned slowly to look in the direction Sadie was pointing to with the beam from her flashlight.

"What?"

"Can't you see her?" Sadie asked, her voice trembling with fear. "It's Penny Torrez."

Penny Torrez's spirit wore the same blood-soaked blue sundress and the same casually demented facial expression. She was standing, almost floating, in the grassy field and moving slowly toward them.

Sadie swallowed thickly as the apparition stopped and pinned Sadie with dead eyes.

"My master told me you'd be back. I thought he was wrong. I told him you were too smart for that."

Her voice was a low growl that made the hairs on Sadie's arms prick up with fear.

"Are you okay?" Maeva asked Sadie, concern cutting her tone.

"She's talking. Can't you see or hear her?" Sadie asked.

"Only those of metaphysical talent can actually see me," Penny said, sounding bored.

"I see a small swirl of mist or smoke right here," Maeva said.

She took a step forward and waved her arm right

through the apparition of Penny. Briefly, the ghost's eyes sparked red as she shot Maeva a look of impatience.

"Knock it off," Penny hissed.

"She—she doesn't like you doing that," Sadie shrieked.

"If my master were here, I'd ask him to get rid of your friends. Then you and I would have ourselves a nice little chat." She threw back her head and laughed maniacally.

"Who is your master?" Sadie demanded, fighting to keep her voice calm. "Is it Satan? The devil?"

"The devil is a figure invented by Christians," she said, chuckling lightly. "We are so much more than that ridiculous imagery. See? No horns." She bent her head and took a step closer. Sadie jumped back.

"Louise, hurry up!" Maeva shouted across the field.

Penny glanced at Maeva like she was a pesky bug.

"Let's cut to the chase," Penny said. Her dead eyes felt like they were drilling into Sadie's. "You. Took. What. Was. His." Each word was punctuated with the spirit's finger stabbing the air in Sadie's direction.

"The money?" Sadie asked in a small voice.

"I'm talking about the child!" Penny snarled viciously. "He was mine to give to the Alliance. He was going to be great. You ruined everything!"

"Oh my God." Maeva jumped back. "Smoke. Lots of smoke."

"That baby was my gift to Witigo. He would've been raised in the order. It was a privilege I gave my life for."

"But what about Jake?" Sadie asked, taking a step backward. "Didn't he have any say about your child?"

She flicked that away with a snap of her wrist.

"Snake was nothing. Less than nothing. He was only good for his sperm and even that took too many tries for me to count. Good news, I have been told that one newborn can replace another, and one with an inherited power would be even better. With my own son in your arms you talked about your sister's pregnancy. My master was very pleased to hear about it. A baby born in a family of your power would make him richer still. It's what he always wanted anyway."

Sadie balled her hands into fists as potent fury boiled inside her gut.

"You and your so-called master stay away from my sister! If you touch Dawn or her baby, I'll—"

"You'll what?" she challenged.

A rustle of hurried footsteps sounded behind them.

"I got the smudge burning," Louise announced breathlessly from a few feet away.

Penny raised her hands high above her head and smiled wickedly.

"You and your little pals thought the smoke from a few herbs was stronger than me? More powerful than Witigo?" She laughed loudly and the sound of it was vile and dark.

Suddenly the spirit of Penny Torrez was directly in front of Sadie, and she reached and embraced Sadie in a tight hug.

The pain was excruciating. Sadie felt like her arms were on fire and she could smell the acrid scent of her own burning flesh. In the distance, she could dimly make out her friends' shouts, but the world around her swirled to black and the ground rushed up to meet her.

When Sadie came to, Maeva and Louise were screaming for her to get up as Penny Torrez stalked angrily toward them. Maeva seemed to hold her off with sprays of the holy water. Sadie got unsteadily to her feet. She had an idea.

"Brutus!" she screamed as loudly as she could.

Penny Torrez inched closer. Maeva's holy water had slowed but not stopped the spirit. Penny Torrez no longer had fingers, only long flames that snaked out from her palms.

"Who the hell's Brutus?" Louise shrieked.

"She's delirious," Maeva responded. "Sadie, we've got to get the hell out of here!"

Just then an angry Rottweiler came charging through the tall grass. Brutus was snarling, his big powerful jaws snapping at the image of Penny Torrez. The spirit of Penny shrank away from the dog before her image began to dissipate. Before she totally dispersed, Penny flung a long drop of liquid blue fire toward Brutus. The dog yelped in pain, then disappeared. Penny's image vanished too, leaving real flames licking at the tinder-dry field at the spot where she'd stood.

"We have to hurry!" Maeva shouted.

The three fled the field for the car.

Sadie glanced back over her shoulder and was horrified to see flames six feet high devouring the tall grass. By the time they reached Sadie's car, the entire acreage was engulfed with a blaze that lit the night into day.

Sadie barely recalled the ride back to Maeva's home. She was afraid to speak until they were all sitting around Maeva's kitchen table.

"I need to call Dawn," Sadie said, getting to her feet. "I don't know how to explain what just happened, but she needs to be warned."

"Sit down. We need to figure things out first," Maeva insisted.

Reluctantly, Sadie sat back down.

"Maeva's right," Terry said, handing Sadie a hot cup of decaf with a shot of some kind of liquor in it. "Try to relax a moment."

"My sister's in danger!" Sadie cried. "How can I relax?"

"We don't know that Dawn is in any real danger," Maeva pointed out. "The dark force that is Penny Torrez spoke with you at that location both times, correct? It's not like she's wandering Seattle looking for your sister. We have to be realistic."

"An evil ghost fueled a five-alarm blaze after threatening my sister's unborn baby. I think being afraid is *very* realistic. Besides, she may not be wandering Seattle, but other Witigo crazies are and they're very much alive!" Sadie's hands flew in the air animatedly. "The guy she called her *master* will be whoever cut open her belly to take her baby."

Sadie wrapped her hands around the coffee cup for warmth. Even though it was probably eighty degrees in the kitchen, Sadie felt chilled.

"Maeva's right. You're overreacting," Louise said, scraping a chair closer to the table.

"I didn't say she's overreacting," Maeva said. "I doubt when Penny Torrez was alive, she could talk to spirits. So Sadie's right that it's a real live person who convinced her to donate the baby to a satanic cult. Besides, you're just annoyed that your smudging didn't work," Maeva stated, smiling a little. "You did your best. Don't sulk."

"I'm not sulking," Louise said, but she folded her arms like a young child when she said it.

"You three never should've gone there without telling me," Terry grumbled.

"I'm sorry," Maeva said, taking his hand in hers. "I know you have no supernatural powers, but your macho presence would've been enough to protect us."

"Damn straight." He lifted her hand and pressed his lips to her palm.

They talked in circles for over an hour but were not able to formulate a plan on how to handle the dark force that was Penny Torrez or how to protect Dawn, if protection was needed.

"I think I need to call it a night," Louise said.

Good-byes were said. Ever the good host, Terry walked Louise to the door. When he came back into the kitchen, he paused between Sadie's chair and Maeva's.

"Well, tonight sounded scary. I'm just glad everyone's okay."

Terry patted Sadie and Maeva on the back affectionately. Sadie flinched as though she'd been struck.

"What's wrong?" Maeva asked, getting to her feet and coming around the table. "Are you hurt?"

"My back stings a little," Sadie said.

It stung *a lot,* but she'd been too worried about Dawn to give her physical pain much thought.

Terry peeled up Sadie's shirt and sucked in a breath. Maeva muttered a loud curse.

"What is it?" Sadie asked. She craned her head to see over her shoulder but couldn't see what they were looking at.

"Baphomet," Maeva whispered.

"Bapho who?" Sadie asked. She got abruptly to her feet and ran out of the kitchen and down the hall, almost stepping on Hairy in the process.

Maeva and Terry followed her into the main-floor bathroom. Sadie stripped off her T-shirt, beyond caring what Terry could possibly think of seeing her in her plain cotton bra. She turned her back to the large wall mirror and Maeva handed her a hand mirror.

"What the hell?" Sadie cried.

Her eyes grew wide at the angry welt on her left shoulder blade. A five-inch diameter circular shape had bubbled with painful blisters. Sadie squinted as she got a closer look. There was a shape singed into the center of the circle.

"Is that . . . is that the shape of a goat's head burnt into my back?" Her jaw dropped.

"Yes, that's Baphomet," Terry said seriously.

"A goat's head in an upside-down pentagram," Maeva explained. "It's a satanic symbol."

"How the hell . . . ?" Sadie searched for words, but none came.

Maeva looked her in the eye.

"You've been branded. They think they own you."

13

Despite Maeva's and Terry's protests Sadie left their house and drove back to Dawn's. She let herself into the house using her spare key. It took two trips to carry in her overnight bag, Hairy in his carrier, and all his food and his litter box. Sadie checked on Dawn, who looked like a beached whale taking up her whole queen-sized bed. Then Sadie fell into a fitful sleep on the futon in the nursery.

Sadie was woken by Hairy's fuzzy butt against her face. He had decided to make himself comfortable and had no trouble hopping onto the low futon bed.

"Get lost," Sadie mumbled, pushing the rabbit to the floor.

She tried to pinch her eyes shut, but it was pointless. She swung her legs out of bed and reached for her cell phone. The glowing display announced that it was five thirty in the morning and she had five missed calls. She checked her voice mail and discovered the first message was from Scott Reed.

"Hey, Sweets, call me."

The next four voice mails were from Zack. One, just checking in. Number two, did she get to Dawn's house safe, because he'd tried Dawn's house at eleven and she wasn't there? Number three was a rambling message about a fire in Kenmore and instructing Sadie to call him back *right now*. She didn't listen to his fourth message.

Sometimes it sucked having an ex-cop as an employee. He had too many connections willing to fill him in on such trivial things as an inferno at a house where she'd helped uncover a couple bodies and one baby with a goat.

Sadie got to her feet and stretched. Her T-shirt pulled against her shoulder blade and she winced.

You've been branded. They think they own you.

Maeva's words rang in her ears. Terry had gently covered the burn with antibiotic ointment and a strip of gauze, but Sadie could tell that the wound had already fused to the bandage. She didn't want a scar. Especially not one in the shape of a goat head in a pentagram, thank you very much.

Suddenly the room she was in and Dawn's entire house felt too confining. She wanted to be home. To set her shambled house to rights again and to try to regain control of her life. But she didn't want to leave her sister.

She heard the flush of a toilet down the hall and realized she wasn't the only one awake. Sadie dug into her overnight bag for clean clothes. Once she was dressed in shorts and a T-shirt, she headed down the hall toward the kitchen and the smell of coffee. Hairy caught up with her, his nails click-clacking on the hardwood as he hurried along, probably hoping for some kind of treat.

She was surprised to find Aunt Lynn at the kitchen table with the newspaper. She looked up and smiled.

"Coffee's made," she said.

Sadie took a mug from the cupboard and filled it.

"I didn't know you were staying here," Sadie said, grabbing a seat across from her.

"When I called to chat with your sister last night, she mentioned John was out of town and you had house trouble. I didn't like the idea of her being home alone so big and pregnant, so I came for the night."

"My mother's driving you crazy, isn't she?"

"Just a little," Aunt Lynn admitted.

"Sorry to hear about your place getting broken into. That's terrible. I should count myself lucky that rarely happens in my town." She took a sip of her coffee. "Dawn said it looked like a hurricane hit your place."

A hurricane of assholes, Sadie thought, but she didn't know exactly what Dawn had told her, so she didn't offer details.

"Well, if you're not busy today, I'm sure Dawn would love to have you keep her company," Sadie said.

You can make sure no satanic fiends try and cut her baby from her belly. Sadie's hands shook a little at the thought.

"I've got work to do, but I'd like to go home first and start the cleanup process," Sadie said.

"We could help if you want," Aunt Lynn offered.

"Thanks, but I've got it under control. I'd much rather have you taking care of Dawn, helping her relax."

"Oh, there won't be much relaxing going on," she said. "I'm sure Dawn will have me folding baby clothes or out shopping for baby stuff. She's got the nesting bug big-time."

"So I've heard."

Sadie finished her mug of coffee and washed it out. Then she fed and watered Hairy before making sure she showed him where she'd placed his litter box.

Before she left the house, she went to say good-bye to Aunt Lynn.

"I'll see you two later. Could you do me a favor and keep Dawn's alarm activated, even when you're home?"

"Well, sure, but you'll have to show me how. I don't have one of those darn things myself."

Sadie showed her aunt over and over how to activate and deactivate the alarm, and then she wrote out the step-by-step process on a large sheet of paper and pinned it to the wall next to the keypad.

Twenty minutes later she steered her Honda up her driveway and parked inside her garage. Before she opened the door, she steeled herself for the carnage inside. Her plan was to make a pot of coffee and drink her way through it as she methodically picked up all that had been dumped from drawers and cupboards.

When she walked into the house, the first thing that hit her was the smell of coffee. She froze where she stood in the mudroom until she gathered the courage to open the door leading to the rest of the house. Definitely coffee smells. Then the sound of a closet opening and Sadie wished her gun was in her hand instead of on the top shelf of her closet.

"Are you just going to stand there or what?" a male voice called from the kitchen.

"Zack?" Sadie let out a whoosh of a relieved breath and hurried toward his voice. As she walked into the kitchen, her feeling of relief was followed quickly by annoyance.

"What are you doing here?"

"Nice to see you too," he grumbled. He took the drawer he'd been filling and slid it effortlessly back into the gaping hole in the counter.

She looked around and realized the kitchen had already been cleaned. All the cutlery on the floor and the broken dishes had been tidied.

"Guess you didn't listen to my message? I said I'd be here to help you clean in the morning." His hair was mussed, there were dark circles under his eyes, and his chin was in need of a shave.

"It's six thirty," she said drily. "In my world it's not officially morning yet." She pointed to her coffeepot. "A couple cups of coffee might help. Oh and I did listen to your other messages. I just must've missed that last one."

He sat down at her kitchen table and sipped coffee from her "I ♥ Seattle" mug.

"Thanks for helping out." She grabbed a mug from the cupboard and filled it with coffee. When she walked past him, she noted the faint smell of booze. It gave her pause. With her back to him she said, "I don't want you to think I'm not grateful."

"You sure as hell don't sound grateful," he drawled. "You sound pissed."

"And you sound like you're hungover." She sniffed the air. "Or maybe you're still drunk."

"I'm fine, but, yeah, I had a few last night."

"And yet here you are at the crack of dawn cleaning up my place. I'd say that's above and beyond the call of duty."

"We're friends, right?" She heard him get up and walk behind her. "Why wouldn't I help out a friend if her place gets trashed?"

He stood only inches away and she turned to face him.

"About when you kissed me. I don't want things to be awkward between us."

He nodded and placed his hands on either side of her on the kitchen counter, pinning her in.

"So that means I can't help you out in a crisis? Help you tidy your house after you've had a break-in?" he asked, his voice low, and his sexy dark gaze sank into hers.

She ducked under his arm and grabbed her coffee mug.

"I got lots on my mind," she said.

"Like setting fire to the Kenmore crime scene?"

She whirled to face him, trying to hide the guilt that was no doubt all over her face.

"I don't know what you're talking about."

"Like hell you don't," he said, his lips tightening into a straight line. "Let me guess. You and Maeva decided to go out there and confront an evil spirit that tried to burn you alive, and figured the best way to handle it was to set an entire community on fire?"

"It wasn't like that," she said quickly. "We didn't start the fire. Louise suggested a smudging would help and—"

"Who suggested a what?"

"It doesn't matter."

"Yeah, it does," he said, grabbing her by the hand and pulling her close. "Everything about you matters to me, Sadie."

He cupped her chin in his hands then and kissed her. His mouth was warm and insistent. It would've been easy for Sadie to lose herself, but she shoved him away.

"You can't keep doing this. Maybe before . . . last year . . . after we, you know . . . damn." She crossed her arms across her chest and simply glared at him. "You're a year too late, Zack."

Zack combed his fingers through his dark hair.

"Look, things were different then. It wasn't the right time. You came to stay with me because someone had just tried to kill you. You needed comforting and I dragged you into bed. It was wrong. I should've at least waited until you were stronger."

"Oh, and now that I'm being chased by bikers and hunted by satanic ghosts, it's time to pick things up where we left off?" Sadie asked with bite. At his defeated look she continued. "I don't remember you holding a gun to my head last year. As a matter of fact, I remember being pretty damn willing." She allowed a small smile at the memory. "But, God, Zack . . . we've worked together nearly every day since then and you've barely looked me in the eye. Any time we accidentally touched, you jumped like you were in pain. And now, now you suddenly make a move for round two?!"

"I guess I figured if I left you alone, things would work out. That I could go back to the way we were before."

"And?"

"First you nearly passed out at that shed after we got the baby. After that, that evil spirit, or whatever the hell it was, hurt you, and then Curly almost killed you, and now this!" He waved his arms to encompass the house.

"So you're not exactly coming to the conclusion that

what's between us is bigger than the both of us, right?"
Sadie said quietly. "This is about you needing to protect
me. Be my rescuer. Again."

"It's not just that. It's—"

She put her hand up to stop him and took a moment
to swallow the lump in her throat.

"It looks like since you're not a cop anymore, you
can't help but rescue the damsel in distress."

"I've tried to get you out of my head!" Zack shouted.
"I tried because I thought it would be a disaster, but . . ."

"But what?"

"But, yeah, I guess it's bigger than both of us," he
said, his voice low. "At least it's bigger than me."

He hooked his finger in the waistband of her shorts
and pulled her body to his. Then he lowered his mouth
and kissed her slow and passionately until she was
breathless. When he released her mouth, he pressed his
lips to her neck and traced a line of kisses down her
throat while his hand slid under her shirt and found her
breast. The feeling of his hands on her was new and yet
familiar. Like she'd been holding her breath and waiting
for it forever.

Somehow they found her bed among her tossed belongings and they couldn't remove each other's clothes
fast enough. When he discovered her bandaged shoulder, he didn't ask—he just murmured, "Poor baby," and
placed gentle kisses all around that spot. She lost herself
in the feel of his hands as they roamed her body.
Thoughts of protest bloomed in her head, but Sadie
pushed them away. She only wanted to feel. When he
entered her, it was as though every nerve in her body
sang with pleasure.

Afterward she lay curled against him. His head rested
on the top of her head and they didn't speak. It would've
been great to just fall asleep together, but the world was
not going to allow that.

A cell phone rang and she recognized the ring as hers. Sadie rolled over and searched their pile of clothes for her phone but couldn't find it.

"It's probably Jackie," Sadie said to Zack. "She'll be looking for work today. I'll just let it go to voice mail and call her later."

She rolled back toward Zack, but immediately after her phone stopped ringing, Zack's started.

"Jackie must be trying you now." Sadie had always told Jackie to try reaching Zack for information about jobs if Sadie herself was unavailable.

"Leave it," Zack said, his voice tight.

But Sadie already had his phone in her hand. She was handing the cell phone to Zack when she noticed the display. The incoming number said that the call was coming from Zack's own home. Sadie's breath caught. She answered the call before she could stop herself.

"Hello?"

"Hello . . . um, Sadie?" Jackie's voice, sounding half-asleep, answered. "I'm sorry, I thought I was calling someone else."

"He'll call you back," Sadie replied, unable to keep the hurt from her voice.

She hung up, got to her feet, and flung the phone at Zack. He caught it deftly before it could hit him square in the face.

"I can't believe this! You left her in your bed to come into mine?" Sadie shouted.

The misery in Zack's eyes was evident. But he didn't deny it.

"Do me a favor and talk to your lover *after* you've shut my door behind you," Sadie said, storming out of the room and heading for the shower.

14

Sadie forced the ache in her heart into fury and used that emotion to propel her into cleaning her house at a fevered pitch. She took her gun from the upper shelf of her closet and kept it within arm's reach, just in case the bikers decided to make another visit. But her mind wasn't on bikers. As she waded through the debris, her mind continuously drifted to Zack.

Within three hours she had drunk her way through another pot of coffee and managed to sweep and pick up most of what had been dumped from closets and cupboards. She'd used nearly a dozen trash bags to contain the debris.

She turned on her kitchen radio and welcomed the annoying arrogance of a local announcer as she wiped down a smudge of ketchup that Zack missed. The sound of the disc jockey cracking jokes was better than the sound of her own labored breathing as she cleaned. And better than the murderous thoughts inside her own head. Soon the biggest telltale sign that something bad had happened was the fingerprint powder that offered smudged marks, most likely all her own, throughout the house. Fingerprint powder could be difficult to remove, but Sadie had more than enough experience cleaning up worse substances.

Dawn called as she was put away her cleaning supplies.

"Aunt Lynn and I have decided to come and help you clean."

"You're too late. I'm all done."

"There's no way you could be finished so soon," Dawn exclaimed.

"Well, I am."

"Okay, then I guess we'll go to the mall. Want to come?"

"Why don't you stay home today? Put your feet up and relax." Sadie nibbled her bottom lip with concern.

"I don't want to hang around the house all day," Dawn protested. "I've still got lots of stuff I need to get for the baby."

Sadie thought about it and realized being surrounded by a throng of shoppers would probably be a safe place for Dawn.

"Okay, but call me later," Sadie told Dawn.

"Are you sure you don't want to come?"

"Thanks, but I've got my own shopping to do. I'll probably go and pick up a new computer monitor."

"I don't like you hanging around that house. It's dangerous."

"I won't be hanging around here. I'm almost done," Sadie said.

"Are you okay? You sound kind of, I don't know . . . sad."

"Just tired. Could you make sure you give Hairy some food and fresh water before you go out?"

She said good-bye and then surveyed her surroundings. She'd done good for a woman scorned, but she definitely needed a second shower.

When she emerged dripping and pink from the hot water, the first thing she heard was raucous laughter. Her heart skipped a beat, but then she realized it was only the radio. She shook her head at her own skittishness. She dressed and walked into the kitchen to make toast. The radio morning man was cracking jokes about the heat.

It's so hot in Seattle this week, the trees are whistling for the dogs.

Sadie rolled her eyes at his lame joke and turned down the radio just a bit before dropping a slice of bread in the toaster. Just as the toast popped, the phone rang and Sadie snatched it up without checking the incoming caller.

"Hi, Sweets," Scott Reed's voice smoothed into her ear.

"What do you want?"

"Besides your body next to mine, you mean?"

"Yeah. Besides that," she snapped.

"The Bellevue meth house is ready to be scrubbed spick-and-span and I'm anxious to do the walk-through with you."

"Yes, the out-of-town owner called their insurance company and got approval for me to proceed when the cops gave the place a go-ahead. But I haven't heard the property is ready," Sadie said. "Sorry if I have to go by more than just your say-so."

She really did not want to clean another meth lab and she sure as hell didn't want Scott Reed tagging along.

"Hey, my sources tell me it's a go."

"Your sources don't mean squat to me, Scott. Besides, I'm really not in the mood—"

"Yeah, sorry to hear about your place getting bulldozed, Sweets. Too bad the bikers think you've got some of their cash, but, hey, you know sometimes having contacts in the media can be a good thing. . . ."

"What do you mean?"

"Maybe I could, you know, talk to a friend at the *Seattle Times* and hint that the cops believe Jake the Snake hid more cash somewhere else and not in that house, or something."

"I doubt it would work. Those goons probably don't even read," she said, but Sadie couldn't help but like the idea.

"Don't underestimate these guys," he warned. "They're

a lot more educated and business savvy then you give them credit for. You've only met the soldiers. The guys on the street with their tattoos, skullcap helmets, and bad teeth straddling Harleys. The Fierce Force leaders are respectable businessmen who wear suits and work in offices. Organized crime is organized for a reason. They're not amateurs. They're as good at what they do as you are at what you do." His tone lightened. "Speaking of what you do, what do you say? I make a couple calls to the *Times* for you, and you call around and see how quickly you and I can walk through the property for me?"

"Okay, I'll make a phone call," Sadie said.

"You're not calling Zack or Jackie to join us, are you? I'd rather it just be us two."

"The last person I'd call would be Zack," Sadie said.

She hung up and dialed David Egan's number.

She got his voice mail and hung up without leaving a message.

Sadie thought about the situation while eating her toast and washing it down with another cup of coffee. If Egan came back into town, she could happily turn the next meth clean over to him. Of course she could always refer it to another cleanup company, even one of the guys who'd gone solo after leaving Egan. That didn't seem right considering Egan had stood by her when her own company's name had been dragged through the mud last year.

She ate the last bite of her toast and redialed David Egan's cell. She was prepared to leave a detailed message and was really surprised when he picked up.

"Hi, Twisted Sis, how's it hanging?" he sang into the phone.

"You're up bright and early," Sadie replied. "I was preparing to leave you a Dear John message."

"Dear John?" Egan asked.

"Yeah. I'm breaking up with you."

"Meaning?"

She could hear a commercial jingle playing in the background and it was loud and annoying, so she spoke up.

"Meaning, I hope you're about to tell me you're coming back into town to resume your work as chief cook and meth washer for Scour Power, so that I can get Scene-2-Clean back on track as a blood 'n' guts cleaning company."

"Aw, Sadie, I appreciate your holding the fort for me. I know this has been tough on you, but seriously, couldn't you hang on a few more days?"

"There's this job that came in and I really don't want to take it on, Egan, so I was hoping—" She stopped herself short when she realized something.

It's so hot Seattleites are flocking to Mama's Mexican for jalapeño chili to cool themselves off.

Sadie reached and turned the power off on her radio, only to hear the same morning DJ cackling over the joke in the background on Egan's end of the line.

"You're in Seattle!" Sadie cried.

"What? Why would you think that, Sis?" he babbled quickly. "I'm tied up with a family emergency out of town. Just like I told you."

"I can hear King County Ken in the background, Egan. I'm listening to the same friggin' station here!" Sadie growled. "Know what? I'm done covering for you. These last few days have been hell on wheels, so, yeah, I'm just . . . done."

"Ah, c'mon, please? Just a few more days," he begged. "I'm in trouble here and I need more time to, um, fix things." He paused. "You know I'd do it for you." She could hear the sincerity and emotion behind his pleading tone when he finished. "Please, Sadie? Give me a few more days. I'm in trouble, but I'm just needing space to sort it all out. I'll make it worth your while. I'll pay you for the jobs you've lost."

Sadie blew out an exasperated breath.

"Whatever you got going on, I expect you'll have your

act together soon. Real soon. Like in three days. I'm taking on only one more job for you and that's it."

She hung up the phone and reluctantly called Reed back.

"I have to wait until I verify clearance," she told him. "But if the house has been cleared, we can meet there this afternoon."

"That's great," he enthused.

"But afterward, I want to talk with you about everything you've got on the Witigo Alliance and Fierce Force, okay? Everything."

"You got it, Sweets, but can you handle satanic shit without falling apart on me?"

"I mop guts for a living, Scott. I think I can handle a few satanic symbols without totally losing control," she said sarcastically.

But after Sadie hung up the phone, she closed her eyes and drew in a deep cleansing breath. She felt like she was playing with fire.

15

"Is all of this gear really necessary?" Scott made a childish face at the blue hazmat overalls Sadie handed him.

"Nope. Not necessary at all." Sadie leaned against the Scene-2-Clean van she'd picked up from Zack's parking lot and she zipped up her own coveralls. "If you don't want to wear the gear, you can walk right through that door and breathe in the wonderful cocktail of benzene, toluene, acetone, chloroform, lye, and hydrochloric acid, and if you're lucky, you'll only experience a headache, nausea, and dizziness. Of course if you're in there more than a few minutes, you can expect chest pain as well as chemical irritation and burns to your skin, eyes, mouth, and nose."

"Fine, but it's not what I'd call comfortable in this heat." He rolled his eyes and wriggled the suit on the rest of the way.

"Welcome to my world," Sadie replied.

She didn't like the idea of having Scott Reed with her in a meth lab he claimed had held a satanic ritual. She was anxious to get it over with.

Once he was covered and they were both sweating in the heat even in the shade of the bungalow's carport, she handed him his respirator.

"After we've got the face masks on, it's difficult to communicate unless we're right up close and nearly shouting."

"Hey, I don't mind getting up close to you." He winked and Sadie couldn't help but laugh.

Scott looked utterly ridiculous in the getup. Of course, most people did look silly outfitted in hazmat gear.

Not Zack, Sadie thought with a combination of regret and anger. *Yes, Zack pulled off wearing a hazmat suit fine. Yup. If possible, he looked even more macho in hazmat gear.*

"Why do you suddenly look like you're about to punch me in the face?" Scott asked.

Sadie shook thoughts of Zack from her head and stabbed a finger at Scott's chest.

"You're not going to touch a thing in there, got it? You'll look around, but looking does not involve touching, is that clear?" Sadie demanded.

"Sure."

"Good. Now, I'm going to be busy taking my before pictures for my records. Do you have any idea what you're looking for? 'Cause I don't want this to take all day."

"Signs of satanic rituals," he replied. "If I point to something in particular, will you take the pictures for me?"

"Yeah, but we're getting in and getting out and you're not allowed any souvenirs."

She helped Scott with his respirator before pulling on her own, then snagged her camera and the house keys. She opened the door from the carport entrance and Reed was right behind her.

The carport door opened into a laundry room. The washer and dryer looked dilapidated and coated with a thick layer of grime. A soaker sink between the appliances looked painted with a dark red phosphorous stain. Sadie snapped photos of the room and continued down the hall to the kitchen. As she took pictures of counters loaded with debris and chemical stains, she also kept one eye on Scott. He walked around looking curiously in every corner.

The kitchen was the area heaviest in debris. There was red chemical staining on the counters, walls, and floor as well as burn marks in several locations. The people from *Better Homes and Gardens* would've had a coronary. Sadie busily snapped photos in a routine fashion and nearly forgot about Scott entirely until she heard a door open down the hall. Sadie finished her shots of the kitchen before going after him.

She found Scott standing in the corner of one of the two bedrooms. He pointed to black stuff on the floor and said something that sounded a lot like "camel fax."

"Camel fax?" Sadie shouted. Obviously translation was lost through his respirator.

Sadie glanced at where Scott pointed and realized he'd probably said "candle wax," and not "camel fax." She nodded and took a picture of black wax that had melted, then hardened in the corner of the room. Drips and dribbles of it crossed the short shag carpet and led across the room to a closet. She followed the trail and opened the door.

The closet was tiny and completely bare with the exception of a couple wire hangers that dangled from the bar and a two-foot symbol drawn on the back wall. The crude picture done with a black permanent marker caused Sadie to suck in a gasp of air, and she braced her knees so she didn't collapse.

Baphomet.

The goat drawn in a downward-pointed pentagram seemed to have eyes that looked right through Sadie. She froze to where she stood. She could feel all the color drain from her face, but Scott didn't notice her panic behind her face mask; he was excited and just wanted pictures.

"Pifure! Ake a pifure!" he called out through his respirator.

Sadie lifted the camera as if in slow motion and snapped a few shots. Her heart was thumping wildly in her chest and Sadie began feeling woozy.

Scott was feeling just fine and, in fact, was on his knees and tracing the outline of the goat-headed figure in the pentagram with his gloved finger. Angrily, Sadie flicked the back of his head with her own gloved hand and when he looked over his shoulder, she nodded to the door.

"Let's go!" she shouted, and yanked him up by his arm.

Once they were outside the house, Sadie couldn't wait to strip out of the gear. Her breath came in adrenaline-laced gasps and she concentrated on not passing out or throwing up.

"Fucking A!" Scout shouted after he tore off his respirator. "Did you see that pentagram? Did you see all the black wax? There was a Black Mass here for sure. Isn't that awesome?" He punched the air with enthusiasm.

"Whoopee."

He was grinning from ear to ear as he slipped out of the rest of his gear and stashed it in the waste bin where Sadie had instructed him to.

"Isn't it cool?"

"Cool?" Sadie blinked at him and felt the heat of anger flood her pale cheeks. "Cool is beating your personal best jogging time, or winning an eBay bid, or finding Kate Spade knockoff sandals half price and they fit. Cool is not—I repeat, *not*—finding a vandalized meth house with a drug addict's rendition of Baphomet in a closet!"

He grinned, walked over, and draped an arm over her shoulders.

"First, can I just say I find it a tiny bit interesting you know the actual name of what we saw in that closet, and"—he leaned his head to the side until it touched hers—"second, there is no way feet as gorgeous as yours should ever be in knockoffs. Stick with me and I'll get you the originals." He turned and planted a wet kiss on her cheek.

"Jesus," she muttered. "Let's just go."

She stomped over to her van and prepared to get in when he stopped her.

"Wait a second, I really want to get the pictures you took."

"I can't give them to you," Sadie said. "You weren't even supposed to be there, remember?"

"I won't say the house where the pictures came from. They're just for my file." He added hurriedly, "Look, I live less than fifteen minutes away. How about we go to my place? You can use my computer to print off the pictures. Just the ones from inside the closet. I don't need any of the others. That closet could be anywhere."

"Am I going to see those pictures on the six o'clock news? Because here's the thing. The cops have already got their own pictures of this place from when they shut down the lab, so they know about the drawing. If you put your pictures on the air, the cops will know exactly where they were taken. They'll realize the pictures came from me and my credibility will be shot."

"Sweets, I'd never do anything to hurt you or your biz," he said, doing a damn good job of looking offended. "I swear, the pictures are only for my file. For research."

She frowned and paused, deep in her own thoughts. She wanted more of an opportunity to talk to him about the Witigo Alliance and what power they might have. Especially considering Penny Torrez was willing to burn their symbol into her back and threaten Dawn's baby.

"I'll follow you to your place," Sadie said.

"Babe, I've been waiting an eternity to hear you say that."

"No funny stuff," she said quickly. "And no kissing, because this is not—I repeat, *not*—a date."

He only smiled.

Sadie got behind the wheel of her van and followed Scott's convertible for a few miles until they were parked in the driveway of a pleasant-looking Cape Cod–style home.

Huh. Well, lookie how Mr. Wild Reporter lives just like Mr. Middle America, she thought.

"I had you pegged for more of a downtown-loft kind of guy," Sadie told him as she met him at the front door.

"Nope. I like a little bit of space between me and my neighbors," he said with a wink. "That way they don't hear the ladies moaning all night long. Well, except for the screamers." He tilted his head and grinned at her. "I bet you're a screamer."

Sadie only rolled her eyes.

Scott opened the front door to more surprises. The rooms were filled with heavy wood furniture, mostly antiques, and had basic off-white walls. Sadie glanced around, feeling disconcerted.

"Are you sure you live here?"

"Yup." He chuckled. "Got a great view of Lake Sammamish from my bedroom. Want to see?"

"I'll take your word for it."

With camera in hand, Sadie followed him down the hall to his office. She stopped in the doorway and looked around the room. On the far wall was a massive bulletin board with pins nailing hundreds of notes, articles, and pictures. Next to it was a whiteboard that listed dates and a timeline that looked like a list of deadlines. The other walls had half a dozen framed magazines, including a *Playboy* that looked like it was from the fifties. Tall bookshelves were jammed with a mixture of music CDs, books, and stacks of newspapers. In the corner was a huge white desk littered with paperwork as high as the computer monitor in its center.

"Now, this is more like it," Sadie said, stepping inside.

"What do you mean?"

"More you."

"Sorry, I know it's a mess."

Sadie looked over and was surprised when she spied someone standing behind Scott.

"Hey, my bedroom is me too." He winked at her. "Come on upstairs and I'll show you."

"So, this is a fair-sized house—you must share it with someone, or do you live alone?" Sadie did not take her eyes off the elderly woman with wiry curly gray hair and wearing a loud purple housedress who stood smiling in the doorway of the den.

"Yeah, Sweets, the whole place is mine. Nobody to disturb us. We could have sex in every room in the place."

Sadie sighed because she was tired of Scott's constant sexual innuendos and because she'd now have to deal with his ghosts on top of everything else.

"Could I get a glass of water?"

"Sure you don't want something stronger?" Scott asked. "I've got beer, wine . . . a fully stocked bar."

"No thanks. It's still early and I've got work to do. Water is fine. Ice if you've got it."

He nodded and left the room, walking nonchalantly through the old woolly-haired woman, confirming her ghostliness.

"Okay, so who are you? A relative or just a previous owner?" Sadie asked, carefully lowering her voice so Scott wouldn't hear.

The woman blinked in surprise and looked around to see who Sadie was talking to. Then she carefully approached Sadie before replying.

"You can see me?"

"Yeah. Lucky me," Sadie said sarcastically. "So, are you going to answer my question?"

"I'm Scott's *baba,*" she replied, nodding her little head.

"His what?"

"It's Ukrainian for 'grandmother,' but my name's Ruby, so you can call me that." She looked wistful. "It feels like years since anyone called me by my given name."

"Okay, Ruby." Sadie walked to the corner of the room and sat down at Scott's computer. Her back was to the door, but the old woman followed, shuffling her feet quickly to where Sadie sat.

"So how is it that you can see me, in this god-awful purple dress, but nobody else can?" The woman's tone had grown loud with excitement. She sat on the edge of the desk and reached as if to hold Sadie's hands.

"Don't touch me." Sadie shrank back. "Sorry, but it creeps me out. I can see the dead. At least, those who haven't moved on," Sadie said, making sure to keep her voice a low whisper. "I can help you move on to where you should be."

And suddenly Sadie was desperate to do so. She hadn't been able to help Penny Torrez, Bambi, or Jake the Snake. Helping ghosts gave her a rush of pleasure. Not helping them made her feel useless and weak.

"You can help me, huh?" The old woman's eyes sparked with amusement as she pinched the material of her dress in her fingers and lifted it up a few inches. "Can you help me out of this ugly purple dress Scott made me wear?"

"What do you mean, he made you wear the purple dress?"

"Well, my mind left before my body followed," Scott's grandmother said sadly. "In the days near the end, I didn't have much use for clothes."

"So you walked around naked?" Sadie smiled a little. Poor Scott.

"Yes. Not a smart thing to do when your doting grandson is living with you and trying to take care of you during the dementia," the grandmother scolded herself. "Alzheimer's is evil!" she shouted, waggling a bony finger in Sadie's face.

Sadie nodded in agreement.

"Anyway, when I had a stroke in the middle of the kitchen wearing nothing but my birthday suit, Scott ran and grabbed this ugly purple nightmare and dressed me in it." She looked down at the fabric with distaste. "He gave it to me that Christmas and I know he wondered why I'd never worn it. Even though I'd lost my mind, I still had a little taste for fashion left in me."

"So he gave you the purple dress and he liked it enough to re-dress you when you died?" Sadie said with a smile. "That's kind of sweet, Ruby. You shouldn't be annoyed. It's beautiful that Scott had enough respect and love that he didn't want them to find you naked in the kitchen."

"I guess," she replied. "You've always liked purple, haven't you Scotty-boy?"

The old woman was staring at the entrance to the den. Sadie turned just in time to see Scott drop Sadie's glass of water with a crash. Splinters of glass spread across the hardwood on a small wave of water, but Scott just stood staring at Sadie with a look of utter astonishment on his face.

"Sorry," Sadie said hastily. "Guess I was talking to myself."

"Really? 'Cause I've been standing here a while and it sounds an awful lot like you're talking to my dead grandmother."

16

"Ha!" Scott's *baba* shouted. "And here I always thought he was a little slow."

Sadie resisted the urge to tell the old biddy to shut up and instead faced Scott.

"Talking to your dead grandmother?" Sadie raised her eyebrows and smirked with amusement. "Are you sure there isn't a paranormal novelist buried in your journalist heart?"

"You called her Ruby."

"You're hearing things."

"You said I re-dressed her in a purple dress. Nobody knows that except me. And you." His voice was louder than necessary and vibrated with emotion. "How could you know that? Shit. I never believed the stories about you."

"What stories?" Sadie said, fighting to keep her voice calm. "If I was mumbling something about a purple dress, it was because I'm debating what to wear to my sister's baby shower."

He wasn't buying her denial.

"I've heard things about you." He pointed a finger in Sadie's direction, and his eyes were big and the look on his face was just plain mean.

"What kind of things?" Sadie asked sharply.

"Things like how some cops say you whisper at crime scenes when you think nobody else is listening. I heard

Detective Malone say that last year when he returned to that shotgun scene in Renton, you were seen chatting away in the garage where the murder happened, and he was pretty sure you were talking to the victim."

"So what!" Sadie shouted back. "It was an ugly scene and it took me two days to mop up the decomp. I've heard the coroner talks to the bodies when he's doing an autopsy too!" She didn't know if that was true. She was reaching. "So forgive me if I talk to myself when I'm trying to keep my mind off the fact that I'm scrubbing away someone's sloughed-off skin! Excuse me if I chat away to keep my mind off the fact that there are maggots having a drunken party in a pool of bodily fluids! I've known other trauma cleaners who whistle a happy tune when they're cleaning a scene."

Sadie's tone was huffy with indignation. She needed to convince Scott. The last thing she wanted was a television reporter who knew her deepest, darkest secret.

"It's why all the cops call you Twisted Sister, isn't it? It's why the others want me to—" He stopped himself. "This is too weird."

Sadie used her most reasonable tone. "Look, they call me Twisted Sister because David Egan from Scour Power gave me that god-awful nickname and it was better than some of the others that were being tossed around, so I didn't discourage it. Think about it. If I were psychic, I'd use my powers to buy a winning lottery ticket." She shook her head and started to giggle. Her giggles turned into full-out guffaws until she was doubled over and tears blurred her vision.

He just watched her.

"Now, let's get back to work," she said. "I'm giving you these pictures, but I was hoping you'd give me some information on that crazy group you told me about when we met for coffee. What did you call them? Wintergreen or something?"

"Witigo. The Witigo Alliance," he said quietly as he walked over to join her by the computer. "When I tried to tell you about WA on our coffee date, you had no interest."

"Yeah, well, I was curious enough to do some of my own research on the Web. They seem like a whacked-out bunch. If, like you say, they were involved in what happened to that baby, and if they're having Black Masses in Seattle meth labs, I figure I'd better find out more information about them, since I'll probably be cleaning up their crap."

The photos Sadie took of the Baphomet and candle wax filled Scott's monitor, and Sadie shuddered before saving them to a file for Scott before disconnecting her camera.

"So if they're just a bunch of crazy Satanists, why are they moving into meth labs?" Sadie asked him.

"I don't know," Scott said, but he sounded like he did know. He just didn't want to talk to her about it.

"You know what I think? I think Penny Torrez was both a member of WA and an FF biker chick," Sadie said.

"Yeah. Maybe." Scott seemed to really consider that. She was just grateful he was no longer talking about her conversation with his dead grandmother.

"Good job. Looks like you convinced him," Ruby said with a throaty giggle.

The old woman patted Sadie's shoulder and Sadie fought back the sudden feeling of nausea from her touch. She bit the inside of her cheek and willed herself to ignore the grandmother, even as the old woman began dancing a jig behind Scott as if taunting him. Sadie focused on sending the photos to the printer.

When Sadie looked up, the grandmother was standing behind Scott and then she vanished. Sadie knew the old woman's spirit hadn't gone for good, though, because there'd been no shimmer and fading to the apparition that signaled Sadie the spirit had moved on to the next dimension. Nope, *Baba* would be back and Sadie was hoping to be long gone before that happened.

When she retrieved the pictures from the printer, she

handed them over to Scott without looking at them. She'd had enough of Baphomet for one day.

Scott barely glanced at the pictures. Although he hadn't brought up the *Baba* incident again, every time he glanced her way, it was with a look of uncertainty. Sadie thought the answer might be to get him drunk.

"You know, I think I'll take that beer now," she told him, getting to her feet. "Or something stronger if you'll join me."

"Okay." He nodded sharply.

This time when he left the room, Sadie followed him, stepping over the broken glass and water on the floor. She hoped *Baba* would stay in the den or remain invisible.

In the old-style country kitchen Scott reached into the cabinet and pulled out a bottle of Canadian whiskey.

"Neat?" he asked.

"Water and ice," she replied.

As she'd hoped, he downed his own glass before he even finished plunking a couple of ice cubes in hers. With any luck he'd wake up in the morning with only the vaguest memory of her mentioning re-dressing his dead grandmother in the infamous purple dress.

"I'm going to go clean up the mess in my office." He grabbed a roll of paper towels and a broom.

When he left the room, Sadie took the drink he'd handed her to the sink and poured almost all of it down the drain. She sat down at the kitchen table and had the glass, with the remaining booze in it, pressed to her lips. When he came back, she pretended to finish off the rest and handed him her glass.

"Okay, so we've got Fierce Force, a biker gang with all the connections and criminal crap of the Hells Angels. And then we've got Witigo Alliance"—she shrugged her shoulders to indicate the little she knew of the group—"um, crazy Satanists who like to baptize babies in the carcasses of goats." She made a face. "Do you think I'm right about Penny Torrez?"

He poured them both another drink and joined her at the table.

"The FF is all about money-making rackets and general lawlessness like prostitution and drugs. WA isn't about money. They're about power. If there was one FF member, or his babe, who liked to dabble"—he shrugged his shoulders—"that could be the connection."

"Like Snake and Penny."

"Right."

He was on his third drink now and they weren't small. He didn't seem to notice Sadie was only sipping from her glass, barely consuming anything. When his cell phone rang and he went in search of it, she dumped her liquor into his glass. When he came into the kitchen, still talking on the phone, Sadie was back at the table examining her fingernails casually.

After he ended the call, he brought the bottle with him to the table.

"Sorry about that," he said. "I have another story I'm supposed to check on later."

He was about to pour himself another drink but noticed his glass was full. He downed it and winced.

"I appreciate you talking to me about this Witigo Alliance thing," Sadie said. "It's good to be prepared in my business."

She bit her lower lip, worried about Dawn. As soon as Scott was safely intoxicated and no longer thinking about Sadie talking to ghosts, she'd make her escape and check in to make sure Dawn was still shopping with Aunt Lynn.

"The WA are bigger than you think." Scott's voice was slurred and louder than necessary. "Hell, they could be living down the street. They could be your neighbors." He pointed his glass at her. "I'll tell you a secret."

"What?" she asked, hoping that secret wasn't something to do with what he had going on inside his Fruit of the Looms.

"It's all about the *O*." He took a big gulp from his glass.

"The *O*?" she repeated. "As in 'orgasms'?"

"I'm talking about the *O*s in the letters." Then he shook his head. "Never mind. I shouldn't talk to you about this stuff."

She gave him a line about orgasms and he hadn't even used it to make any lewd suggestions? They took their drinks into the living room.

Sadie's cell phone rang. It was Zack. She took a deep breath and answered.

"Hello?"

"Sadie, about Jackie—"

"I don't want to talk about it," she snapped.

"Fine."

"If you're going to talk to me, it has to be about work."

"Okay." He was quiet a moment. "Has Thuggy called you looking for work?"

"No. Why?"

"If you hear from him, let me know," Zack replied, sidestepping her question.

"Okay. I did a walk-through on a Bellevue meth lab today. If we start on that one, I guess I could call him in for it."

"Good." He paused before adding, "We're going to have to talk about it eventually."

She told him she had to go, and when she hung up, her phone rang again.

She didn't recognize the incoming number and assumed it was business.

"Scene-2-Clean, how may I help you?" she answered.

"This is Tim."

"Tim?"

"From Onyx House. Joy looked up your sister's number in the phone book, and Dawn gave us this number to reach you. I hope that's okay?"

Sadie sat a little straighter.

"Sure," she replied uneasily.

"I'm so sorry we didn't get more of a chance to chat when you visited yesterday."

"Um. Yes. I'm the one who's sorry. I didn't know Joy worked there or that you two were married," Sadie said quickly.

"Joy?" Scott squinted his blurry eyes at her and she shushed him.

"When Joy mentioned later who you were, of course I felt terrible about treating you and your sister so formally."

Sadie didn't know how to respond to that.

"I mean, after all, Joy was practically a member of your family and just because we got married after what happened to your brother, well, that's no reason for us not to welcome you and Dawn like relatives yourself."

"It was just nice to see Joy and your place. You've got a nice B and B. Maybe I'll check in sometime myself," Sadie said without meaning it.

"Actually, that's why I'm calling. I guess with the brochures you took, you know that Onyx House offers all kinds of workshops and retreats to heal the mind, body, and soul. We've got one tomorrow, as a matter of fact, that's all about healing after the loss of a family member. I know it's been six years since you lost Brian, but I'm sure you'd find it helpful and soothing."

Sheesh! That was the last thing she wanted.

"To tell you the truth, Tim, I don't think I'm interested. Like you said, it's been six years since Brian died. I've come to terms with what happened. Really." She quickly added, "But thanks for thinking of me."

She thought of Rhea and the silver ID bracelet, and Sadie had a dozen unanswered questions. Maybe going back to Onyx House wasn't such a bad idea.

"Well, maybe you'd like to come over for breakfast, then. I'll be making my famous cinnamon rolls. Then, if you feel comfortable, you could stay for the session."

Sadie liked the idea of talking more to Joy and somehow finding out if Rhea was Brian's child.

"I won't take no for an answer," he said firmly. "It would mean a lot to Joy."

"Okay, then. What time?"

"We'll expect you at nine for breakfast and the workshop starts at ten thirty."

Sadie agreed. When she disconnected, Scott was eyeing her with a strange look.

"Life's a bitch," he said.

"Yup. It is."

"So how about you stay the rest of the day and night, Sweets?" His words were slightly slurred. "Forget FF and WA. I'll give you better Os than you've ever had."

He's baaaack, she thought.

"I really should get back to work."

"Stay and have another drink with me first." "Another" came out as "a nudder" and Sadie figured one more straight whiskey should put enough of an alcohol haze of doubt across his memory that Scott would truly wonder about any recollection of Sadie conversing with the dead.

"Okay, but just one more. How about I make you a sandwich too?"

She walked into the kitchen and put both their glasses on the counter. She opened the door to a surprisingly well-stocked fridge. She knew Scott was physically fit and obviously took care of himself, including with what he ate. She took out a package of low-fat smoked turkey as well as some light mayo and a jar of Dijon mustard. She put it all on the counter and found the bread in a cupboard. Once she got the sandwiches made, she worked on the drinks. She added tap water and lots of ice to the whiskey in her glass and poured the remaining drops of the whiskey in his.

She decided to look for a new bottle. She opened the cupboard she thought he'd kept the booze in, but oops! It was the wrong one. This cupboard didn't hold liquor, only a hodgepodge of loose photos. She reached with her other hand for the next maple cabinet door, simultaneously closing the first one she'd opened, but stopped short when the picture on top of the pile caught her eye.

Sadie reached and pulled out the photo, and her blood heated. It was a picture of Sadie cradling her bunny, Hairy, in her arms. She was in the kitchen of her home. Wearing nothing but the long Mariners T she slept in. She thanked God the T-shirt was long enough to cover the bare essentials. She snagged a handful of the pictures and they were all of her, some of them going back a month.

Why the hell would Scott be taking pictures of her? Was he doing some sort of documentary on the life of a trauma-clean woman? Fury rolled through her. She was going to kill him!

With the photos in hand she stormed back into the living room to tear him a new asshole. When she entered the room, though, she stopped short. Scott was slumped over on the sofa and snoring softly. Damn. It was the perfect opportunity for her to leave. Still, how could she let him get away with such an invasion of her privacy?

She couldn't. But there would be time in the future to exact revenge. Today she just needed to make sure Scott Reed wouldn't be blabbing on the news about her talking to the dead.

So instead of throttling Scott, she made her way back into the kitchen and carefully retrieved all the pictures from the cupboard. Behind the stack of pictures was an impressive camera. Without hesitation Sadie took the camera, opened a few compartments, then took some apple juice from the fridge and drizzled some inside. Not enough that it was dripping wet, but enough that it should seize up working mechanisms of the camera. She knew it wouldn't stop him for long because he could easily pick up another camera, but Sadie felt much better exacting a little revenge.

Sadie walked away and cut through the living room on her way to the front door.

"Yanno," Scott murmured, opening one droopy eye. "I'm gonna win an award with my Witigo story."

Sadie didn't reply. When he drifted off again, she stuffed the pictures he'd taken into her purse and headed for the door. She was slipping on her shoes when Ruby appeared again.

"You'll come back again, won't you?" she asked Sadie. "It's kind of lonely with nobody to talk to."

Sadie slipped her feet back out of her shoes and nodded for Ruby to follow her to the kitchen.

"You don't have to stay here in this in-between state," Sadie told her in a soft tone. "How long have you been dead?"

"It'll be two years next month," she answered. "It's been great not having Alzheimer's kicking me around, but it's been lonely with nobody to talk to. Can you show Scott how to talk to me? I miss him."

"It's not a skill I can teach," Sadie said. "But like I was telling you, it's time for you to leave this place. Go to be with those who went before you. You must have family who have passed?"

"They've forgotten me." She sniffed. "Norman, my husband, and my mom and dad."

"Ruby, I think they are there waiting for you, but you haven't moved on because you have unfinished business here."

"Like what?" She looked skeptical.

"If you don't know, I can't guess," Sadie said. "Maybe there's a message you want me to give to the family remaining?"

"Scott's mother and father live in California." She blew a raspberry at the thought of them. "Couple of nitwits, the two of them. Scotty-boy doesn't have a thing to do with them since they told him he was wasting his life going into journalism. The only thing right my son and his good-for-nothing wife ever did was give birth to that boy."

"Scott doesn't have any brothers and sisters?" Sadie asked curiously.

Ruby looked at Sadie and shook her head.

"I know what it is," she said suddenly. "I've got a message to give to Scott. You need to tell him he's good enough. He doesn't need to dig so deep in his stories that they bury him and suck him down. He's good enough without that. He doesn't need to lower himself." She frowned at Sadie. "You gonna write this down? It's my last wish."

Sadie took a pen and scrap paper from her purse and scribbled down, "You're good enough."

"Anything else?" Sadie asked.

Ruby shook her head.

Sadie thought of the pictures in her hand. She didn't want to give Scott any message, but she told Ruby she would. Then Sadie told her it was time.

"The best way is to allow a kind of peace to come over you," Sadie instructed. "Close your eyes, envision all those loved ones who have gone on ahead of you, and visualize yourself reaching for them."

The essence that was Ruby Reed began to shimmer around the edges. Within seconds, the ghost faded until Ruby was completely transparent. The woman blew Sadie a kiss before she was totally gone.

It felt good. More than good. Great. Sadie felt giddy for helping Ruby Reed move on spiritually. She'd missed that feeling and the delight of it carried her until she'd left Scott's house and was in her van. Then she looked down at the scrap paper in her hand. Ruby's last message to Scott.

Sadie had never ignored a spirit's request. There was a first time for everything.

17

Back at Dawn's house, Sadie waited for the women to return from their marathon shopping. Then she oohed and aahed appropriately over all the cutesy baby purchases. It was evening and they were deciding on pizza or Chinese when Aunt Lynn announced she'd go back to her sister's house for the night. Sadie and Dawn didn't push her out the door but didn't beg her to stay either.

Once their aunt was gone, they decided on pizza and an evening of doing their nails and watching a chick flick. Dawn fell asleep ten minutes into the movie. Sadie watched the rest of the romantic comedy, all the while scowling at the hero, thinking that he was probably a two-timing creep like Zack.

It took her a long time to fall asleep. When Sadie woke up the next morning, her first thought was that sleeping on Dawn's futon was killing her back. Her next thought was how much she was dreading going to Onyx House and asking Joy if she'd had Brian's baby and just failed to mention it.

Sadie found Dawn in the kitchen eating a large portion of fresh fruit and toast and sipping a glass of milk.

"There's coffee in the carafe," Dawn said. "I'm dying for some, but it's not good for the baby."

Sadie poured herself a full cup and sat with Dawn. "I'm doing breakfast at Onyx House this morning. Why don't you come with me?"

"And watch you ask our dead brother's ex-fiancée if she had a baby who died?" She wrinkled her nose. "I'd rather go into labor right here and right now."

Dawn scooped Hairy into her arms and snuggled him under her chin for a minute before he wriggled free and she let him down to skid along the floor to his food bowl.

"I don't feel good about leaving you home alone," Sadie said.

"I appreciate you telling me that some ghost has threatened my baby, but I think I can fend Casper off with a vacuum cleaner and some garlic," she giggled.

"I'm not joking about this, Dawn."

"I know you're not, but c'mon, you can't expect me to take this seriously."

Sadie stripped off the shirt she was wearing and turned around.

"What are you—?" Dawn began, and then she gasped. "What the hell is that thing on your back?!"

"A satanic mark put there by Casper, or should I say Penny Torrez."

"The woman who was killed when they took her baby?"

"Yes. She's not like any spirit I've ever dealt with before, Dawn. As you can tell." Sadie tugged her T-shirt back over her head. "Whoever took Penny's baby from her and killed her is not a spirit. They're a live person living in Seattle who knows that you're pregnant and has threatened to take your baby, since we interrupted their ritual."

"Shit." Dawn's eyes were wide. "You didn't tell me that part before."

"I didn't want to scare you."

"Well, I'm scared now!"

"Good. Hopefully that means you'll be careful. If you won't come with me to Onyx House, how about if I drop you off at Mom's?"

Dawn stuck out her tongue.

"Mom loves to dote on you and try and figure out if

you're having a boy or a girl. You could torture her by saying you found out what the ultrasound results were and keep her guessing. When you get tired of that, you can start whining and whimpering about how nobody's thrown you a shower yet because everyone's too busy, and watch her swallow her tongue as she tries hard not to blow Saturday's surprise."

"That *does* sound like fun." Dawn grinned. "In the meantime, you'll find out about that ghost girl—what was her name?"

"Rhea."

"Yeah. Rhea." She ate the last bite of her toast. "I'd like to know if I used to have a niece."

Within a half hour they'd both dressed and were on their way out. Dawn was careful to set her house alarm before they locked up. When they arrived at their mom and dad's place, Aunt Lynn was also there and both the women were thrilled with the prospect of spending a few hours with Dawn.

On Sadie's drive over to Onyx House she checked her phone messages. No new calls asking Scene-2-Clean to come mop up a loved one. No messages from Zack. Her phone rang just as she was tucking it back in her purse.

"Hello?" Sadie answered.

"Any new jobs you need me for?" Jackie asked a little too cheerfully.

"I did a walk-through of a new meth job yesterday," Sadie said in a clipped, businesslike tone. "I'm busy this morning, but I'd like us to get started on it later today." Sadie gave her the address. "I'll call you when I'm on my way over there, and the two of you can meet me. I take it you'll tell Zack about the job."

"Tell Zack? Sure," Jackie replied. "I can do that if you want."

"I just figured it might be easier for you to talk to him, since you two are a thing and all." A thing? Sadie rolled her eyes at her own inability to put it better than that.

"A thing? You mean because—"

"Because you're sleeping together. Yes." She snapped the words off.

"You sound pissed," Jackie said. "I mean, you have every right to be ticked off if there's a Scene-2-Clean policy about employees dating, but, you know, you never said anything about that and—"

"I guess since I run a company of only three employees, I didn't know I had to have a dating policy!" Sadie was stopped at a light. She leaned forward to rest her forehead on the steering wheel. She'd wanted Jackie to deny everything. Instead she'd confirmed Sadie's fears. She took a deep breath and forced herself to calm down. It wasn't Jackie's fault. She probably didn't know Zack and Sadie had had a thing of their own last year or that he'd just recently lured her back to his bed. "I'm sorry. It's none of my business and I have no right to be pissed off. I'm just . . ." Hurt. "Surprised. That's all. What you two do on your own time is your own business." She quickly finished, "Just make sure it *is* on your own time, okay?"

"Yes. Of course. Um. This probably isn't a good time, but I was wondering if I could get an advance on my paycheck? I've had some unexpected expenses this month."

"You're right. It's not a good time."

Sadie said good-bye. Instead of placing her cell phone neatly in her purse, she angrily flung it to the floor.

As she drove closer, Sadie focused her energy on how she'd ask Joy about Rhea. Traffic was lighter than she expected, and she debated circling the neighborhood before going inside. Then she spied the same two girls that had been jumping rope in the driveway. They had their backpacks on and were just boarding a school bus.

After the bus pulled away, Sadie saw Rhea. She had her arms out wide and was spinning round and round. When she stopped, she had her head tilted back, laughing as she stumbled unsteadily on her feet. Finally she fell and lay there, hovering a few inches above the ground.

Sadie smiled. She remembered the joy of spinning around like that as a kid. Fun times. Simple times. Her hands were tight on the steering wheel as she brought her car to the curb. She watched Rhea get to her feet and wave. Brian's bracelet dangled from her tiny wrist. She was eyeing Sadie curiously as if unsure whether to approach.

Sadie felt the same uncertainty.

She could be my niece, Sadie thought. *My own flesh and blood and my last connection to Brian.*

Sadie turned off the ignition and frowned. Another idea was quick on the heels of that one.

Rhea could just as easily be Tim's child.

Sadie looked at the girl with the huge eyes and bouncy pigtails, but nothing about her features gave a clue either way.

Sadie picked up her cell phone from the floor of the car and spent a few seconds checking for voice mail messages. Still no calls from Zack. When she put the phone away and glanced up, Rhea was standing outside the driver's side of the car.

Sadie emitted a sharp squeak.

"Sorry. You scared me," Sadie explained as she rolled down her window.

The little girl offered her an amused smile.

"I knew you'd come back."

"You did, huh?" Sadie smiled in return. "How old did you say you are?"

"I'm old enough to count," she shouted. "One-two-three. And I'm ol' enough to bounce—one-two-three. . . ." She hopped up and down on the balls of her feet. "And I'm ol' enough to pounce!" She made her hands into catlike claws and lunged at Sadie's car, then dissolved into a fit of giggles.

When her laughter subsided, Sadie asked her, "So did

you know I was coming because you heard someone saying I was coming for breakfast today?"

"Yeah, I heard Dad tell Mom you were coming."

"Your dad . . . that would be Tim?" Sadie asked.

"They had a fight about it," Rhea said sadly, ignoring Sadie's question.

"About what?"

"About you coming. Mom said it wasn't the right time for you to visit. She called you a dog." Rhea made a *woof woof* sound and giggled.

"She's no prize herself," Sadie grumbled.

Rhea put a finger to her lips and looked up at the sky thoughtfully.

"I think she said you were a sleeping dog, so Dad should let you sleep."

"Maybe what she said was 'Let sleeping dogs lie'?" Sadie asked.

"Yeah!" Rhea nodded enthusiastically.

Well, that was kind of better than being called a dog.

"I wonder why she'd say that."

Rhea shrugged.

"Maybe 'cause Dad wants to talk about my real dad and Mom doesn't wanna."

Aha!

"Real dad?"

"Yeah, I call Tim Dad 'cause my real dad is an angel in heaven from before I came out of my mom's tummy." She looked over at the house. "They're watching for you."

Sadie glanced quickly through the trellis and could see the drapes parted slightly. When she glanced back out her car window, Rhea was gone. Sadie put her cell phone to her ear and pretended to talk on it. Let them think she needed to make a phone call before making nice-nice over breakfast. She needed a moment to get her blood pressure under control.

"Why would Joy have Brian's baby and never tell us?" Sadie asked her quiet cell phone.

She thought of Joy back then. Twentysomething. Her

fiancé breaks up with her and then goes home and kills himself. She packs up to live with her mom and dad in California and maybe just then discovers she's pregnant. She would've been confused and overwhelmed.

"I'll cut her some slack for not telling us in the beginning," Sadie mumbled to herself. "But to not tell us even after she has the child, our flesh and blood, living with her here in Seattle?"

She tried to make a new start with a new man, Sadie reminded herself, but she still felt cheated.

A sidelong glance told her someone was still watching for her and waiting. She put her phone in her purse and then it rang for real. She answered before checking the incoming number.

"Jackie called me about the meth job this afternoon," Zack said.

Did she call you over the phone or call your name in her bedroom? Sadie thought vehemently.

"Right," Sadie said, going for an all-business tone.

"I know you're upset but—"

"Upset?" she shouted. She could feel tears clog her throat. "Why should I be upset except that you climbed into my bed while you left Jackie still warming yours?!"

"About that. We'd had too much to drink and—"

"I don't want to hear all the gory details, thank you very much."

"Well, you're just going to have to listen up, Sadie, because there's more."

"More?" she asked, struggling to keep a tearful tremor from her voice.

"Yeah. I screwed up."

"I think we already established that."

"It's worse. I told Jackie."

"Told her what?" But even as she asked the question, she already knew. "Oh, God. You told her I see the dead?"

"I'm sorry. I had too much to drink, and, well, what can I say? I fucked up."

She felt hurt and betrayed and now kicked while she was down.

"I've got to go."

"We should talk about this," Zack said. "Even if you decide to fire my ass, we should still talk about it."

"I'm busy. I have to go into a wacky new age workshop and confront my ex-future-sister-in-law about having Brian's child, who fell out of a window."

She hung up the phone before he could even respond to her convoluted statement.

It felt like there was just too much going on in her world to sit down now and have a polite breakfast. Still, Sadie realized that was exactly what she needed to do.

She left her car and began walking toward the front door of Onyx House. She ducked through the ivy-covered trellis and up the path and then stepped up the stairs of the wooden porch. She raised her hand to knock and paused momentarily as the decorative wooden plate once again caught her attention.

ONYX HOUSE, it read. Burned into the block of wood. And the *O* had spokes. But the sign was worn and faded with age. She reached to touch it, but her fingers recoiled at a sound. She whirled on her heel to find Tim standing just beyond the screen door watching her.

"H-hello," Sadie stuttered. "I was just about to knock."

"It was a gift," Tim said, nodding toward the carved sign. "At first I found it a little backwoodsy, you know? Like something you'd hang on the door of your cottage. But Joy thought it was a quaint thing to hang at the entrance." He opened the door wide. "Come in."

Sadie pasted a smile on her face and stepped inside. A thick aroma of home baking reached her. The smell of cinnamon and fresh coffee.

"I'm early," Sadie said apologetically.

"You're perfectly on time," he said with a grin. "I'm just about to take the cinnamon rolls from the oven." He closed the heavy wood door behind her and it sounded with a thud of finality. "You can have one hot out of the oven."

He motioned for her to follow him down the hall and into the kitchen. The room was huge with a massive table, or possibly two or three pushed together in a long rectangle, covered with one long emerald green cloth and surrounded with a dozen dark wood chairs.

He poured her coffee into a beautiful blue ceramic mug and put it on the table in front of her.

"Is milk okay? I'm afraid we're out of cream. Joy just left for the store to pick some up."

"Black is fine," Sadie said.

"I know it must've been a shock for Joy when Dawn and I just showed up here out of the blue."

"Not really."

He pulled out the chair across from her and sat down with his own cup of coffee.

"I've tried to convince her to call you for years but she didn't want to deal with things. I knew you can only put off things for so long. Eventually you were bound to show up or run into each other, I mean."

"Yeah, sure, but like I told Joy, I just found a brochure for this place in a box of Brian's things, so when I saw he'd been here just a few days before . . ."

"You were curious. I don't blame you." He sipped from his coffee.

"So you two got married after Joy returned to live in Seattle?" Sadie asked.

"Yes, I'd offered her a job, and well, things progressed from there and—"

"Any kids?" Sadie blurted before she could stop herself.

"A daughter." He looked down into his mug before his gaze lifted to meet hers. "She died last year. She was only five."

"I'm sorry," Sadie said, feeling the wave of sorrow that left him. "It must be horrible to lose a child."

She wanted to talk to him about Rhea but decided that was a can of worms to open with Joy instead.

A timer went off and Tim was on his feet removing cinnamon rolls from the second oven. He was a regular Betty Crocker.

He put some of the buns onto a plate and brought them to the table.

"Please help yourself," he said. "They're great when they're still warm."

"Delicious," Sadie said, and meant it. One bite and the roll had melted in her mouth.

They ate in silence for a moment before Tim began to speak.

"Although we get a lot of guests here, I want you to know that I remember Brian. He seemed like a sincere guy. Very serious."

Sadie shook her head. "That's interesting. I don't remember seeing his serious side too often. He was the jokester in the family. To tell you the truth, I find it hard to believe he'd ever consider coming here, let alone taking some of your sessions." She swallowed the last mouthful of her cinnamon bun and added, "No offense."

"Some people come here out of curiosity and some come just to relax. Brian, well, I got the feeling he was . . . searching."

"For what?"

"Answers."

"To what?" Sadie asked, her eyes firm on Tim's.

"I'm not sure. . . ."

Sadie got the distinct impression he was lying.

"You must've talked about this with Joy," Sadie pushed. "What did she say he was looking for?"

"Joy always found it extremely painful to talk about your brother. I'm sure you understand that."

He got up from the table and brought a carafe over to refill their mugs. As he topped off Sadie's coffee, he looked sincerely into her eyes.

"I just wish we could've done more to help him. If only we'd known he was so troubled . . ."

"Yes," Sadie said abruptly.

Tim sat with his back to the large kitchen window that had a view of the picturesque yard. It would've been more scenic if Rhea weren't bouncing up and down on the rear porch and occasionally pausing to make faces at Sadie through the window. She stopped now and held up fingers—one-two-three—and bounced up and down, then made clawlike finger action as she jumped around on the deck.

Sadie could hear her shouting in a singsong voice.

"I'm old enough to count, one-two-three, and I'm ol' enough to bounce, one-two-three, and I'm ol' enough to pounce!"

She stopped to make a snarling-tiger face at Sadie, her fingers in claws against the window.

At least she was a happy ghost.

"How did she die?" Sadie murmured.

"Who?" Tim asked, putting down his coffee and tilting his head quizzically at Sadie.

"Rhea."

"I don't remember telling you her name." Tim looked at Sadie oddly, then followed her gaze over his shoulder. He opened his mouth to say more, but just then the front doorbell rang.

A look of annoyance crossed his face as he excused himself to get the door. Sadie made shooing motions with her hands, but Rhea still made funny faces in the window. This one had her tongue sticking out and her eyes rolling to the back of her head. Obviously the little girl enjoyed an audience. A jokester. Like Brian.

Sadie decided to get up on the pretense of walking around admiring the kitchen. If she was no longer looking out the window, she could think without Rhea's distraction.

When Tim returned, it was with a woman who looked

like a throw back to the sixties in a long peasant skirt, a tie-dyed shirt, and dreadlocks.

Tim introduced her as Lulu, who'd be running the session that morning.

"So you're here for the workshop on healing after loss?" Lulu asked, her voice sounding spacey, like she'd smoked a joint outside.

"Yes," Tim answered for her.

Only if I can't figure out a way to escape before then, Sadie thought.

"We'd hoped for a quiet breakfast together first. You're early." Tim looked pointedly at Lulu.

"Sorry, Tim." Lulu giggled. "It's those cinnamon buns. It's like they call to me."

"I'll get you one to take into the meeting room while you set up." He walked toward the counter.

"Joy told me about your loss," Lulu said. "Have you tried to get in touch with him? It could help you move forward with your life."

"I have moved on," Sadie said with more bite than she intended. She took a breath and softened her tone. "It's been six years. Time heals all wounds, right?"

"Time has nothing to do with it," Tim insisted, returning with a roll on a small plate lined with a paper napkin, and coffee in a travel mug. He handed the items to Lulu and she thanked him.

"Am I setting up in the basement room?" she asked. Tim nodded.

"Did you ever meet Rhea?" Sadie blurted.

Lulu opened her mouth to speak, but Tim put a hand on her arm to stop her.

"Lulu has to go set up. We'll be expecting more guests soon."

Sadie noted a tattoo on Tim's hand between the thumb and forefinger. A small circle with wiggly lines extending from its circumference.

"Interesting tattoo," Sadie said, nonchalantly pointing to it.

Sadie thought Tim and Lulu exchanged a knowing look, but Lulu excused herself to leave.

Tim refilled their coffees and Sadie asked again about the tattoo.

"Is it a symbol of something?"

"Yes, it's symbolic of a college dare after a keg party in my younger days." Tim winked.

Sadie laughed politely and then her cell phone rang. She answered the call, determined it was business related, and excused herself to finish talking in the other room. The caller was an insurance adjuster Sadie had been dealing with on a prior job. It was a routine follow-up call about some paperwork, but Sadie took the opportunity to use it as an excuse.

She returned to the kitchen and almost bumped right into him by the door.

"I'm sorry, but I have to leave. Something's come up at work." She looked at Tim evenly. "I wish I could stay and talk with Joy, but I need to get started on this immediately."

"I understand," Tim said. "But how about a quick tour?"

She almost relented, but her phone rang again.

"I really should go," Sadie said.

"Another time, then," Tim said with a flicker of annoyance in his tone. He walked her to the door.

The second she'd pulled away from the curb, Sadie took out her cell phone and dialed Zack. She didn't want to talk to him and she really didn't want to look at him either, but this wasn't high school. She was a grown woman with a business to run and she wasn't going to let a convoluted romantic love triangle screw with her job. It was time to put on her big-girl panties and do what was right.

"Hi," he answered, obviously recognizing the incoming phone number. "I'm glad you called. We should talk about—"

"We need to talk about work. I just got a call for a

decomp scene in North Queen Anne," she interrupted. "It would help if I had both of you on board to get the job done." Sadie paused for effect. "That means I want us all focused on the job." *Rather than on each other,* she thought, and finished, "Let's just meet for coffee and talk so we can get beyond this."

"Great," he said, sounding simultaneously relieved and apprehensive. "We can sit, the two of us, and I'll explain—"

"Not just the two of us. I want Jackie there as well." She fought the touch of annoyance that flared through her, causing those big-girl panties to pinch painfully. "I don't want explanations, Zack. I want assurances."

"What kind of assurances?"

"The kind that tells me the two of you are still able to work with each other and with me."

"That's not going to be a problem."

"I also need to know that Jackie can keep her mouth shut and be a professional no matter what she thinks about my conversations with dead people."

Zack didn't respond.

"So call her up and tell her I'd like to meet with both of you at El Diablo's in an hour."

Sadie used that hour to drive back to get the Scene-2-Clean van and load it up with equipment from her garage. She climbed into the van and pressed the garage remote to roll up the back door. She was just backing out of the garage when she spotted someone walking up her driveway.

"Damn. Thuggy," Sadie said.

She realized she should've called him like she promised. The last thing she needed was to deal with him today. Sadie didn't get out of the vehicle, but she rolled down her window when he approached.

"Sorry I didn't call you back," Sadie said.

"Have you talked to Egan?" he asked.

"Not lately."

He looked disappointed.

"I know I promised you a meth clean, but I've got another job I need to work first."

"Then I'll help with that," he said.

"It's a decomp scene. Two women left to rot in their home for a couple weeks in this heat." She raised her eyebrows at him in question.

"Yeah, well, think I'll pass." He blew out a breath. "I could do other things, though. I heard your place got trashed. I could give you security. I've done lots of security before."

Sadie could believe it. Thuggy's muscles had muscles. It gave her an idea.

"You know what? My sister could use security." Sadie reached for her purse and slipped out a photo of Dawn. She held it up to Thuggy.

"Your sister?"

"She's very pregnant and I've been staying with her, but I can't be with her every second. Fierce Force threatened her because of me. I need to keep her safe." She looked for a pen but couldn't find one.

"I'll call your cell phone in a few minutes and leave you the address for my mom and sister. Dawn's at my mom's now, but you can pick her up and bring her back to her place. Then just stay with her until I get there."

"You said she needs protection from the FF?" Thuggy asked.

"Yeah. And the devil," Sadie replied, and at Thuggy's taken-aback expression she added, "Some weird cult. Just make sure nobody gets near my sister, okay? I'll pay you full wages for your time."

He agreed. As he turned to walk away, Sadie reached out and stopped him.

"Thuggy, if anything happens to Dawn, you'll never work in this business again. Ever."

18

After Thuggy left, Sadie adroitly backed the behemoth van out of her driveway while punching in her mother's phone number on her cell.

"Can I talk to Dawn?" she asked her mother.

"Hello?" Dawn greeted.

"How's it going?" Sadie asked her sister.

"Great. It's been really nice visiting like this." Her voice was light, but Sadie could hear the underlying tone of desperation. Spending time refereeing their mother and Aunt Lynn could make a person crazy.

"Aunt Lynn's not so bad," Sadie said.

"Auntie Lynn is a real hoot," Dawn replied with forced cheeriness.

"That's me," Aunt Lynn shouted in the background. "I'm a hoot."

"Stop shouting," Sadie heard her mother's voice hiss.

"And that's your mother," Aunt Lynn shouted again even louder. "The wet blanket."

"Tell me you're coming to rescue me," Dawn said through clenched teeth.

"Not unless you want to come with me to a double-death decomposition scene."

"Even the words make me feel like losing my lunch," Dawn replied. "But it might be worth it to get out of this place," she added on a whisper.

"I'm sending someone to keep an eye on you," Sadie said.

"Really? Who? Is it Zack? Man, I could use some eye candy right now. Just looking at that man makes my insides all gooey."

"It's not Zack. It's Thuggy."

"Thuggy?"

"He's kind of a coworker and he's done security before. Zack said he's okay, so I'm trusting him. He'll be keeping an eye on you."

"Is he cute?"

Sadie thought about that.

"If you find refrigerators or small mountains cute, then, yeah, he's a real cutie-pie." She gave Dawn a description of the muscled man. "He'll give you a ride home and stay with you until I get there."

"Fine, but if he's not here shortly, I'll leave without him and you're going to owe me big-time," Dawn said. "I'm talking back rubs and foot massages and loads and loads of free babysitting and diaper changes."

"Don't get carried away," Sadie said. "I'll offer to babysit when the kid hits puberty and understands what I do for a living."

"Great. You're already a pillar of support."

"Sorry. Tell Mom that Terry is trying out new recipes for a wedding, and she may want the recipes because the food would blow her socks off."

"Why would I tell her that?"

"Help me out. I need brownie points here. You're having her grandbaby, so you can do no wrong. I've done wrong based on everything else in my life. It'll help if she thinks I'm actually working on this shower thing."

"Fine. Gotta go. I have to pee. I always have to pee. Oh, Auntie Lynn wants to talk to you." There was the rustling of the phone changing hands before Sadie's aunt came on the line.

"I was just telling your mom and sister about how

Uncle Glen really loved spending time with you girls when you'd come for two weeks every summer."

"Uncle Glen usually made us play board games for three days straight," Sadie said with a smile, and she bit her tongue so she wouldn't add, *Then in the middle of the night I'd hear him talking to himself as he paced the floors and he scared me to death.*

"He never forgot those days," Aunt Lynn said. "Even just before he passed away, when he had one of his clearer moments, he said he wanted a rematch of your Monopoly game."

"It was a nice weekend," Sadie said. "It was just before he . . ." Sadie's voice trailed off.

"Yes, before I locked him in the loony bin." She sighed. "Sometimes I think that was what sent him over the edge. Just because a person hears voices doesn't mean they have to be locked up. I wish I'd kept him home."

Sadie thought of the voices of the dead in her own life and shuddered. She hoped nobody got it in their head to lock her up.

"You did everything you could," Sadie assured her. "The doctors said it was for the best."

"Maybe."

"I have to go now. I've got a meeting with my staff," Sadie replied quickly, and they said good-bye as she steered the van into the neighborhood of Queen Anne.

The heat was unbearable. She had the AC on high and still it seemed to make little impact inside the large expanse of the van. She dialed Thuggy's cell and got his voice mail. She gave him all the addresses he needed and told him to hurry his ass over to her mom's.

When she parked the vehicle a block down from the El Diablo coffee shop, she was fifteen minutes early. Sadie glanced in the rearview mirror and cringed as she caught sight of her reflection. She looked like she'd already sweated a bucket and then dumped it on her head. She dug around in her purse for a comb but came up empty. Ditto on the lipstick. She ran her fingers through her short-cropped hair, hoping to spike it and give it some lift. It lay limply against her scalp as if she'd just stepped out of the shower.

This was ridiculous. Why did she give a rat's ass what she looked like?

Sadie gave up and climbed from her van, hoping the air-conditioned coffee shop would remove some of the sweaty gleam from her face. She walked through the wall of heat up the street to the coffee shop and noticed Zack's Mustang parked at the curb. He was early too.

This is good, Sadie thought. *We'll have a chance to talk before Jackie gets here. I can tell him that I honestly don't care if he's sleeping with her.*

"Where he unzips his pants doesn't matter to me," she murmured as she pushed open the door to El Diablo's.

A blast of icy air hit her and goose bumps immediately cropped up on her forearms, but it felt good. She stepped into line behind a few others in need of their coffee fix, and she scanned the clientele for Zack. She finally spotted him perched on a stool at a counter near the wall that boasted the devil-girl mural, the shop's mascot. Between Zack and the devil sat Jackie. Both had their backs to Sadie.

Sadie's teeth clenched at the sight of them together. She repeated a mantra of *it-doesn't-matter, it-doesn't-matter* in her head while she waited in line to order her coffee.

She wanted a Cubano coffee, but she needed to cool off and not just because the thermometer said ninety outside. She ordered a piña colada *batido* and stepped aside to wait for it.

From the corner of her eye Sadie watched them. Zack was leaning left and speaking intently in Jackie's ear, but it didn't look cozy. He looked pissed. When he stabbed her shoulder with his index finger, Jackie flinched and nodded curtly in response.

It almost looked like Zack was telling her off about

something. Then again, there was a very good chance they were just comparing stories and trying to decide how to handle Sadie and the impending meeting.

The barista handed Sadie her icy fruit shake and she stirred it once before taking a big breath and walking toward Zack and Jackie.

Be calm, she told herself. *You need them to stay on as employees. Things will be fine as long as you don't reveal your inner jealous bitch.*

With an impassive look pasted on her face to hide her anger and trepidation, Sadie was at their counter before either of them looked over.

"Good. You're both here." Her voice was clipped. "How about we move to a table."

"Sure," Jackie said swiftly, swinging her long legs off her stool and snagging a nearby empty table.

"Good choice," Zack said, nodding at Sadie's fruit shake. "It's hotter than a ten-dollar pistol out there."

They sat then, the three of them sipping their various drinks. Sadie knew she had to be the one to break the silence.

"I just want to say," Sadie began, pulling her chair closer to the table, "that I'm okay with . . ." She stumbled a little and used her hand to motion from Zack to Jackie. "With the two of you doing . . . I mean, being together." She cursed the blush that crept up her neck, and sipped her shake.

"Look, it was a onetime thing," Zack said. He looked at Jackie, his eyes challenging her to say otherwise.

"He's right," Jackie said, and added hurriedly, "I was at the bar and had too much to drink and I called Zack to come and give me a lift, but then I convinced him to have a few drinks too, and, well, one thing led to another and we shared a cab." Her face reddened as she spoke and she fluffed her hair with her fingers to distract from her embarrassment.

"Could we please skip the details?" Sadie said, blinking away the repulsive visual of a drunk Zack and equally inebriated Jackie slobbering all over each other.

"Sorry. I just wanted to make sure you knew it was, like, you know . . ."

"A onetime thing," Zack said.

"Right," Jackie agreed.

God, this was positively painful!

"Look, I'm not a prude," Sadie said. "I'm not going to fire either of you for, um, ending up together and—"

"It's over." Zack's voice was louder than it should've been and other people turned to look over at them curiously.

"Um, okay." Sadie was feeling increasingly more uncomfortable and struggled to regain control of the conversation. "Actually, what I really thought we should talk about was what Zack told you about *me*." Sadie looked pointedly at Jackie.

"We don't need to talk about it," Jackie said. "I'm good."

"No. We really do need to talk about it. Zack told you about my . . ." She groped for the words and lowered her voice to a mere whisper. "My way of dealing with spirits."

Jackie's lips threatened a smile, but Zack looked positively miserable.

"What's done is done. It couldn't have stayed a secret forever, but I can at least answer any questions you have," Sadie said to Jackie. "I'd rather you hear it from me, and it would be good if you at least didn't feel like you were working for a complete lunatic."

A quick flash across Jackie's face said that no matter what Sadie said, Jackie already had made up her mind Sadie was crazy. However, Jackie recovered her facial expression and changed it to bland.

"It'll just take some getting used to," Jackie said with a shrug. "But, hey, you can do whatever you do with, um, ghosts, and it doesn't change what I do, right?"

"No. Of course not," Sadie said quickly. "Your job doesn't change. Zack's job has never changed because of my, um, ability. I don't know that he's ever gotten used to it, but at least he's stopped complaining about me talking to spirits around him when he's working a scene."

"It still freaks me out when she starts talking out loud and we're on a scene," Zack replied, his tone half-joking.

Sadie shot him a don't-push-your-luck look.

"I don't expect you to believe in ghosts or that I speak to the dead. I hardly believe it myself sometimes," she said ruefully. "So if it'll make you feel better to think you're working for a nut or somebody who's eccentric, I'm okay with that."

Jackie offered her the first glimpse of a smile.

"But here's the thing, and it's a big thing," Sadie said seriously. "This topic does not go beyond the three of us. I mean it. I need you to promise you won't talk about this to anybody. You can understand how damaging it would be to Scene-2-Clean if this kind of thing got out."

Jackie looked like she was about to say something, then thought better of it, and shook her head.

"Well?" Sadie demanded.

"I get it," Jackie replied, looking down at her hands. "You don't have to worry. It's not like I'm going to run around telling people I work with a ghost whisperer." She snorted and downed the rest of her coffee.

"Okay, and I'll make sure you get that advance on your pay you asked about," Sadie said, slurping from her drink. "Now let's move on. We've got a big cleanup ahead of us. You probably heard about the case in North Queen Anne? The one with the eighty-year-old twin sisters who shared the house?"

"Sure. They both died at home and nobody noticed for almost two weeks," Jackie said. "It'll be nasty."

"I've got the van loaded up," Sadie informed them. "Let's go."

They drove the two miles until they were winding down the narrow street and Sadie parked her van in the sloped drive of an old Victorian home. On either side of the house stood modern multileveled homes squaring off for the best views. Zack and Jackie each parked at the curb and came to help her unload the van.

An old man across the street ran over to greet them just as Sadie was about to take supplies out of the van.

"I'm Bill," he shouted, thrusting his hand at Sadie. The old man had a full round face layered with so many wrinkles he looked like a Shar-Pei dog.

"Bill Doyle?" Sadie asked as her hand was enveloped in a hardy handshake.

"Yes." He nodded. "I called your company to do the job."

"Nice to meet you, Bill. I didn't know you would be meeting me here today. Do you live in the area?"

"Right there." He pointed proudly across the street to a small, old cottage-style house.

Sadie made introductions.

"Zack and Jackie will be working with me on this house," Sadie explained to Bill. To her employees she explained, "Bill is the heir to the twins' estate. He was their good friend and, apparently, neighbor."

"Wanda and Jean had nobody else," Bill admitted, looking terribly sad. "It's a shame what happened to them." He shook his head slowly from side to side. "A real shame. If I hadn't been visiting my daughter in Maine, I would've noticed they hadn't left the house. Every single morning Wanda and Jean would be out in their garden tending the roses."

He pointed to the dense, thorny bushes that lined the drive so close they nearly scratched Sadie's van.

"They're beautiful," Jackie said, smiling warmly at him.

"I just can't believe they're both gone at the same time. The medical examiner said Wanda fell down the stairs and the fall killed her instantly, and then Jean's heart gave out, probably after she saw her dead sister, and Jean fell over the railing." He sighed and shook his head. "I guess they were meant to be together forever."

Sadie was an expert at handling the bereaved, but even she found this one a little hard to take.

"Yes, I guess we should be glad that they're still together, right?" Sadie stepped aside and Zack opened the van door to take out supplies while she dealt with their client.

"Yeah, everyone's been telling me that it's nice they went at the same time, since they lived together for nearly fifty years. I guess that's a good way to look at it, but it doesn't sound right. Near the end they were talking about each getting their own place. They'd finally gotten fed up with living together."

Guess Mr. Death put an end to that idea, Sadie thought drily.

Sadie put her hand on his shoulder.

"How about if we go over to your place and I'll get you to sign the documentation and get the insurance papers from you, and we can chat while Zack and Jackie do the initial walk-through?"

"Good idea," Zack said. "We can get started."

"Jackie, would you mind taking the pictures? My camera's in the van," Sadie asked.

She left them then and walked across the street to the small home directly opposite.

Bill made tea and Sadie forced herself not to feel overly nauseated as she drank it. She hated tea. Why did grieving people always drink tea? He put a plate of stale cookies in front of her too, and Sadie politely took one.

"So you were away visiting your daughter?" Sadie asked as she delicately nibbled a cookie and watched as Bill looked over the Scene-2-Clean contract.

"Yes. She's going through a divorce and wanted me there to tell her everything would be okay." He looked up sadly. "Since my wife passed on a few years ago, it's been up to me to make sure the whole damn family doesn't fall apart. I do my best, but, hey, they're spread all over the entire country. One in Maine. Two in Portland." He sighed and sipped his tea. "Of course they all want me to move to where they are, and nobody gives a rat's ass to the thought that this is my home!" Then he looked apologetic. "Sorry. You don't need to hear about my garbage."

"That's okay," Sadie assured him. "It must be hard without any relatives nearby."

"We moved in on our wedding night." He nodded across the street. "Wanda and Jean were already living across the street." He picked up his mug and downed the remaining fluid. "They used to exchange recipes with my wife, Marge. When she passed, they took over feeding me too. Of course that was mostly Wanda. Jean never liked to cook." He got up and opened the freezer portion of his fridge to reveal stacks of neatly labeled casserole dishes. "I've prolly got twenty meals still in here from those gals." His voice broke with emotion. Bill closed the freezer door and sat back down. "It's not the food I'm worried about. I can open a can when I need to. It's just that nobody else in the area is very neighborly at all. Mostly Chinese and who knows what else living in these houses now. Some of them don't speak a word of English, and they keep tearing down small houses like mine and building monster-sized mansions. They have families of three and four people living in five thousand square feet!"

"I'm sure if you reached out to your neighbors, you'd find a lot of them are really friendly," Sadie said.

"Screw 'em," he replied angrily, then added, "Pardon my language."

"I understand you really miss Jean and Wanda. It must've been great to have ladies your own age to talk to."

Suddenly Bill looked kind of flustered. He made a big show of getting up to get another pen when his didn't work. Then he signed Sadie's contract and ushered her out the door after she promised she'd let him know when the place was cleaned and ready for him to list for sale, if that was his choice.

When Sadie crossed the street to her van, Zack and Jackie were just stripping out of their hazmat suits and Zack handed Sadie the camera.

"It's ugly," he said, but he smiled when he said it. "Is it wrong for me to be glad we're mopping up decomp from two old ladies instead of cleaning a meth lab?"

Sadie didn't respond.

"The sites are close together. One at the bottom of the stairs," Jackie said, "and the other a few feet over. I guess from the one who went over the railing. Lots of glass embedded in the hardwood there. Something broke."

"I was told there was a large antique console table with a glass top under the landing. They figure Jean was standing looking over the railing at her sister dead at the bottom of the stairs. She keeled over the railing and landed on the glass console when she had her heart attack," Sadie said matter-of-factly.

"Wow, they lived together all these years and then died together," Jackie said. "Makes you think that they were just always meant to be together. It's kind of sweet really."

"Yeah, well, when I go, I don't want it to be in ninety-degree heat and then left to rot at the bottom of my stairs for two weeks," Sadie replied as she glanced through the digital display of the photos Jackie had taken.

They all suited back up just inside the back door. Sadie wished she'd had a chance to go through the house on her own. She told herself that it really didn't matter. That she was going to be fine. But the minute she stepped inside the old house, she knew she was not going to be fine at all. Things were going to be more than a little stressful on this scene.

"Oh, for damnation, Wanda, just shut the hell up!" came a shout from down the hall.

Sadie, Zack, and Jackie walked toward the scene. They were in full hazmat gear including face masks. The pungent stench of death would've curled their hair otherwise.

"You don't tell me to shut up, Jean! You're the one who should shut up. For fifty years you've been telling me to be quiet and I'm not going to do it anymore!" squeaked an elderly lady's voice.

When they reached the spirits making the noise, Sadie saw the two ladies just as clearly as she could see Jackie and Zack standing in front of her.

One of the eighty-year-old women was in a floor-length nightie, her neck was bent at an odd angle, and the left side of her head was smashed in with blood caked to her wiry silver curls. The other ghost had on merely a pantie girdle of some kind. Her steel-colored hair was in rollers, her face was peppered with embedded glass fragments, and her left arm was dangling uselessly at her side.

"Great. Just great," Sadie murmured behind her respirator.

Sadie usually saw the dead as they appeared when they passed. When we're talking eighty-year-old twin ladies with pendulum breasts swinging to their navels and no bras on to hold 'em up, it wasn't pretty.

Jackie and Zack had brought in the medical waste bins. Zack was in the foyer using emulsifiers to soften dried tissue and decomp fluid by the front door, and Jackie was taking a utility knife to the carpet at the base of the stairs.

"Shit," Sadie mumbled behind her respirator.

She tried to ignore the two ladies, but they were bickering loudly. Sadie grabbed a bin and began picking up glass, while Jean, the old lady with glass in her face and rollers in her hair, shouted at her sister.

Sadie concentrated as best she could. She carefully

picked up shards of blood-covered glass with her gloved hands. Maggots protested and crawled after the pieces as she removed them. Maggots were determined little buggers. They were already annoyed that the main source of food, the bodies, was gone, but they would've happily gone on to swim in the decomp fluid and multiply as long as possible.

"Just look what you did to that console table," the old woman referred to as Wanda complained. "I looked all over for one that fit that spot perfectly, and your big ass blew it to smithereens!"

"It wasn't my fault," Jean exclaimed. "I fell from the second floor. If you hadn't hidden my heart medication, ya crazy ol' bitch, my heart wouldn't have given out just after you fell down the stairs!"

"I didn't fall down the stairs, you stupid ninny. You pushed me!" Wanda screeched. Her broken neck had her head tilted in an odd angle like she was looking up at the ceiling.

"I wouldn't have pushed you if you hadn't said you were going to go and move in with Bill!" Jean shrieked. "How could you do that to me after all these years together?"

"For God's sake, I just wanted to live! Is that so wrong? We've been together for all these years. . . . I just wanted a chance to be with a man. You robbed me of that!"

The two women wailed and screamed at each other like toddlers having a temper tantrum. Sadie pointed a gloved finger at first one and then the other.

"Knock it off!" Sadie hissed. "Stop it right now or so help me, I'll leave your beautiful home a disaster."

They stopped cold and looked at Sadie.

"Is she talking to us, Wanda?"

"Why, I believe she is, Jean."

Both women inched toward Sadie, who looked over her shoulder at Zack and Jackie. They too had stopped what they were doing and were staring at her. Sadie cleared her throat and got back down on her knees to begin tossing out glass. The old ladies crouched down to Sadie's level.

"How can you see us?" asked Jean.

"Maybe we're not dead," suggested Wanda hopefully.

"Have you looked in the mirror, honey?" Jean said, exasperated. "Trust me. You're dead."

"You don't have to get so snippy," Wanda sniffed. "I tried looking in a mirror, but there isn't nothing looking back. Guess that says it all, then. Oh, Lord, I don't wanna be dead!" She covered her face with her hands and began sobbing.

Jean went over and began patting Wanda's back.

Sadie ignored them, or did her best to. When they'd been at the cleanup job for close to three hours, Zack suggested they all take a break.

They doffed their gear quickly. Sadie's T-shirt was nearly soaked through with perspiration. Jackie looked like she had a fine mist on her.

"Want to grab a bite to eat and come back?" Zack asked.

"It's too hot," Sadie said. "Let's finish tomorrow. They aren't going anywhere."

"Who?" Jackie asked.

"I mean this job. It's not going anywhere," she added quickly. "Why don't we pick up where we left off in the morning bright and early before the heat hits? I've got lots of paperwork to do on the next meth lab and I want to try and talk to Egan again."

"What's up with Egan?" Zack asked. "Is he ever coming back?"

"Soon," Sadie said.

She took her time putting her gear away. Jackie and Zack were gone and she considered leaving herself, but there was only one way she'd be able to come back tomorrow and that was if she dealt with the women today.

She suited back up and went into the house to deal with Jean and Wanda. The problem was, it was difficult to speak to them through the respirator. The dead liked to hang where they passed. They didn't travel well unless they'd been left for some time. Then they sometimes got more limber. Using some elaborate hand gestures, she was able to convince Wanda and Jean to step out the back door and onto the deck. Sadie knew she was taking a chance the neighbors would see, but the yard had the protection of a lot of mature trees.

Removing her headgear, she got down to business.

"You two are dead," Sadie said matter-of-factly. "I can see and talk to the dead and I can help you move on."

The spirit known as Jean crossed her arms, thankfully blocking the view of her droopy breasts, and shook her head full of curlers.

"I'm not going anywhere. If I go, Wanda will just haunt Bill and I'll be all alone."

"Isn't that a fine how-do-ya-do?" Wanda snorted. She turned so that she could glare angrily at Jean, but with her head twisted at her broken-neck angle, she only looked like a pretzel. "Even after you kill me, you still don't let me have my way!"

"I didn't kill you on purpose!" Jean shouted. "You've always worn your nightdresses too long. Look!" She pointed at Wanda's feet. "You're stepping on it right now. It should come to your ankles so you won't step on it. I told you I'd hem it, but no-o-o."

"I wouldn't've stepped on the damn thing and tripped down the stairs if you hadn't pushed me!" Wanda shrieked.

"Okay, enough!" Sadie shouted, then cleared her throat and tried to regain some calm. "Neither of you can stay in this house forever."

"Well, I'm not leaving," Jean insisted.

"Me either," stated Wanda.

Sadie groaned.

"Okay, let's start from the beginning. From what I've heard, you were in love with Bill." Sadie pointed at Wanda.

"He made me all tingly," Wanda replied, pointing low in her nightie. "Down there."

Sadie thought of Bill, the old guy who looked like a

Shar-Pei dog, and tried to shake the visual of the two old fogies together.

"She was making a total ass of herself," Jean hissed. "Always going over there with food morning and night. Suggesting they go off together for a weekend." She clucked her tongue. "It was disgusting!"

"Why?" Sadie asked, holding up a hand in a stopping gesture.

"Why what?" asked Jean.

"Why was it disgusting?" Besides the obvious that they were as old as dirt and shouldn't be thinking romantic thoughts. "Why would it bother you if your sister got some happiness in her golden years?"

"Because she's not my sister. She's my wife!" Jean spit, and her anger dissolved into tears.

Sadie just stood there with her jaw hanging open.

"It's true," Wanda said quietly. "We lived together for over fifty years in that way. We had no living relatives, so, well, to the world we were sisters. The twin spinsters who never married." She turned her body so that her tilted head could look Sadie in the eye. "We don't even look alike but nobody ever questioned it. We weren't like you young people nowadays all living free with gay pride, you know. Things were different then. If you were a woman who liked other women, it wasn't like you'd tell the world. You'd become a spinster. We would've been run out of this neighborhood back in our day."

"Oka-a-ay," Sadie said, unsure of what else she could say.

"We were happy. Then after fifty-three years you decided to throw yourself at another right in front of me as if I meant nothing. And, of all things, you went after a man!" Jean wailed.

"There. There." Wanda put a hand on Jean's back and patted it gently. "I just didn't want to go to my grave never having experienced a man. Can't you understand that?"

"No," Jean replied stubbornly. "I can't. You were my everything. I never wanted anybody else."

They clung to each other then, a mess of silver hair, bloodstains, and undulating breasts. Ugh.

Sadie cleared her throat to get their attention.

"Look, since we can't change what happened," Sadie said, "how about we just change the future. You two won't be happy here." She looked at Wanda. "Bill can't see you and he certainly can't"—she waved at Wanda's broken body—"satisfy you in any way."

Wanda nodded reluctantly.

Sadie turned to Jean. "Can you accept the fact that Wanda loves you but wanted to try, um, a different flavor before she died? That doesn't make what you had for all those years any less, um, special."

"I guess," Jean replied.

"I'm sorry," Wanda said, reaching her hand out to her mate.

"Me too," Jean replied, pulling her into another hug.

"Good. This is good. If I'm lucky, I might get home in time to wash this entire day away with a martini." She blew out a breath. "You two are ready to move on. Close your eyes and think of the happy times you've had." Both ladies smiled dreamily and closed their eyes, their hands still locked together. "Now think of living those special times together with all those who've gone before you. You'll be accepted on the other side. No more lies."

"Oh, that'll be nice," Wanda said.

The edges of the couple began to shimmer. Before long they were a luminous and transpicuous shape. Then they were gone in a flash, but the flash was real. Sadie whirled her head just in time to see the glint of the hot sun as it sparked off a camera lens.

"That's all we need," Scott Reed said to his cameraman. To Sadie he shouted across the yard, "Good to see ya, Sweets!"

Sadie felt nothing but a white-hot rage.

19

Sadie screamed and ran after Scott, but he was gone. It was out of her hands. If he wanted to advertise her craziness on Emerald Nine News, there was nothing she could do.

Feeling sad and depressed, she went home to her mother.

"Nice that you could come," her mother said when she answered the door. "I've got a roast in the oven and we're just working on making decorations for the shower."

Sadie followed her mom through the living room, where her dad sat. He waved hello.

"Your sister, she had to go home 'cause some big guy was coming over. She said he works for you," Sadie's dad said.

"He does." She leaned over and gave him a hug.

"Why is he with your sister? Shouldn't he be at work with you?"

It is work. I'm paying him, Sadie thought.

"Yeah, Thuggy's just doing something for me with Dawn," Sadie said vaguely.

"What kind of a name is 'Thuggy'?" Dad asked.

"It's short for 'Thugwold.' "

"Shit. That's even worse. What kind of a name is 'Thugwold'?"

But her aunt rushed into the living room and saved her from answering.

"Sadie, I'm so glad you were able to make it!"

Aunt Lynn snagged Sadie by the hand and pulled her into the dining room, where her mother sat at a table covered in disposable diapers.

"What's going on?" Sadie asked.

"Peggy has a bee in her bonnet about decorating the house for the shower," Auntie Lynn announced, rolling her eyes.

"It's a great idea," Sadie's mom replied. "We're going to use pink and blue streamers as a clothesline across the dining room, and then we're going to use pink and blue clothespins to hang the diapers." She handed Sadie pink and blue Sharpie markers. "You are going to take ten of the diapers and write one big letter on each one so that it says B-A-B-Y-S-H-O-W-E-R."

Sadie thought it was the stupidest idea for a decoration she'd ever heard of and she really hadn't planned on spending her evening coloring diapers.

"I've got a ton of paperwork to get caught up on at home," Sadie began. "I don't know how long I can stay."

She hated the disappointment on her mom's face and immediately regretted the words.

"Sadie, when was the last time you checked your tire pressure?" Sadie's dad griped from the living room a few feet away. "Come outside for a minute. Your tires are looking low."

Sadie closed her mouth against telling her father she was a grown woman who could take care of her own tires, thank you very much. She slipped her feet back in her shoes and followed him out.

"The tires look fine, Dad," Sadie said.

"You can never be too sure." He pulled a tire gauge from his pocket as they approached her Honda, and knelt at the front tire.

Sadie knelt beside him and watched as he spun the

stem cap off. There was a small hiss of air as he pressed the gauge quickly and firmly to the valve and then quickly read the number.

"You know, this shower is real important to your mom," he said, getting up and walking over to the rear tire. "I know you've got your own busy life going on, but, well, family is all she's got." He looked her in the eye then and Sadie saw wrinkles on his face she'd never noticed before. God, when had her parents gotten old?

"I know. You're right," Sadie said. "I should be more involved in the shower."

She followed him around the other side of the vehicle and joined him to kneel beside the third tire. It wasn't the first time he'd used car maintenance to cover a serious conversation. That first time would've been when she was sixteen and had just started dating. He showed her how to check the car's oil and then told her just because a boy had hands didn't mean she needed to let him use them. She should've remembered that little nugget of advice with Zack.

"I thought Mom would want one-on-one time with Aunt Lynn," Sadie said, and the defense sounded weak even to her own ears.

"Having Lynn around is good for your mom, but having her girls around gives her something to show off. Do you get that?"

He walked over to check the pressure on the final tire.

"I get it. I'm sorry. Things have been a little crazy at work, but I promise to try and spend more time with Mom."

"And I don't mind seeing your mug around either. I won't be around forever, you know."

A pang of emotion bloomed in her chest.

"You're not sick, are you?"

"Nah." He stood and dusted his hands on his pants. "My blood pressure's a little high sometimes, but the docs are taking care of that." He put his arm around Sadie as they walked back toward the house. "Why don't you ever bring around that Zack Bowman character? He seems like an upstanding kind of guy."

"It's complicated," Sadie mumbled.

"It always is," he said with a chuckle.

They walked back inside the house arm in arm. Sadie went toward the dining room to join the women, and her dad plopped himself back down on the sofa in the living room to channel surf.

"Looks like I can stay a little longer than I thought," Sadie said, sitting down at the table next to her mother.

"We can use all the help we can get," her mom replied.

Aunt Lynn sat, elbows on the table, chopping away at yellow construction paper.

"What are you making?" Sadie asked her aunt.

"They're supposed to be baby bootees for wall decorations," Peggy said with a look of disdain.

"Hey, I'm doing the best I can," Aunt Lynn said. She held up a crookedly cut yellow bootee that looked more like a deformed cowboy boot. "What can I say? Glen was more crafty than I ever was." She sighed. "Remember all those wooden butterflies he carved and nailed up on our fence?"

"Oh yeah," Sadie said, smiling. She called out toward the living room, "Dad, remember when you tried to show me how to carve one of those wooden butterflies after I got back from a visit?"

"How can I forget?" He held up his index finger. "Five stitches taught me to never assume wood carving was easy just because Glen made it look like it was."

Dad put his feet up on the coffee table and settled in to watch CNN.

"I still have the butterflies up on the fence," Aunt Lynn said wistfully. "They're faded from the weather, but I don't have the heart to bring them down. You know, when I brought him home to die, he told me he'd been dreaming about the butterflies and missed them." She sniffed and reached for a tissue.

"I always thought Uncle Glen died in the, um . . ." She groped for the PC word for lunatic asylum and the best she could come up with was, "Hospital?"

"Nope he was determined as all get-out to go home for a visit. It was like he knew he wasn't long for this world and wanted to pass away at home." Her tongue stuck out of the corner of her mouth as she carefully cut out another lopsided baby bootee. "He was only home a few days before the stroke hit."

"Yes, it's almost as if he knew," Peggy said sadly. "It was nice that Brian happened to be out that way and got to see him."

"They had a great visit too," Lynn stated, finishing off the baby bootee and starting on another. "I left them alone to chat and Glen was having one of his few days when he wasn't talking to the dead."

Sadie's hand jerked and she drew a blue line right across the diaper she'd been working on.

"Wh-what did you say?" Sadie stammered, her gaze fixed on her aunt.

"Look what you've done," her mother exclaimed, snatching the ruined diaper from Sadie's hand and giving her a new one. "Try and pay attention," she said, clucking her tongue.

"Aunt Lynn, what did you say about Uncle Glen talking to the dead?" Sadie repeated, ignoring her mother.

"Well, that's what he always said." She shrugged and held up her yellow construction paper bootee to eye it critically. "He thought the voices inside his head were ghosts. The voices of dead people who had messages for him." She tilted her head and looked quizzically at Sadie. "Oh, you mustn't look so upset about it. He sure wasn't the only one. There was one guy in the institute who thought he was Abraham Lincoln." She shook her head and chuckled at the memory. "He really believed it too, just like your uncle believed people who had died talked to him. He insisted on it even in his last couple hours. Poor Brian sat there and listened to him ramble on, and when he had the stroke, your brother was just so upset. It's too bad he was in the room when it happened, but, you know, it was nice too for Glen to be surrounded by family."

Sadie's head felt woozy. The Sharpie marker she'd been holding slipped from her fingers and rolled onto the floor.

"Are you okay?" her mom asked. "You look pale. I bet you haven't eaten yet today." She got to her feet. "I'll check on the pot roast. It should almost be done."

Sadie got to her feet.

"I've got a bit of a headache. I'll go splash water on my face."

She went down the hall to the powder room. She closed and locked the door and ran the water before tugging her cell phone out of her purse.

"What are you up to?" Sadie asked as soon as Maeva answered the phone.

"I'm sitting back and relaxing with a glass of wine while Terry massages my feet."

"Oh, that sounds tough." Sadie felt a pang of jealousy.

"Well, I had a tough day. The usual skeptics and sincere believers came in for psychic readings, but we had a knock-'em-dead sale on crystals in the store side of the shop and I was on my feet more than I'd like."

"Then how about going on a nice leisurely drive with me tonight?"

"Where?"

"Redmond."

"That's not so bad."

"Redmond, Oregon."

"That's like three hundred miles!"

"Yes, but I'll do all the driving and you can just sit back and relax."

"I'm sitting back and relaxing now *and* I'm getting a foot massage. Did I mention that Terry's got marinara sauce simmering on the stove?"

"You can eat your pasta first, since I'm committed to

consuming a dried-up pot roast at my mom's." She lowered her voice. "Look, I'm willing to massage your feet if you'll come with me."

"You must be desperate. What or who is in Redmond, Oregon?"

"My dead uncle."

20

"I've gotta tell you, Sadie. There's a real good chance this is a complete waste of time," Maeva said, reclining the passenger seat of Sadie's Honda until it was as far back as it would go. "It's been six years and—"

"You talk to spirits all the time that have been dead for a lot longer than six years. Sometimes you reach people from the last century."

"True."

"And you get results."

"Most of the time." She brushed her fingernails against her chest and smirked. "I'm pretty good, aren't I? You were the biggest skeptic I've ever converted."

"Yeah, well, I'm a believer now."

"I just don't want you to be disappointed," Maeva said softly. "I know I've told you before it's possible you inherited your ability from a deceased family member, but it's just as likely that your uncle was simply plain crazy."

"I need to know for sure."

"But it won't change anything."

Sadie didn't reply. It was after ten and not much traffic greeted her on the highway. She checked the speedometer and pressed down a little more on the accelerator.

"If Uncle Glen *did* talk to the dead, I don't believe he passed that on to me," Sadie said seriously.

"Then why are we traveling hundreds of miles this

late, and why did I leave a perfectly good pedi-massage that promised to turn into hot 'n' heavy sex?"

"I think Uncle Glen handed down his ability to Brian."

"What?" Maeva jolted her seat back to the upright position and stared at Sadie for a full minute without speaking.

"You think Brian inherited speaking to the dead from your uncle and then passed it along to you when he killed himself?"

Sadie slid her friend a sidelong glance before turning to stare out at the white lines on the highway.

"Yes. If Uncle Glen had it and he died while Brian was visiting, then it's possible, right?"

Maeva tapped a finger to her chin.

"Yes. I guess it is."

They didn't say anything more.

Maeva drifted off to sleep as Sadie cruised the highway out of Washington and into Oregon. Sadie's mind was more awake than after a Starbucks triple-shot latte. She could hardly wait to get to her aunt's house.

After two and a half hours Sadie was a block from her destination. She steered down a wide residential street lined with quiet middle-class bungalows on spacious lots. Childhood memories flooded her. She remembered riding her bike down these roads, racing Dawn and Brian to the corner store to buy bagfuls of penny candy. She remembered camping in Aunt Lynn's backyard under the stars with nothing in the yard with them except for Uncle Glen's butterfly wood carvings that watched them from the fence boards.

She recognized the butterflies before she even noticed the small house. The one-level home looked half as big as she remembered it, but those damn butterflies, though faded from years of rain and sun, looked the same. There must've been forty at varying heights on the front fence that lined the driveway to the street, and more continued into the backyard. Some of them had lost the wiry antennae glued into their wooden bodies, but Sadie saw them through the eyes of her youth.

"Wake up, sleepyhead," Sadie said, taking her key from the ignition.

Maeva yawned, stretched, and looked around.

"Holy crap. What's with all the bugs?"

"My uncle carved them."

"I don't like bugs," Maeva said, grabbing the tote bag at her feet and opening the car door.

"They're not bugs," Sadie said, opening her own door and closing it softly behind her. "They're butterflies."

In the dark the streetlight glinted off the metal antennae.

"Okay, maybe they're a little freaky looking if you're not used to them," Sadie admitted.

"A little?" Maeva chuckled as she joined Sadie to walk up the stone path to the front door. "Are you sure your uncle didn't think it was dead bugs he was talking to, instead of human spirits?"

At the front door, Sadie stood on tiptoe and ran the tips of her fingers along the top of the doorframe until she found the spare key that had been kept there since her childhood. She slid the key into the dead bolt, and the lock slid open easily.

They stepped inside and felt around for a light switch. The house smelled like lemon furniture polish and floor wax. The smells had her memories working overtime. She half expected her aunt and uncle to run over and give her a bear hug.

"So, what's the plan?" Maeva asked, kicking off her flip-flops and surveying the rooms.

"I'm not sure," Sadie admitted. She walked into the familiar open area that combined a living room and dining room. A country kitchen with rooster wallpaper was down the hall to the left. To the right, overstuffed sofas and chairs boasting faded yellow wagon-wheel patterns sat in front of an old TV.

"God, this place looks just the same as when Dawn and I visited as kids."

"You sound surprised. When was the last time you visited your aunt?" Maeva asked.

"She's come up to Seattle for Christmases, so I haven't bothered to come here," Sadie said, feeling guilty.

Maeva sat down on a sofa and put her feet up on an oak coffee table with a carved wagon-wheel wood inlay.

"This place is like stepping back in time to the age of tacky furniture," Maeva said. "What's the theme here? Circle the covered wagons?"

Sadie didn't reply and she didn't sit. Her butt still felt asleep from the long drive. Plus the more she walked around the small house, the more she felt an excited hum vibrating just under her skin.

"I'm feeling good about this. I think we might be able to reach Uncle Glen." Sadie looked at Maeva. "Let's do this thing."

"Okay." Maeva rolled her shoulders and turned her neck this way and that until the bones cracked. Then she hoisted her small tote bag and unpacked a large pillar candle, a Bic lighter, and a romance novel.

Sadie pointed to the book. "I don't think that's Uncle Glen's kind of reading. I remember him as being more of a Lawrence Sanders fan."

"This is for me. In case Uncle Glen's stubborn about showing up, I don't want to just sit here bored out of my mind."

"Gotcha."

Maeva lit the candle and a mellow vanilla scent wafted through the air. The medium settled back down on the sofa, closed her eyes, and began to hum "We're Off to See the Wizard" from *The Wizard of Oz*. A small smile played on Sadie's lips.

"Still the same ol' song, huh?"

"Why mess with what works?" Maeva replied, and resumed humming.

Sadie knew from past experience that Maeva's humming wasn't about visiting Munchkins in Munchkinland or helping the Tin Man find a heart. It helped Maeva summon the dead.

After about ten minutes Maeva's forehead had broken into a fine mist of sweat despite the fact that Sadie had cranked the air conditioner.

"No luck?" Sadie asked, breaking her friend's spell.

"Not a thing. Sorry." Maeva offered her a tight-lipped smile.

Sadie sat down for the first time and leaned forward, resting her elbows on her knees and her face in her hands. Exhaustion and crushed hope left her feeling an emotional wreck. She bit back tears.

"We're both tired. How about if I make some coffee?" Maeva suggested, getting to her feet and walking toward the kitchen. "An infusion of caffeine will help us decide what we need to do next."

"Maybe what we need to do next is just give up and drive back home," Sadie said to herself.

She heard her friend opening and closing cupboard doors down the hall in the kitchen.

"You always did give up too soon," a male voice spoke from across the room.

Sadie startled and looked to the sound of the voice.

"Uncle Glen!" Sadie exclaimed, wanting to rush over and hug the old man standing next to the television.

"Yup. Even as a little girl. We'd play Monopoly and if I was beating your ass badly, you'd just want to give up."

"Only if you were cheating," Sadie exclaimed, a smile playing on her lips.

"I didn't cheat, unless it was to let you win on account of you being too damn stubborn about losing."

"I beat you fair and square. You never once let me win," Sadie said indignantly. She closed her eyes with relief and let out a long breath. "It's so good to see you, Uncle Glen."

"You too," he replied, his voice tender.

"I'm so sorry I never came to visit you at the, erm, in the—"

"Loony bin?"

Sadie cringed and her discomfort caused him to chuckle.

"That's okay. I didn't want visitors there and Lynn knew that. Damn depressing place what with everyone walking around talking to themselves." He paused. "Me included."

"About that . . ."

"I wasn't crazy, Sadie. At least I don't think so. I just couldn't stop the voices inside my head. They'd only get louder if I didn't reply to them. The docs put me on all kinds of meds. Said I was schizophrenic."

"Were you?" Sadie asked quietly.

"No. The pills didn't help. The docs thought they did, and that's why they convinced Lynn to keep me there on account of she could never get me to take them at home."

"Auntie Lynn never should've put you in that place," Sadie said, feeling angry.

"Whoa, now, it sure wasn't your aunt's fault," Uncle Glen said, and he waggled a finger at Sadie. "And you won't be telling her about any of this, will you? It wouldn't be right, her being made to feel guilty about something she couldn't possibly understand."

"I won't say anything to her. I just wish I'd known that you had the gift and then I—"

"Gift?" He let out a bark of laughter. "Is that what they're calling it these days? A gift?" He sat down on the love seat next to the sofa where she was, or actually he just kind of hovered over the cushions. "I sure as hell never thought of it as any kind of a gift. Listening to the voices of the dead was nothing but a curse. I kept it inside as long as I could. A guy I met in the institute told me when I passed it would go on to my loved ones. I sure as hell didn't want that to happen. Especially not to Lynn." He sighed. "But I should've let it go to Lynn, right? She had a good full life." He looked over at Sadie, his face twisted in pain. "If I'd known it would go to Brian . . . and he'd kill himself because of it, I never would have—"

"It wasn't your fault." Sadie said. "You couldn't help what happened."

She felt a surge of sharp pain in her chest, thinking about how Brian would've thought he was crazy.

"And that's how you ended up with it too?" he asked.

"Yes," Sadie said.

He sighed and shook his head. "I guess I got it from my aunt Emma. They locked her away at twenty and she died inside a sanitarium after living there for nearly forty years. At least I got to live most of my life on the outside." He pointed a finger at Sadie. "Those summers you and Dawn came to visit, those were the best of times for us. Without kids of our own, you were all we had."

"Us and the butterflies," Sadie joked.

"Yeah. The butterflies." He shook his head sadly. "One for every soul I helped go over."

Sadie looked at him with wonder and amazement.

"That's why you made them?"

"To help me remember that besides the fact I looked crazy, I was doing a good thing with my life."

"Wow."

"Now, about your aunt," he said firmly. "She's lonely here. You need to convince her to sell this place and move to Seattle so she can see you girls and your mom and dad."

"But she's happy here."

"No, she's not. She just doesn't want to burden any-one or feel like she's a fifth wheel." He nodded sharply. "Make her feel like you need her there and she'll dump this ol' place in a heartbeat."

"Are you sure?"

"Positive. I want you to promise me you'll work on your mom and dad too, so that they can convince Lynn that's what she needs to do."

Sadie agreed to try.

"I'm sorry about Brian," he said softly. "I tried to warn him before the blood vessel burst inside my head. I told him all about the voices and how they might come for him and that he shouldn't be afraid."

"And?"

"What do you think?" He blew out a low breath. "Your brother was a young stud full of life. He thought I was crazy. And rightly so. Only those living with it know the truth."

"I wish I'd known what he was going through. Maybe I could've helped him to understand. . . ."

"You probably would've thought he was crazy, Sadie." At the look on her face he added, "You don't think so, but I'm sure you haven't told the whole world what you got going on, have you?" At the look on her face he smiled. "Nope. I didn't think so. You know damn well not everyone gets it." He nodded toward the kitchen, where there was the sound of running water as Maeva continued to make a pot of coffee. "You're lucky you found a friend who gets it. The graveyards are full of those who couldn't handle their so-called gift." He got up and walked toward Sadie and stopped directly in front of her. "Wish I could give you a hug," he said, his voice hoarse.

She got to her feet.

"Do it, then," Sadie said, offering him a brave smile.

He shook his head. "Nope. I remember how it made me feel when the dead touched me. I thought I was gonna pass out or toss my lunch. I don't want you to remember me that way." He folded his hands neatly together and regarded his niece seriously. "Sadie, I've been trapped inside this house for six years. I'm tired. I need to let go."

She nodded and tears burned the backs of her eyes.

"I can almost see him," Uncle Glen said wistfully, his eyes distant.

"Who?"

"Brian," he said. The edges of his shape began to shimmer. "He can't come for me because he took his own life, but we can still be together after I let go."

"Then go," Sadie said firmly. "I'll take care of Aunt Lynn. You go and take care of my brother. Tell him I love him."

"Sorry it took me so long," Maeva said, walking into the room with two hot mugs filled with coffee. "I found the coffee grinds, but it took forever to locate where she keeps the sugar, and you know how I hate my coffee without a couple spoons of—" She stopped short. "Shit. Why are you crying?"

It took a while for Sadie to get the words out. Maeva helped Sadie to feel relief and gratefulness that she could help her uncle move on while she got closure for herself. After they finished their coffee and cleaned up, they hit the road again.

"I need to talk to Joy," Sadie said as her Honda rocketed down the highway back toward Seattle.

"You can call her in the morning," Maeva said sleepily.

"I could," Sadie agreed, digging out her cell phone. "But I'd rather talk to her now."

Sadie punched in the number of Onyx House and was grateful that it was Joy who answered the phone instead of Tim.

"Hullo?" came the sleepy greeting.

"Sorry to be calling so late."

"S-S-Sadie?" Joy stammered.

Sadie could hear the rustling of blankets.

"It's nearly two in the morning," Joy said incredulously. "What's up?"

"I need to talk to you about Brian," Sadie said. "About how he acted after he visited my uncle in Oregon."

"That was years ago!" she exclaimed angrily. "And I've got to get up early tomorrow morning. If you really want to talk, we can meet for coffee later. When it's actually daylight."

"Just a couple questions. Do you remember Brian going to visit my uncle?"

Joy sighed.

"He didn't s-s-set out to visit your uncle. He was on his way to S-S-Smith Rock for his annual boys' rock-climbing weekend," Joy said with a snort. She seemed to not approve of the outing. "He went a day early and decided to stay with your aunt and uncle."

"And how was he when he got back?"

"Again, Sadie, that was over s-s-six years ago! How would I remember how he was?"

"Because maybe he came back different. Was he talking to himself, or, um, seeming to talk to people who weren't there?"

Joy was quiet for so long Sadie prompted her.

"Joy? Did you hear me?"

"Look, Brian had a kind of thing going on in those last few weeks," Joy answered. "I don't think it'll come as any s-s-surprise for me to tell you that he was down. Really depressed."

"Depressed because he heard voices?" Sadie pushed.

"All I know is that I tried to get him to go to a doctor, but he wouldn't, s-s-so I brought him here, hoping he'd find peace with himself and maybe find people who understood."

"Obviously that was a big help," Sadie replied snarkily.

"Look, I'm s-s-sorry your brother and my fiancé killed himself," Joy said, biting off each syllable with anger. "But it was s-s-six years ago. I've moved on and you should consider just letting sleeping dogs lie."

And that reminded Sadie of Rhea.

"One more question. Why didn't you tell us that you were pregnant? Why didn't you give us the opportunity to get to know Brian's daughter?" Sadie demanded.

She was talking to air.

"She hung up," Sadie told Maeva.

"Gee, I wonder why." Maeva chuckled. "Ever hear of tact and diplomacy? Ever hear that you can catch more flies with honey than with vinegar?"

"Ever hear that he who hesitates is lost?" Sadie snapped. "I always knew that there must've been a big reason why Brian killed himself, and now I know what drove him to it. If she'd told him she was pregnant, maybe he would've snapped out of his depression. Maybe he would've gotten help or even just accepted that the dead talk to him and that he wasn't going crazy."

"Joy probably didn't even know she was pregnant, Sadie. You can't pin it all on her."

Sadie's fingers were tight on the steering wheel and tears leaked from under her lashes as she gunned the accelerator.

"I know what you're thinking," Maeva said.

"No, you don't," Sadie snapped.

"You are *not* your brother, Sadie," Maeva said quietly. Then she added in a firm voice, "You know why you've been given this gift. You know that you help people go over. If Brian had given it half a chance, maybe he could've learned that too. You help people with your gift."

"My so-called gift was handed down to me because my brother killed himself, Maeva. How can I go around happily trying to move spirits from here into the great beyond knowing that the only reason I *can* do it is because Brian blew his brains all over his bathroom with a gun?"

"How can you not?"

21

"I think I should try to talk to Rhea," Sadie said as she steered the car into the outskirts of Seattle.

"In the morning," Maeva said sleepily.

She fell back asleep and dozed off for the remaining drive until they were parked a few houses down from the bed-and-breakfast and Sadie killed the ignition.

Maeva sat up and looked around.

"Where are we?"

"Parked around the corner from Onyx House."

"I thought we agreed we'd do it in the morning?"

"Technically it is the morning."

"It's like three in the morning," Maeva pointed out. "Okay, we're here. So what's your plan?"

"Um . . ."

"You don't even have a plan?"

"In all fairness your snoring made it difficult to concentrate."

"Hunh." Maeva crossed her arms over her chest and scrunched up her face. "Okay, I've got it. You want to talk to Rhea, right? You've always seen this kid outside, right? So it's not like we have to break in or something. Lord knows we don't want to confront Joy, since she's already not very happy with you. We'll just walk around the gardens outside the house, keeping near the bushes so nobody notices us, and hopefully Rhea shows up."

"Okay," Sadie agreed.

They climbed out of Sadie's car and gently closed the doors. Walking around the corner and slowly up the street, Maeva bent to Sadie as they ducked under a streetlight.

"So what killed your little niece anyway?"

"She fell out her bedroom window," Sadie said.

"Jesus," Maeva muttered.

"Yeah," Sadie agreed. "One of the neighbors said Joy was working in her garden at the time and Rhea landed only a foot away."

"So your brother kills himself and then a few years later his little girl falls out a window. It's amazing Joy is still standing upright."

Sadie thought about how Brian's death just brought her to her knees emotionally. Losing a fiancé would've been awful, but losing your daughter in such a preventable accident would've been murder.

They ducked under the trellis archway and stayed along the cedar hedge as they circled the yard. The house was completely dark and the full shrubs added spooky shadows to the yard. The cool grass tickled her ankles. After a few minutes Sadie was getting discouraged.

"She's a little kid. Maybe she doesn't even come out at night," Sadie said.

"She's a spirit, Sadie. She has no concept of time and space as we know it. She can materialize or not as it pleases her."

They stepped around the back of the house, and outside lights promptly lit the yard.

"Oh shit!" Sadie whispered, and jumped back into shadow at the side of the house. Maeva leapt back with her.

"I think they're just motion-detector lights," Maeva whispered in Sadie's ear.

"What are you guys doin'?" a young voice asked.

Sadie whirled around to find Rhea standing there smiling and eyeing them curiously.

"She's here," Sadie said to Maeva, her voice still a hushed whisper.

Maeva turned and looked where Sadie pointed.

"I can make out only a whitish wisp of smoke," Maeva admitted.

It was no surprise. Maeva's skills were more along the lines of receiving messages from those spirits she herself actually summoned.

"Why are you whispering?" the little girl asked, her own voice lowered and followed by a delighted giggle.

"I don't want your mom or stepdad to know we're here," Sadie admitted.

"You don't have to worry 'bout Dad, on account of he's not home. He went out and he's not back yet."

"So Joy's home alone?" Sadie asked, looking up to the higher windows above them. Maeva's gaze followed hers.

"Yep. 'Cept for she's got a guest."

"Right. I guess this is a B and B," Sadie said, more to herself. She faced Rhea, then dropped down to one knee so that she was looking the little girl straight in the eye. "I want to ask you something important. I want you to think hard and tell me if you ever remember your mom talking about why your real dad died."

"Oh, I know why he died," Rhea said, nodding her head seriously. "I do. It was 'cause of a gun and that's why guns are never, not ever, for kids to touch or play with."

Sadie blew out a long breath and tried a different approach.

"Yes, it was because he got shot with a gun, but did your mom ever say why?"

Rhea pinched her face into a thoughtful look and tapped her pursed lips with the tip of her finger.

"It was on account of voices."

"Voices?"

"Yep. Voices he heard, and then he came here and Daddy Tim told him he was gonna end up loony like his uncle and he'd be better off gone. Mom said his head and heart were all broken inside 'cause of voices."

"Tim told him he was crazy?" Sadie's tone was harsher than she wanted and she saw Rhea flinch away.

"You're mad."

"I'm not mad at *you*. I'm mad that your daddy is dead."

"Tim's my real daddy, you know, on account of Mom said so and since I never knew the other dad."

Sadie sighed and looked into Rhea's sad face.

"I wish I could've been your real aunt when you were alive."

"You need to help her move on," Maeva said, coming to stand next to Sadie. "You're becoming attached."

"She's Brian's flesh and blood," Sadie whispered.

"No, she's not," Maeva said firmly. "Because she's no longer even part of our reality. You need to help her move on, because it's what you are called to do."

"I don't wanna go," Rhea said, her bottom lip beginning to quiver.

"See what you've done?" Sadie demanded. "You're upsetting her."

Maeva opened her mouth to say something, then shut it again, tilting her head as if listening to a distant sound.

"You don't have to move on if you're not ready," Sadie told Rhea.

"You better leave," Rhea said. She looked off toward the front yard and lifted her finger to point. "One of the bad people is coming."

Sadie looked toward the front yard where Rhea pointed. When she turned back, Rhea was gone. Then she heard it.

"A motorcycle!" Maeva and Sadie cried simultaneously.

By the time they heard it, he was already driving up to the front of the house. There was no way to get to Sadie's car without walking right past the biker, so they hunkered down low behind a clump of shrubs that, hopefully, hid them while allowing them ample view of the front yard.

The Harley-Davidson made a final *fwap fwap* growl before it was turned off. Seconds later a man clad in black leather strode purposely through the vine-covered trellis and toward the front door. His leather jacket was new and fitted. The helmet he wore was the modern full-facial type and certainly not the black beanie Fierce Force members were known to wear. At the front door, the motorcyclist simply knocked once.

Sadie found herself leaning forward, her face against scratchy branches, in order to see. She could hear Maeva's heavy breathing next to her.

The front door was opened by Joy. She was wearing jeans and a T-shirt and looked like she'd been expecting someone. When the man stepped inside, he tugged off his helmet. As he reached behind him to shut the door, Sadie saw his face clearly.

It was Scott Reed.

Sadie's hand flew to her mouth to stifle a gasp. Maeva's face had the same look of astonishment.

The door to Onyx House closed.

"Let's wait a minute and then make a run for it," Maeva suggested.

Sadie nodded.

After a minute or two, they got to their feet and carefully threaded their way between the taller shrubs in the garden. Once they were near the trellis, they bolted through the yard, down the street, and around the corner.

Once inside the car, they zipped out of the neighborhood as quickly as possible.

"He could be doing a story," Maeva suggested.

"Maybe . . . ," Sadie said, but it felt wrong to her. She opened her mouth to say more but heard the muffled ring of her cell phone sounding from the bottom of her purse.

Since Sadie was driving, Maeva dug out the phone for

her. She looked at the display before handing it over to Sadie.

"It's Zack."

Sadie frowned. It was the middle of the night.

She took the phone and answered.

"Yeah?"

"Where are you?"

"I'm out," she said huffily. He had no right to demand to know where she was in the middle of the night.

"You need to get your ass to your sister's place. Someone's taken Dawn."

22

Sadie reached Dawn's house in record time, but she didn't remember the drive. Her Honda had barely come to a complete stop at the curb before she was flying out of her car and hurling herself toward the house with Maeva jumping out of the passenger seat and running to catch up.

Zack stopped her in the driveway.

"Tell me everything!" Sadie said, her voice tinged with hysteria. "What are they doing to get my sister back?" She nodded toward a growing police presence in and around Dawn's house.

"I'm sure the police are doing everything they can," Maeva said quietly.

"They've got her, don't they?" Sadie said, her eyes large and brimming with tears. "Those bikers or Satanists or whoever took my sister and they're . . . they're going to kill her and cut out her baby!" The last was said behind her fingers. She felt her knees buckle and Zack grabbed her by her elbow.

"You've got to calm down," he said, his voice coplike in its firmness, and his jaw set in granite anger. "Time is everything right now."

Sadie nodded and bit the inside of her cheek to stop from screaming. The part of her that was insanely angry with Zack got buried beneath the heart-pounding fear her sister could be dead.

"Oh, God, Thuggy was supposed to be watching her!"

Zack's eyes narrowed. "When did you talk to Thuggy?"

"Earlier today. He came to my house and I told him I'd pay him to keep an eye on Dawn until I got here."

"He wasn't here. The cops got a nine-one-one call from your sister. She said someone was breaking into her house, but then the call ended and by the time they got here, she was gone."

"Oh, God! Who do I talk to? What do I do?"

Zack brought her over to the detective handling the case.

"Sadie said Thuggy was supposed to be watching Dawn," Zack said.

"Shit. There was no sign of him," the detective said. He turned to Sadie. "You might as well know that Thuggy—or should I say Ron—is one of ours," the detective said.

"One of yours?" Sadie blinked in surprise. "You mean . . ."

"He's been undercover working for Egan doing meth-lab cleanup and trying to uncover more information about the meth trade. He was doing well until Egan disappeared."

Sadie turned to Zack. "You knew this?"

"I told you I trusted the guy. There wasn't anything else I could say."

Sadie turned to Maeva. She was on her phone explaining things to Terry.

"I need to go inside."

Sadie didn't wait for permission and nobody stopped her. Zack simply fell into step beside her.

Sadie walked past the people dusting for prints and collecting evidence. Zack brought her down the hall to Dawn's bedroom.

The bedsheets were twisted and crumpled as if someone had just woken up and hadn't had time to make the bed. There was a glass of water and crackers on the bedside table and an open copy of *What to Expect When You're Expecting*. The house was hot and smelled faintly of new paint from the newly finished nursery. Sadie thought about Penny Torrez and her blood-soaked dress, and a searing pain knifed through her chest.

Zack tried to hug her, but Sadie yanked away. She sank slowly to her knees and sobbed gut-wrenching cries until Maeva came to coax her out of the house.

"Zack said we should go back to your house. Someone needs to be there in case a call comes in," Maeva said once they were back outside.

"They're giving us the brush-off," Sadie sniffed. "Nobody's going to call. This isn't a ransom situation."

"You don't know that. I'll drive you back home," Zack said, and it wasn't a suggestion. For an ex-cop, he was in full cop mode now, like it or not. He tossed his own keys to Maeva. "You take my Mustang and meet us at Sadie's place."

Sadie's hands trembled as she buckled in.

"This is all my fault," Sadie moaned. "We've got to find her." She covered her face with her hands. "Oh, God, I've got to call John. I've got to call my mom and dad."

"Wait on telling your folks until morning. The officers that tried to reach John at his hotel were told he'd already left for the airport. His plane won't land for a few more hours. By then we'll have good news."

Sadie knew what Zack wasn't saying. That if they didn't find Dawn soon, they wouldn't find her alive.

Once they were at her house, Sadie raced to the answering machine.

"Nothing. No ransom messages." She turned to Zack. "This isn't a kidnapping. They want her baby and they'll kill her to get it." Her voice was thin and high with emotion.

"All of SPD is on the lookout for her, Sadie."

Maeva walked in then, her eyes a question.

"Nothing," Sadie said. "No messages. Not that we expected any. Maeva, I need you to make some calls and find out where the hell this Witigo Alliance group meets. You're the only one I know with those kinds of contacts."

"I've already called Louise, but it went to voice mail. Terry's working on everyone in our address book and everyone we know that was at that session last year."

It wasn't enough. Sadie felt useless pacing the floor.

Her cell phone rang and Sadie jumped. She nearly dropped it in her excitement to answer the call.

"It's Egan," Sadie announced to the room, and she stabbed the button to take the call.

"What?" she demanded.

There was no response.

"Hello?" she repeated. To Zack and Maeva she added, "Listen." And put the call on speaker. Nobody was on the line, but there was the sound of crashing and banging before the call went dead.

Sadie looked at Zack. "The call came from his house. I've got a bad feeling. I think Egan's mixed up in all this somehow."

"I'll call it in," Zack said, already reaching for his own phone, but Sadie stopped him.

"What if it's nothing and we're pulling everyone away from leads that are really important?" she asked him.

"You two go," Maeva suggested. "Terry's on his way over and we'll be making calls from here. I'll let you know if anyone calls the house."

Sadie was already on her way out the door as Zack shouted protests behind her.

"I don't think this is a good idea," he said.

"Then stay!" She whirled and shouted at him. "But I'm not going to sit on my ass doing nothing. I'm going to Egan's and if that turns up nothing, then I'm beating every friggin' bush in this city until I find my sister, got it?!"

"I'll drive," he said, walking toward his Mustang.

Zack steered out of the neighborhood as Sadie impatiently tapped her foot while sitting on the passenger side.

"Can't you go faster?"

"I don't want to get us killed," Zack grumbled, but it was useless. Sadie didn't care at this point who died. As long as it wasn't her sister or her future niece or nephew.

Sadie tried to call back Egan, but there was no answer. She didn't want to tie up her phone, so she gave the number to Zack. He dialed it on his own cell and left it on speaker while it rang and rang.

A few minutes later Zack eyed her curiously when Sadie gave him directions.

"Isn't Egan's apartment just up the road?"

"Yeah, it is, but he wasn't calling from his apartment. He's got a place in Bellevue."

"Why the hell does a single guy need two places?" Zack asked.

"His dad died a few months ago and left the house to him. He plans to move into it eventually, but it needed a lot of work, so he's been doing renos on the weekend. He's there enough he had a phone installed. We've talked on the weekends, so I had the number programmed into my phone."

Sadie cursed as a light turned red. She closed her eyes and muttered a silent prayer.

They drove to the address she had and found themselves in an area of middle-class two-level homes. Each home had a tidy postage-stamp yard and a single attached garage. They pulled up the driveway and stared at the house. It was completely dark.

They walked together to the front door and Sadie pressed the bell, tapping her foot as she waited.

"You don't honestly expect he's going to answer, do you?" Zack asked.

"At this point, anything's possible," Sadie replied. She rubbed her forearms. The weather had finally turned and she could feel moist cool air drifting in off the Pacific.

Zack rapped his knuckles sharply on the door.

A narrow window ran parallel with the front door and Sadie was trying to peer between tight blinds.

"I think I see a light, but it might just be a reflection."

"Wait here." Zack turned to go. "I'll check around back."

After what felt like forever, the front door opened and Zack ushered her inside.

"How'd you get in?" Sadie asked as she closed the front door behind her.

"Looks like someone already beat us to it. The lock on the patio door was broken and the door was wide-open."

The two-level home opened onto a short hall with stairs leading up to the second level. To the right was a closet, and to the left was a spacious living room and beyond that was the kitchen. To Sadie's surprise the place was fully furnished and didn't look like a place undergoing renos.

"Looks like the renovations are done," Zack said drily. "Hell, you should see the stuff this guy's got." Zack led the way through the living room that boasted a massive plasma-screen TV and a new butter-soft leather sofa and chairs cozied up to the fireplace. An amazing multicolored area rug divided the living area from the dining room.

"That rug still has the price on it," Sadie said.

She knelt, lifted the tag from the carpet, and let out a low whistle. "Two thousand smackers for a six-by-eight rug?" She got to her feet and turned slowly, taking in expensive art on the walls.

"Are you thinking what I'm thinking?" Zack asked.

"That Egan's business has done really well?"

"That Egan's got his fingers in other pots besides meth cleaning if he's living this well, and I doubt it's legal. . . ."

"You don't know that," Sadie said, even though she'd been thinking the same thing. "Where's the phone?"

They looked around and found the base for a cordless phone but no handset.

"Must be upstairs," Sadie said after checking the modern-age kitchen with the stainless Sub-Zero refrigerator.

She turned and walked back to the front foyer and took the stairs up to the second level. Zack was right behind her.

"You take the bedroom," Sadie said. "I'll take the den."

Egan's office was a chaotic mess of paperwork, but he had a new fax machine in the corner. On his desk, being used as a paperweight, was a bottle of Carsebridge Scotch whisky. Sadie didn't know much about Scotch, but she knew expensive when she saw it.

Almost hidden under a stack of manila folders was Egan's cell phone. Sadie picked it up and began scrolling through all the recent incoming and outgoing calls from Egan's number. She snagged a notepad and pen and began writing them down.

"Nothing unusual in the bedroom," Zack said. "Unless you count a bedspread that looks like it's spun from gold." He pointed. "Hey, that bottle of whiskey's gotta be worth nearly two hundred bucks. Egan's got expensive tastes." He walked over and picked up the bottle. "Think Egan would mind?"

"Huh?" Sadie was busily checking Egan's calls.

Zack put the bottle back.

"You checking who called?"

"Yeah." Sadie continued to scroll through the list of incoming callers. The last few were from Sadie's and Zack's cell phones. Then she stopped abruptly and she felt her face pale.

She stared, unblinking, at the number on the display and swallowed.

"Two days ago somebody called him from Onyx House bed-and-breakfast," Sadie said. "Small world, huh?"

"It isn't that small," Zack replied tightly.

"What the hell is going on?" Sadie asked quietly. "I'm going to try calling this house again."

She picked up her phone and dialed the number for the house they were in. Her cell phone rang in her ear as they walked back downstairs.

Zack tilted his head. "Do you hear that?"

"What?" Sadie pulled her phone away from her ear but didn't disconnect. A phone was ringing somewhere. "Doesn't this place have a basement?"

Zack had his gun in his hand and headed to a door in the hall. He opened the door and peered into the darkness. The ring of a phone could be heard coming from downstairs. At the same time it went to voice mail at Sadie's end, the ringing sound stopped.

The light was on in the basement.

"Stay here," he told her.

"Like hell."

The basement was small but held a finished rec room that reeked of new smells. New carpet. New paint but no furniture. There were two things wrong with the room.

First, a large hole had been punched into the wall and the drywall torn apart.

Second, David Egan was slumped in a corner with a bullet hole between his eyes.

23

They found the cordless house phone under David Egan's body. Egan must've tried to call her while he lay dying.

Sadie looked at death every day. Mopped up the remains of it and wiped off the grime and slop of it. She could shut down her emotions to do her job, but it was hard when she knew the dead.

"He was one of us," Sadie said weakly.

"Maybe, but he was into other shit that caused this," Zack said.

"He always was the cynical one," came a voice behind Sadie.

She turned around and came face-to-face with Egan's spirit. Standing there clear as day, a large, bloody hole between his eyebrows, just like his physical self on the floor.

"Egan!"

He whipped his head from side to side as if she must be talking to someone else.

"You can see me?"

"Yes, I can see the dead."

"Man, I don't look so good, do I?" he asked, looking at his body against the wall. "How come you can see me?"

"I don't have time to explain. I need you to tell me

what happened," Sadie said, never so glad to see a ghost in her life. "Someone's kidnapped Dawn."

"Your sister? Ah, man, that sucks." He tilted his head at her. "What do you mean, you can talk to the dead?"

"You talking to Egan's ghost?" Zack asked.

Sadie nodded to Zack, and to David Egan she said, "I can see and talk to the dead and I'm happy to have a fun conversation with you about that another time, but I need to find my sister before the Witigo Alliance cuts open her belly and stuffs her baby in a goat."

"That's sick, man." Egan recoiled. "All I know about is the meth money." He nodded toward the hole in his wall. "I'm sorry to get you mixed up in it. When I got clearance to clean the meth house in Kirkland, I did my due diligence. We cleaned the place out. Scrubbed away at it top to bottom, but on the last day when I'm doing my walk-through, I noticed a board in the corner was loose, so I lifted it, and holy shit!" He shook his head. "I figure Fierce Force stashed their money in the house and planned to come back for it. I knew I shouldn't touch it. The last thing I wanted was to get mixed up with bikers, but, hey, I figured they'd never miss a few of those packages of bills."

"What about Jake the Snake?" Sadie demanded.

"I never touched him, Sadie," Egan said, making a cross-his-heart motion. "He came into the house after me and he started looking for the money. I hid in a closet—otherwise they would've killed me then. Curly the Cutter knew Snake was thinking of defecting, so I guess they followed him to the house, and pow! They took care of him. After they walked out, I helped myself to a duffel bag full of bills. I figured they'd think another biker stole from them. I didn't mean for you to get caught up in it. They were planning on moving the cash to another location, but they knew the house was still being watched by the cops. Then the day they planned on making the move, you got the cleaning job and found the cash."

"And they thought I took the money," Sadie said. "Thanks a lot."

"Yeah, but Curly figured it out. He said he found out where I was because he'd been following Thuggy."

"Thuggy was an undercover cop. He must've been watching the house." Sadie looked at Zack for clarification.

"I knew Thuggy from my early days on the force, so I made him right away when I saw him working for Egan. He confided that he'd infiltrated the FF and was watching the Kirkland house," Zack confirmed.

"He probably saw you leave with the cash, but none of this is helping me find my sister," Sadie shouted with exasperation.

"Undercover." Egan's eyes grew wide. "Oh shit. So that's why they . . ."

"They what?"

"Sadie, they killed Thuggy."

"What?!"

"Yeah, when Curly was here, he said they found out where the money was from an undercover pig. They gave him a shot of extrapure heroin to get him to talk. After he told them where the money was, here with me, they waited for him to die and then set fire to the body."

"Shit."

Her mind was reeling with sorrow and guilt about Thuggy, but she still needed to find Dawn.

"Where is she, Egan? The bikers took Dawn."

He shook his head. "They wouldn't do that."

"Why? Because they're so morally above killing a pregnant woman?" Sadie spit sarcastically.

"No, it's because they're done with you."

"What do you mean?"

"One of Curly's henchmen asked about you. He said, 'So what do we do about the cleanup broad?' And Curly told him that was over, since they now had the money and knew you didn't take it. They wouldn't take Dawn to get their money back if they already got their money."

"The ones connected to Witigo would," Sadie said.

"Witigo." His eyes grew wide. "I heard about those dark dudes. The ones hooked up with the devil." He shook his head. "Snake's girlfriend . . . Penny something or other, she turned some of the FF on to that devil-worship shit, but most of them didn't want anything to do with it. As far as I know, they backed away. Except for Snake's girl. Pretty bad when it's too scary even for bikers."

"Okay, but why are you talking to Onyx House?" Sadie demanded. "I saw somebody from there called you."

"That freaky fake B and B?"

"What do you mean, fake B and B?" Sadie asked.

"I don't know what they do in that house, but I know that Penny's friend Joy sure doesn't make beds there."

"Penny's friend Joy?" Sadie's mouth went dry.

"Yeah, they were buddies. The seminars Joy has, they're just a cover-up for those crazy devil worshippers. The workshops are how they recruit more people. At least that's how Penny got hooked."

"I've called this in," Zack said. "Cops are on their way, so I've gotta wait here and somehow explain what I was doing inside this place."

Sadie held out her hand. "Give me your keys. I don't want to be tied up talking to the cops about Egan. I've got to go look for my sister."

"No way. If you go out on your own, then you'll get yourself killed. Wait until the cops get here and I'll go with you."

Sadie nodded in agreement and headed for the stairs.

"I'll send the cops down here when they show up," she said calmly.

As soon as she got upstairs she headed for the front door and took off at a dead run. She knew Zack couldn't leave the scene, but there was no way she was waiting one second longer. A block away she hailed a cab and gave him the address of Onyx House.

It took all of two minutes for Zack to call her on her cell.

"I'm sorry," she said as a greeting when she answered. "When the cops get there, you need to find a way to tell them Thuggy is the guy buried with Bambi under the tree. The burned body. It was his. I guess the reason he wasn't watching Dawn is because he was already dead. He doesn't know he's dead. He's still working undercover. I'll deal with that later, but right now, there's no way I can spend the rest of the night talking to police about Egan when I need to be looking for Dawn."

"You need to be letting the police look for Dawn!" he shouted. "Don't do anything stupid."

"When have I ever done anything stupid?" she demanded, and hung up before he could start listing days and times.

When the cabdriver was within a block of Onyx House, Sadie asked him to drop her off. She paid him and stepped out onto the dark tree-lined street, immediately feeling vulnerable. For the first time she wished she'd listened to Zack and carried her gun. But she had no talent for shooting. The only talent she had would have to do. Hopefully, a certain five-year-old ghost was available to help her get inside the house.

Sadie ducked inside the yard and crept to the edge of the bushes.

"You shouldn't've come," Rhea whispered. She was glancing around and nervously fading in and out.

"Why? Is that other man still here?" Sadie asked, standing in the shadow.

"They will hurt you."

"I'm not going to get hurt," Sadie insisted. "But someone's taken my sister and I have to find her. Have you seen a pregnant lady?"

Rhea nodded sadly.

"Where is she?!" Sadie insisted, her voice rising, and

she reached for the girl in spite of herself, but Rhea was gone.

Suddenly, she felt the bite of cold metal as a blade pressed against her larynx.

"Make a sound and you're dead," said a firm male voice.

She was brought into Onyx House through the back door.

"Keep going," snarled the man with the knife still at her throat. "Through the kitchen and down the stairs."

He pushed her along and the edge of the knife made tiny cuts into her throat, making her afraid to even swallow. The stairs to the basement of the old home were extremely steep and there was only a faint glimmer of light coming from below. Once she reached the bottom of the stairs, he turned her around and pushed Sadie forward into a larger room.

"I told you if we waited long enough, she'd come to us."

Sadie recognized the voice as Joy's, but when she turned toward the sound, she spotted her sister.

"Dawn!" Sadie screamed.

Her sister was gagged and tied to a straight-backed chair. Sadie lunged to be with her, but a hand clamped on her arm and held her firm.

"Make sure she's s-s-secured," Joy said, sounding almost bored. "She's a s-s-slippery one."

Sadie was forced into a wooden chair not far from Dawn.

"You're going to be fine. Everything's going to be okay," Sadie assured.

She hated the naked fear in Dawn's eyes and she planned on making everyone in the room pay for putting it there. Unfortunately, her hands were immediately restrained behind her back with plastic cable ties that dug into her flesh. Then her ankles were each bound to a leg of the chair.

"Please don't gag me," Sadie pleaded. "Let me talk to my sister."

"Just go along, Sweets. It'll be easier."

Sadie spun her head in the direction of Scott Reed's voice.

"You!" she spit. "You did this!"

But he looked just as afraid as Dawn.

"Shut up," Joy said to Reed. "You have no power here."

She looked around the room for the first time. There were about half a dozen people in the room. They looked at Sadie with a mixture of revulsion and excitement. A coffee table was pushed into the center of the room by a young man with a goatee that was similar to Tim's. But where was Tim?

"Keep me and let my sister go," Sadie said. "Please."

"You're both needed for the ritual. Trust me, this wasn't my wish, but Tim s-s-said one day you would come to Onyx House and he was right!" She shouted the word "right" and the room erupted in applause.

"We had our doubts," she admitted when the claps died down. "Even I began to wonder. Especially after our dear Rhea died." Pain flashed across her eyes, but when it was gone, all that remained was madness. "You are the proof," she said to Sadie. "You and your powers. You are what made today possible."

There was more applause.

"You should actually feel quite honored," Joy said.

"Oka-a-ay," Sadie said. "If it is all about me, let my sister go."

"Oh, we will be letting her go all right," Joy said.

"They only want her baby," Reed spoke up.

"Shut up," Joy hissed. "Nobody has given you permission to s-s-speak. You did your investigation into S-S-Sadie and you got proof for Witigo Alliance that she had the power we hoped, but now your work is done. Now you are useless to us."

"You were investigating me for this bunch of wackos?" Sadie called out to Reed, but he slunk off to stand against the wall with the others. Sadie could see him break out in a sweat.

"If you continue to s-s-speak, I'll have you gagged," Joy barked at Sadie.

Just then the door to the basement opened and everyone was silent as someone came down the stairs. Sadie prayed it was Zack. With his gun and maybe a couple dozen trigger-happy cops.

Unfortunately it was Tim.

"Greetings, Master," the crowd murmured together as if on cue.

He was carrying a large cloth sack that he dragged behind him. He walked over to the coffee table and turned the sack upside down. The body of an eviscerated goat tumbled out. Its white belly hair was matted with fresh blood.

Sadie glanced at her sister and saw Dawn's eyes were wide with fear.

"Don't look at it," she whispered to Dawn. "Close your eyes."

Tim turned to look at Sadie and he clapped his hands.

"Wonderful!" he exclaimed, obviously delighted to see her. He walked over to Joy, embraced her, and planted a long wet kiss on her mouth. When he finally released her, Joy's face was absolutely radiant. She looked drunk with pleasure.

"You have redeemed yourself," he told her, looking into her eyes. "Producing me a powerless, worthless heir is all forgiven now."

"He calls me that only 'cause I didn't have power," Rhea said.

Sadie twisted around to see the ghost of the little girl just behind her.

"Please help me," Sadie said. "Think of a way for us to get out of here."

"I can't help you," Rhea whispered back. "I don't

know how, but I'll help your friends." The little girl folded her arms over her chest angrily. "It's not my fault Daddy's power went to you and not to me," Rhea continued with a pout. "I wasn't even born yet. If Daddy didn't die so early—"

"They would've killed him," Sadie murmured. She turned away from Rhea and looked at Tim with hatred in her eyes. "If Brian hadn't taken his own life, you planned on killing him anyway. That's why you told him he was crazy. You didn't want him to know he had a gift, because you wanted his power for yourself. When Joy told you she was pregnant, you knew that Brian's power would go to her baby."

Sudden realization hit her.

"So that's why you need both me and the baby. When you kill me, the power will go to the baby and you'll have your heir, but actually it isn't about having a child. You want to use that child to connect you to the dark forces. To be your bridge to the other side and give you power to communicate with the dead."

"Not the way you do," Tim said slyly. "My communication with spirits will be on an entirely different plane." He chuckled and the entire room erupted into laughter to join him.

"Did you kill Rhea too, just because she had no power?"

"Of course not!" Joy said.

"Why isn't she gagged?" Tim asked heatedly, and two or three men leapt forward to do the job.

"She wasn't even Brian's child!" Sadie screamed out. A big burly guy succeeded in thrusting a rag that reeked of damp and mildew into her mouth, but Tim shoved the man aside and yanked the rag from Sadie's mouth.

"What did you say?" His eyes were narrowed to slits.

"I said the reason why Rhea had no power wasn't because of *me*. It was because she wasn't Brian's blood." Sadie looked beyond Tim to nod to Joy. "Tell him, Joy.

Tell him that Rhea wasn't Brian's child." Sadie looked up at Tim. "Rhea was your flesh and blood, not Brian's."

"What?!" His eyes bulged and Tim whirled to face Joy. "You lying whore! You told me you were pregnant with Brian's child. You knew that was the only reason you would gain entry into the order, and you knew it was the only reason I chose to take you as my bride!"

Joy shrank back until she was flat against the wall.

"She's lying!" Joy said.

"Oh yeah? Rhea herself told me," Sadie shouted hurriedly. "I speak to the dead, remember? And they speak to me, but there's something that you don't know—the dead also talk to each other. Rhea had a nice chat with Brian and reported back to me."

Sadie turned to offer an apology for the lie to Rhea, but the little girl was gone. Sadie turned back at the sound of Tim's fist slamming into the wall an inch from Joy's face. Sadie thought Joy would flinch or move away, but she merely stood there as if prepared to take whatever punishment he dished out.

Suddenly, Tim took a deep breath and turned away.

"What's done is done," he said. "The past doesn't matter anymore. Today's ritual is what's important. The only way Witigo can move on is to have the power of both the living and the dead. After tonight, we'll have both."

Sadie thought she heard a sound upstairs. She strained to listen but realized it must be her imagination or the sound of her own heart pounding painfully in her ears.

Tim stepped forward and unrolled the satchel and laid the contents out on the table. There were six knives with ornate black and silver handles that he spaced evenly on the table. Next, he added a clear bottle of red liquid and a chalice.

For two weeks the heat wave had made Sadie feel overheated, but now her blood ran like ice in her veins. *Please, God,* she prayed. *Oh please, no.*

She thought back to her Catholic roots and began to recite the prayers of her youth. She could almost smell the incense. Then she opened her eyes and realized it was incense. Incense and smoke.

I'm losing my mind.

"What's that smell?" Tim demanded. He nodded to Joy. "Did you leave something cooking in the kitchen?"

"I—I don't think s-s-so."

"Go check," he ordered.

Joy hurried up the stairs. When she reached the top and opened the door, she screamed.

"Fire!"

It was pandemonium. Everyone scrambled up the stairs at once. Even though Tim shouted for all to remain calm, nobody listened. Apparently, the wrath of their master was nothing compared with the thought of burning alive in the basement of an ancient B and B.

Dawn and Sadie were left in the basement. Dawn's face was white as paste and her eyes were wide with fear.

"We're going to be okay," Sadie said.

She made hopping and wiggling motions until her chair was right next to her sister's.

There were chaotic shouts upstairs and the sound of gunshots. Followed by the joyful sound of Zack's voice as he screamed, "Sadie!"

He bounded down the stairs and ran to her, lifting her, chair and all, right off the floor. Then he went to Dawn and removed her gag.

"Are you okay?" he asked her.

"I really need to pee," she said.

Zack looked around, saw the knives, and used one to cut away her ties first and then Sadie's.

"We've got to get out of here." Dawn coughed. "What about the fire?"

She tried to get to her feet but stumbled. Zack caught her and pushed her back onto the chair.

"There's no fire. Not really. Let the cops do their

thing upstairs and paramedics will come down and examine you."

"But the smoke?" Sadie asked.

"Maeva and her friend Louise did something they called smudging. They started it before the rest of us got here. It turned out to be a great idea. Everyone was afraid we'd end up in a standoff with you two as hostages. This way, the bad guys all ended up running right into the arms of the cops."

"We heard shots," Sadie said.

"Tim tried to make a run for it. I think he took one in the leg."

"Between the legs would've been better," Sadie grumbled.

She grabbed her sister in a hug.

"I'm sooo sorry you got dragged into this."

"You can make it up to me by helping me to the washroom."

They found one down the hall and Dawn waddled quickly inside. When she reappeared, she breathed a sigh of relief.

"That shower tomorrow had better be frigg'n awesome. You owe me."

"You still want the shower after all this?" Sadie asked incredulously.

"Especially after all this!" Dawn exclaimed.

The paramedics looked Dawn over and pronounced her and her baby healthy despite the trauma, but they insisted she go to the hospital anyway. Sadie promised to be along shortly. As soon as she spoke to the police and gave her statement no less than half a dozen times. It was par for the course.

Louise and Maeva were pleased as punch that they'd taken matters into their own hands.

"Rhea helped show us where you were," Maeva said.

"What would you have done if everyone came running out of the house assuming there was a fire, but the cops hadn't arrived yet?" Sadie asked with a smile.

"Actually, we hadn't thought things out that far," Maeva admitted.

"Like hell we hadn't." Louise lifted the front of her shirt to reveal a revolver tucked neatly into the waistband of her pants.

"If you don't have a license to carry concealed, you're going to want to get rid of that thing before you give your statement," Zack said with a pained expression on his face.

"Oh. Right," Louise said, and she hustled off to her car.

"Terry threatened not to let me hang out with you anymore," Maeva said. "You should be prepared for a lecture."

"He can yell at me all he wants after the baby shower," Sadie said.

"The shower's still on?" Maeva asked, her eyebrows raised in surprise.

"Yep. It's still on."

"Awesome. I've got my present all wrapped and ready to go."

"Please tell me you didn't get the baby a miniature tarot-card pack or something like that," Sadie groaned.

"Of course not," Maeva exclaimed, but the twinkle in her eye promised the gift would have Maeva's special touch. She rubbed her arms with her hands. "Is it finally cooling off or am I hallucinating?"

Sadie took a deep breath of the cool, damp air, enjoying the smell of the ocean.

"I think Seattle's finally getting back to normal."

It was at least another ninety minutes before Sadie was free to go. Maeva and Louise went home. Zack offered to bring Sadie to the hospital to be with Dawn. On the drive over to the hospital, they sat quietly, each buried in his or her own thoughts.

"I'm sorry I left you at Egan's house to deal with all that crap," Sadie said.

Zack stopped his car at a red light and glanced over at her.

"You had to rescue your sister. I get it. While we're apologizing, I'm sorry for everything that's happened too, but I didn't sleep with Jackie."

"What?" Sadie whirled and gaped at him. "What do you mean, you didn't sleep with her? Why would you tell me you did if you didn't?"

"I was drunk. She was supposed to sleep on my couch and I told her I'd drive her home in the morning. When I woke up, she was naked in my bed and I just assumed . . ."

"And who corrected that assumption?"

"She did. When I put a gun to her head earlier tonight."

"What?" Sadie shrieked.

"She was feeding information to Scott Reed in return for cash. Her gambling problem was bigger than I thought. Guess she was back to owing a lot of money and didn't want to lose any more fingers. Jackie also admitted that I wasn't the one who told her about your ability to speak to the dead. Reed was trying to get in good with the WA for his story, and he knew WA wanted proof of your abilities. For what it's worth, I don't think Reed realized he was putting you in danger. He told Jackie that Witigo were a bunch of nuts, but he didn't think they were dangerous. She believed that."

"She was willing to believe anything for the cash," Sadie grumbled.

"Yeah. In the beginning, Jackie just told Reed the cleanup jobs where we were working, so that's why he always seemed to be around."

"And he was photographing me at home too."

"Reed asked Jackie to see if she could confirm your ability." He looked at Sadie. "Unfortunately, I did."

The light turned green and he punched the accelerator.

"I had a feeling something was up with her," Sadie admitted. "But I thought that feeling was all about how she looked at you." Sadie thought about things a minute.

"I don't blame you for thinking she was hot. I mean, c'mon . . . you're a man after all."

He reached and put a hand on her leg.

"You're the only woman who can turn me on by wearing a hazmat suit."

Sadie laughed.

"Well, you know what this means, don't you?" she said after a while.

"What?"

"I've gotta put another ad in the *Times* for an employee."

"Maybe we can handle the cleans just the two of us for a while."

"Yeah. Maybe."

"I want to be more involved," he said, steering the car into the hospital parking lot.

"You're my right-hand man. The only way you could get more involved with Scene-2-Clean is if you bought me out and ran the company." She snorted.

"I don't mean with the company." He steered his Mustang into an open parking stall and put the gearshift in park. "I love you, Sadie. I want to spend more time with you, outside of work. I want us to really give this thing a chance."

"Okay." She swallowed thickly. "Maybe we can try dating. Like normal people."

"Or maybe you could just move in." He turned and looked at her seriously. "Dating would be included, but you wouldn't have to go home after you said good night."

"Wait a second, you want me to sell my house and move into your apartment?"

"You're right. It's a bad idea." He took his keys from the ignition. "Let's go see Dawn."

24

The next day Sadie brought Dawn over to her mom's house, where a crowd screaming *"Surprise!"* greeted them.

Dawn squealed with delight and acted like she really was surprised, even though all the surprises had happened the night before.

Sadie's mom and aunt were impressed with Terry's creative appetizers and elaborate stork cake. Terry cornered Sadie in the kitchen, held a spatula to her face, and threatened her with bodily harm. He backed off when Maeva promised she'd never go midnight Satanist hunting again without him.

Dawn sat down and opened her gifts and was thrilled with the coupon for free babysitting Sadie provided.

She opened Maeva's gift last and pronounced it the loveliest nursery decoration she'd ever seen.

"What a perfect mirror for the wall," Dawn exclaimed, holding up the circular mirror with the engraved carvings around the white wood frame.

"That's not a normal mirror, is it?" Sadie whispered in Maeva's ear.

"It's a scrying mirror," Maeva whispered back. "You know, for seeing into the future. I figured we'd better get him or her started early."

Sadie could only laugh.

Once the last guest had gone home and all the dishes

and decorations were put away, Dawn sat on the sofa with her feet on the coffee table.

"Careful with that cranberry juice," Sadie's mom told Dawn. "We just had the sofa cleaned." She sat down next to her daughter.

Sadie and Aunt Lynn each grabbed a chair.

"That was really nice," Dawn said with a contented sigh. She took a long sip of her juice.

"Yes, it was. See, Peggy, you were all stressed for nothing. It all went off beautifully," Aunt Lynn said. "I guess I should start packing soon," Aunt Lynn said wistfully. "It's been a lovely visit, but I can't exactly hang around forever."

"Why not?" Sadie asked.

"Yeah, Auntie Lynn, why don't you stay in Seattle?" Dawn suggested.

"Oh, you don't want me hanging around," she said quickly. "Besides, I've got my house. I've been there so long I wouldn't know where to begin packing everything up."

"I'd help you pack," Sadie offered. "I'd even let you put up some of the butterflies on my back fence."

"You'd do that?" Lynn asked, dabbing at her eyes quickly and then waving her hand. "Oh, forget it. It's a silly thought."

"No, it isn't," Peggy insisted. "It's time you sold that house and moved to where the rest of your family is."

Dad walked into the room along with John. The two men had been hiding from the shower by watching sports in the back bedroom. Now they came into the living room with plates heaped with shower leftovers.

"You should definitely move here," Sadie's dad said.

"Sounds like it's final," Sadie said. "You can stay with me until you find a place."

"No, she'll stay here," Peggy insisted.

"Well, I think she should stay with me," Dawn said. "She can help with the baby."

"That's a great idea," John agreed. "Dawn could use

an extra pair of hands when I'm at work." He looked pointedly at Sadie. "And it needs to be someone responsible."

Sadie figured it was going to take a lot of diaper changes and free babysitting to win back her brother-in-law.

"Oh no! Mom, I'm so sorry. I'll pay to have your sofa cleaned again," Dawn said.

"You spilled your juice?" her mom exclaimed, leaning forward to look.

"No. My water just broke."

Chaos ensued with everyone fighting for a chance to drive Dawn to the hospital. John won that battle, with Mom, Dad, and Aunt Lynn piling into a separate car to follow.

"I'll be there soon," Sadie promised. "There's something I need to do first.

"My sister is on her way to the hospital to have the baby," Sadie told Zack over the phone. "If you're not doing anything, do you think you can sneak me onto a crime scene?"

"A florist might be a better idea," he said.

"Yeah, but first things first."

Zack met Sadie at the curb, parking outside of Onyx House.

"You're not going to try and go inside the house, though, right?" Zack asked. "I'm still catching flak for breaking into Egan's house."

"What I've got to do is just outside in the yard," Sadie promised. She started to walk away, leaving Zack leaning against the hood of his Mustang. She was ducking under the arbor when she stopped short, turned around, and walked back to Zack.

"I don't think I was clear before," Sadie said.

"About what?"

"About this." She stood on tiptoe and kissed him fully on the mouth.

"I love you, Zack Bowman," she whispered against his mouth.

Then she reached into her pocket and pulled out a single key and pressed it into his palm.

"Your apartment's too small. Hairy and I need our space, but if you'll still have us, I'd love you to come and live with me."

"I'd like that," he said gruffly.

She took him by the hand then and nodded.

"C'mon," she said, tugging him toward the yard. "If you're with me, you might as well be all the way."

They walked together under the vine-covered trellis.

Sadie found Rhea sitting cross-legged on the grass under the window where she'd fallen the year before.

"Hi," Sadie called out, and the little girl jumped to her feet and frowned.

Almost immediately her essence began to fade away.

"Don't go," Sadie called out. She released Zack's hand and reached out for Rhea.

"You can't touch me, remember?" Rhea smirked. "It'll give you cooties."

"It won't give me cooties," Sadie said, laughing. "It'll just make me grossed out. Kinda like fingernails on a blackboard."

"Oh, I hate that sound!" Rhea exclaimed with a shudder. "Why did you come back?"

"Because I wanted to say I'm sorry for lying."

"About what?"

"About Brian not being your dad."

Rhea fully appeared then and began toying with the ID bracelet. She spun it around and around her wrist. Her eyes were wide and bright with unshed tears.

"Brian really is your dad. I just said he wasn't because—"

"Because you wanted Tim to get mad at Mom?"

"Something like that," Sadie said.

"So that means you're my aunt too."

"Yes." Sadie swallowed the emotion that clogged her throat, and nodded. "And I wish I'd known you were here. Maybe I could've stopped everything that was going on and maybe then you wouldn't have fallen out a window."

"Tim pushed me," Rhea said quietly, and fat tears rolled down her cheeks.

"I thought so," Sadie said. "I'm so sorry."

"It's not your fault."

Sadie took a deep breath.

"I really wish you could stay here so that we could talk all the time."

"I can," Rhea insisted. "I can stay here forever and you can come and visit and we'll talk. Just like now."

"I know you *can* stay, but you need to think about if that's what you really want," Sadie said softly. "You have other choices."

Sadie heard Maeva calling from the front yard.

"Over here!" Sadie called over her shoulder.

Maeva and Louise appeared from around the side of the house. Each of them carried a small tote bag.

"Wh-what's going on?" Rhea asked, jumping away. "You're going to make me go, aren't you?"

"Only if you want to," Sadie said.

"Well, I *don't* want to," Rhea insisted with a stomp of her foot that was like a pouf of talcum powder. "And you can't make me. Hmph."

"If you stay here, it's going to be awfully lonely most of the time," Sadie said. "But if you go, you can be with your dad. Your real dad."

Rhea looked skeptical.

"Nope. I tried once and it didn't even work. I tried to go and nobody was there."

"He didn't know about you then," Sadie explained. She nodded toward Maeva and Louise. "That's why they're here. I can't contact Brian because of how he died. But they can. They can call him here and then you can decide what to do. Maybe the two of you can go together."

"Really? Cross your heart?"

Sadie nodded and made the heart-crossing motion with her right hand.

They sat in a circle on the grass, Sadie, Maeva, Louise, and Zack, with Rhea in the center. Maeva lit a vanilla-scented candle and began humming. Louise murmured a chant. Sadie closed her eyes and held her breath, afraid to do anything.

After a minute Maeva abruptly stopped humming and Louise suddenly stopped chanting.

"There's a mist," Maeva murmured.

"White smoke," Louise added. "It's Brian."

"I see him," Rhea said, her voice soft with wonder. "He has nice eyes. Friendly eyes like you, Sadie."

Sadie opened her eyes to see Rhea looking up and smiling.

"Brian, I don't know if you can hear me, but this is your daughter, Rhea," Sadie said. "Joy was pregnant when you left. Rhea needs someone to take care of her now." Sadie's voice was choked with emotion. She turned to Maeva. "I don't know if he can hear me."

"He can," Maeva said, and she nodded toward the center of the circle. "He has a message for you. He says thank you." She blinked away tears and appeared to be listening before she spoke again. "He also says he loves you very much and he hopes you can move on now and let him go."

Sadie's throat was tight with emotion. She could only nod.

Rhea's form became slightly transparent. She reached her hand up over her head and suddenly Sadie saw a cloud of smoke form the shape of a hand. The misty fingers reached out to lock with Rhea's hand.

"I think I'm going to go," Rhea said softly. The edges around her shape were shimmering. "He wants me to come with him."

She looked over at Sadie as if asking permission.

"You need to take care of each other," Sadie said firmly. "I love you. Both of you."

"I love you too," Rhea said.

The little girl's shape was suddenly engulfed in arms of white mist. Both shapes shimmered before dematerializing. They left behind only a fine wisp of mist that washed away as fat raindrops fell from the sky like tears.

Read on for a sneak peek at the next
Ghost Dusters Mystery,
coming from Obsidian in December 2009.

The cemetery had smelled of freshly mowed grass. Sadie would've preferred the pungent stench of body decomposition. She had shifted uneasily from one foot to the other and skipped her gaze over the cluster of family and friends, then glanced upward at the gunmetal sky. She had looked everywhere but at the casket that rested on straps waiting to be lowered into the gaping hole beneath it.

The priest's voice had droned on about how the human body was merely a shell.

Tell me about it, Sadie had thought, swallowing a thick lump of emotion.

If anyone knew souls weren't attached to their bodies, it was Sadie. She lived that truth nearly every day. While Scene-2-Clean, her trauma-clean company, mopped up the physical mess of death, Sadie dealt with the spirits who needed help moving on to the next dimension.

In the back of her mind Sadie thought her firsthand knowledge of spirits and the ethereal dimension should give her comfort at the funeral of a loved one. It hadn't.

Sadie had let out a small, sorrowful sigh, and then Zack's hand found hers. She had tensed at first, then relaxed and linked her fingers with his, offering him a grateful smile before turning her gaze to the crowd. Her sister, Dawn, balanced her one-year-old son on her hip and leaned into the embrace of her husband, John.

When Dawn's eyes met Sadie's the pain was so raw that Sadie had to look away.

The priest had wrapped things up by offering solace to the bereaved, and then everyone walked back to their cars. A few paused to comment softly to Sadie, but their words of comfort had dropped like stones at her feet.

She had been eager to leave the cemetery, but once they'd arrived at her mom's house and mourners arrived for the wake, Sadie just wanted to escape. A couple hours of small talk had felt like a lifetime. Finally, when they were down to just family, Zack tracked down Sadie as she sipped coffee alone in the kitchen.

"Your mom's asking where you are. Why don't you come into the living room with everyone else?" Zack asked.

"I'll be in there in a minute. I need to use the washroom first," Sadie replied.

She quickly walked down the hall and wondered how long she could successfully stay hidden in the main bathroom before someone came looking for her. She'd successfully held her emotions together all day. It was a constant battle not to break down, but she just didn't want to lower her wall. Not yet.

She used the toilet, flushed, and walked to the sink to splash cold water on her face. She glanced up at her reflection in the mirror and took in the dark circles under her eyes, and then ran damp fingers through her short-cropped hair.

"I liked it better when you had it long," a deep male voice said quietly from behind her.

Sadie squeaked in surprise and whirled to face the man.

She gasped. "Wh-what the hell are you doing?"

"Oh, I know," he said, holding up a hand. "You're a grown woman. I shouldn't be sneaking up on you in the bathroom. It's unseemly."

"It's not that. . . ." Sadie said. She slowly shook her

head from side to side and tried to come up with an easy way to say what needed to be said. "Dad, you're dead."

Her father tossed back his head and laughed with a throaty guffaw that reminded Sadie of childhood Christmas mornings and Sunday picnics. Tears burned her eyes but she blinked them away.

"It's true, Dad. You're dead. Gone. We just put you to rest at Memorial Cemetery."

"I didn't raise you to be a fibber, young lady."

Sadie sat down on the toilet seat and blew out an uneasy breath. "You had a heart attack watching Leno."

"I always knew Jay's monologue would kill me," he said with a snort. At Sadie's deadpan face he took a step forward and reached for her. His hand dropped straight through Sadie's shoulder, but he didn't appear to notice. Sadie shivered with the revulsion that always coursed through her body when spirits attempted to physically touch her.

"Have you had a hit to the head? A fever?" he asked.

Sadie looked up into her father's gray eyes and shook her head.

"No, Dad." She locked eyes with him. "I'm serious."

"That's ridiculous! How can I be dead? If I were dead, we wouldn't be able to have this conversation."

"So you'd think," she commented drily. At his confused look she took a deep breath and blurted out, "I can see and talk to the dead. Those who haven't gone over. It's a little gift I adopted after Brian died. I see a lot of spirits doing trauma cleans. I try and help them."

"You've been hanging out with that weird psychic friend of yours too much," he growled, shaking an angry finger in her face. "Or you've been working too long cleaning up crime scenes. What kind of job is that for a young woman, anyway? Who on earth has ever heard of a pretty young thing like you mopping up people's bodily fluids after they've been left to rot and—"

"Stop," Sadie pleaded quietly. She pinched her eyes

shut. "Please. Just stop. Don't make this harder than it already is."

"You need to talk to someone. A shrink or something. Guess we should've gotten you some help after your brother killed himself, but—"

"This isn't about Brian. This is about you!" Sadie shouted. "You're dead! Haven't you wondered why you haven't been able to talk to anyone for days, not even Mom? All the people that have been in the house for the last few hours were here for *your* wake."

"That's crazy talk." He puffed out his cheeks and walked over to the small bathroom sink. "You're saying I'm a ghost. Well, according to all the old movies I've seen, if I were a ghost I wouldn't be able to see myself in the—"

He stopped short because there was no reflection staring back at him in the mirror. The look on his face was first one of astonishment, then fear. His reaction knifed painfully through Sadie's chest.

"I'm sorry, Dad."

"But—but how can this be?" he murmured.

He reached his fingers out to touch the mirror but they simply passed right through. Then he looked back over at Sadie and quickly vanished. Sadie knew her father's spirit wasn't gone for good. There'd been no shimmer. When the spirits she met left for the next dimension permanently, their shapes always shimmered around the edges before slowly dissipating. A quick disappearance like this only meant he'd left the area or was no longer visible to Sadie.

Sadie spent a moment gathering her thoughts. She'd naturally assumed she'd never see her father again.

"You okay in there?" Zack's voice called from the other side of the bathroom door.

"I'll be right out," Sadie replied.

She heard Zack walk away, then waited a beat to see if her dad would return. When he didn't, she stepped out of the bathroom and walked into the living room to find Dawn hoisting one-year-old Jacob into her arms while John snagged the diaper bag and various toys off the carpet. All the other guests were gone.

"You're leaving?" Sadie asked.

"It's time for his nap," Dawn replied.

"He could nap here," Sadie said.

"It's just easier if he's in his own bed," John explained.

"Maeva and Terry did a great job catering the wake," Dawn said, shifting Jacob onto her other hip. "They said to say good-bye to you. They were in a hurry because Terry has to cater a wedding in a few hours and Maeva was holding a séance at her psychic café at four o'clock. She said she'll call you later."

"Where's Mom?" Sadie looked around for her mother.

"She went to lie down," Dawn said. "I think she took one of the sedatives the doctor prescribed."

At Sadie's worried look Dawn added, "She's going to be fine."

"Her husband of forty-eight years just died. I don't think 'fine' is the word that covers it," Sadie said, snarkily.

"Easy." Zack placed a warning hand on her arm.

"That's not what I meant," Dawn said reproachfully.

"What your sister meant was that we've been with your mother practically every second since your dad died. We know she's hurting, but she'll have to be alone eventually," John stated softly.

"But she shouldn't be alone today," Sadie insisted.

"We can stay longer," Zack said. "We're not in any rush."

But Sadie *was* in a rush. She didn't want to deal with the naked grief that shimmered in her mom's red-rimmed eyes. Mostly she didn't want to deal with her dead father, whose ghost was for some reason camping out in the bathroom.

"You've been avoiding spending one-on-one time with Mom since it happened," Dawn said accusingly.

"I have not," Sadie protested, but at Dawn's piercing glare she relented. "Okay, maybe I have, but—"

"Look, I get it," Dawn said huffily. "But we *all* miss him and we're *all* hurting. You don't have the market cornered on pain."

"I never said I did."

"Well, then don't act like it."

"You two knock it off," Dad chimed from the hallway. "Your squabbling will wake up your mother."

"Shut up," Sadie hissed.

"You shut up!" Dawn retorted angrily.

"Let's go," John said, taking a now whimpering Jacob from Dawn's arms and heading for the door.

"I wasn't talking to you," Sadie protested lamely, but she didn't want to follow that up with, *I was talking to our dead father, who finally decided to come out of the bathroom.* It wasn't until Dawn and her family had left in a huff that Zack spoke.

"So your dad's ghost is here with us, huh?"

"Yup. This day just keeps getting better and better," Sadie said sarcastically.

"Wait a second," her dad spoke up. "You mean to tell me that this guy knows about you being able to talk to ghosts, but you didn't bother telling me or your mother?" His voice was colored with hurt.

"Sorry. It's not the kind of thing I felt comfortable talking to you about," Sadie said to her father. To Zack she said, "He's miffed that I never told him about the talking-to-the-dead thing."

"Hell, sometimes I wish you'd never told *me,*" Zack said, slumping into an overstuffed chair. At Sadie's angry glare Zack cleared his throat. "I'm kidding. Really. I love everything about you. Your whole communicating-with-ghosts thing makes life, um, interesting."

"Huh." Sadie said.

"Tell him to get out of my chair," Dad said. "I'm dead a few days and that man thinks he can just sit in my chair."

"That man is Zack Bowman, my boyfriend, whom I live with. You don't have to act like you've forgotten who he is," Sadie retorted.

"Your dad never did like me," Zack said, folding his arms angrily over his chest.

"He's right," Dad said.

"Oh, for Pete's sake, he just didn't like the idea that we were living together without getting married," Sadie said to Zack. "Right?" she said to her dad.

"And I don't like him sitting in my chair."

"It's not like *you're* sitting in it," Sadie said with exasperation.

"Oh yeah?"

Dad walked over and sat right on top of Zack. Of course, Zack had no idea that Ron Novak was sitting sort of *on* him and kind of *through* him. Sadie looked over at her father and could see right through him to Zack. It was a surreal image that gave her an immediate headache.

"I've got to get out of here," Sadie said with a sigh. "I just can't deal with this right now. Maybe I'll get home and find there's a message from a nice simple suicide to clean up. That would be nice."